P9-DCP-589

IN
Times
Gone By

Books by Tracie Peterson

www.traciepeterson.com

GOLDEN GATE SECRETS
In Places Hidden • In Dreams Forgotten
In Times Gone By

HEART OF THE FRONTIER
Treasured Grace • Beloved Hope
Cherished Mercy

THE HEART OF ALASKA***
In the Shadow of Denali
Out of the Ashes

SAPPHIRE BRIDES
A Treasure Concealed
A Beauty Refined • A Love Transformed

BRIDES OF SEATTLE
Steadfast Heart
Refining Fire • Love Everlasting

LONE STAR BRIDES
A Sensible Arrangement
A Moment in Time • A Matter of Heart
Lone Star Brides (3 in 1)

LAND OF SHINING WATER
The Icecutter's Daughter
The Quarryman's Bride • The Miner's Lady

LAND OF THE LONE STAR
Chasing the Sun
Touching the Sky • Taming the Wind

BRIDAL VEIL ISLAND*
To Have and To Hold
To Love and Cherish • To Honor and Trust

STRIKING A MATCH
Embers of Love
Hearts Aglow • Hope Rekindled

SONG OF ALASKA
Dawn's Prelude
Morning's Refrain • Twilight's Serenade

ALASKAN QUEST
Summer of the Midnight Sun
Under the Northern Lights
Whispers of Winter
Alaskan Quest (3 in 1)

BRIDES OF GALLATIN COUNTY
A Promise to Believe In
A Love to Last Forever
A Dream to Call My Own

THE BROADMOOR LEGACY*
A Daughter's Inheritance
An Unexpected Love
A Surrendered Heart

BELLS OF LOWELL*
Daughter of the Loom
A Fragile Design • These Tangled Threads

LIGHTS OF LOWELL*
A Tapestry of Hope • A Love Woven
True • The Pattern of Her Heart

DESERT ROSES
Shadows of the Canyon
Across the Years • Beneath a Harvest Sky

HEIRS OF MONTANA
Land of My Heart • The Coming Storm
To Dream Anew • The Hope Within

LADIES OF LIBERTY
A Lady of High Regard • A Lady of
Hidden Intent • A Lady of Secret Devotion

RIBBONS OF STEEL**
Distant Dreams • A Hope Beyond
A Promise for Tomorrow

RIBBONS WEST**
Westward the Dream
Separate Roads • Ties That Bind

WESTWARD CHRONICLES
A Shelter of Hope
Hidden in a Whisper • A Veiled Reflection

YUKON QUEST
Treasures of the North
Ashes and Ice • Rivers of Gold

---

*All Things Hidden****
*Beyond the Silence****
House of Secrets
A Slender Thread
What She Left for Me
Where My Heart Belongs

*with Judith Miller **with Judith Pella ***with Kimberley Woodhouse

GOLDEN GATE SECRETS

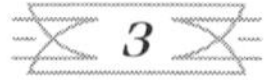

TRACIE PETERSON

a division of Baker Publishing Group
Minneapolis, Minnesota

© 2018 by Peterson Ink, Inc.

Published by Bethany House Publishers
11400 Hampshire Avenue South
Bloomington, Minnesota 55438
www.bethanyhouse.com

Bethany House Publishers is a division of
Baker Publishing Group, Grand Rapids, Michigan

Printed in the United States of America

All rights reserved. No part of this publication may be reproduced, stored in a retrieval system, or transmitted in any form or by any means—for example, electronic, photocopy, recording—without the prior written permission of the publisher. The only exception is brief quotations in printed reviews.

Library of Congress Cataloging-in-Publication Data
Names: Peterson, Tracie, author.
Title: In times gone by / Tracie Peterson.
Description: Minneapolis, Minnesota : Bethany House, a division of Baker Publishing Group, [2018] | Series: Golden Gate secrets : 3
Identifiers: LCCN 2018020565 | ISBN 9780764219016 (trade paper) | ISBN 9780764231230 (cloth) | ISBN 9780764231247 (large print) | ISBN 9781493413812 (e-book)
Subjects: | GSAFD: Love stories.
Classification: LCC PS3566.E7717 G56 2018 | DDC 813/.54—dc23
LC record available at https://lccn.loc.gov/2018020565

Scripture quotations are from the King James Version of the Bible unless otherwise marked.

Scripture quotations marked (NIV) are from the Holy Bible, New International Version®. NIV®. Copyright © 1973, 1978, 1984, 2011 by Biblica, Inc.™ Used by permission of Zondervan. All rights reserved worldwide. www.zondervan.com

This is a work of historical reconstruction; the appearances of certain historical figures are therefore inevitable. All other characters, however, are products of the author's imagination, and any resemblance to actual persons, living or dead, is coincidental.

Cover design by LOOK Design Studio

Cover photography by Aimee Christenson

18 19 20 21 22 23 24 7 6 5 4 3 2 1

To Kimberley Woodhouse,

with thanks for all you do and for the friendship you've given me over the years. I cherish working with you, but even more, I cherish the honesty and love between us.

CHAPTER 1

April 1906—San Francisco

Everything smelled like smoke. Tasted like smoke. No matter how many times Kenzie Gifford washed her clothes, her hair, even her hands, the acrid scent lingered. Would it ever change?

She looked up from her work to gaze north. A good portion of the city had burned to the ground. The charred frames of buildings stood like blackened ghosts of what had once been a vibrant, beautiful town. Surrounding those were the crumbled stones and cracked foundations that the earthquake had left behind. San Francisco as many had known it no longer existed.

Early on the morning of the eighteenth, the earth had shaken with such tremendous force that Kenzie had actually thought the world had come to an end. Didn't the Bible speak of such things? Earthquakes, stars falling from the sky, the earth burning. Of course, the world hadn't ended, although the end had come for hundreds—maybe thousands—of poor souls.

She shuddered and tried to push aside the images of things she'd seen. Forgetting the earthquake and its aftermath was impossible, especially when everyone seemed to gauge their existence from that day. It was almost like a strange rebirth. No matter where she went, people were talking about where they were and what they were doing when the "big one" hit.

San Franciscans were no strangers to earthquakes. Often they occurred with hardly more than a passing nod of acknowledgment. But not when they came with the intensity and length of this quake. Even the old-timers were saying it was the worst they'd ever known.

Kenzie returned her attention to the cast-iron kettle. Soon she would rinse the bed linens and hang them on the makeshift laundry lines. For a few minutes they would smell of strong lye soap and then revert to the familiar smoky stench. She took up her paddle and bent to stir the linens.

"This is the last of them," Judith Whitley said, depositing a large wheelbarrow overflowing with sheets and pillowcases. "Mrs. Andrews said she and the other ladies would be out to take over as soon as they've finished their breakfast. Oh, and they said they'd hang the woolen blankets and pound the dust from them too."

Kenzie put aside the paddle and straightened. "It's good to see everyone pulling together."

Judith pushed back her long blond braid, then wiped her forehead with the back of her sleeve. She glanced back at the warehouse. "Caleb said disaster brings out the best and the worst in people. I'm glad we seem to have those with better dispositions."

Caleb Coulter, Judith's fiancé, had purchased the large warehouse shortly before the earthquake. He and his sister Camrianne had intended to create a shelter for displaced women and children. They called it Solid Rock as a reminder of Christ being their firm foundation and of their desire to provide such a refuge for the downtrodden. They had arranged with Camri's fiancé, Patrick

Murdock, a talented carpenter, to ready the building for residents. No one had anticipated they would need it so soon.

"I've heard all sorts of terrible stories about the relief camps," Judith continued. "Of course, everyone is still in such a state of shock and disarray. So many people are still missing. Mrs. Gimble said she and her husband can't find their children. Imagine, entire families just disappearing."

"Like yours did," Kenzie said, hoping her tone was more sympathetic than agitated. She didn't like to think about so many people being dead.

"Yes. Like mine, although I hardly had a chance to know them." Judith shook her head. "Sometimes I wonder if it would have been better to never have known them."

Judith had come to San Francisco to find her long-lost family, only to lose all but one in the earthquake. Kenzie felt sorry for her friend. Not only for the loss of life, but for the threat that had come against Judith.

"Well, if you'd never known them, your cousin Bill wouldn't have tried to kill you. On the other hand, had he not tried to kill you, then you wouldn't have been rescued by the man you love." The wind came up, and Kenzie wriggled her nose. "I'll be so glad when we get rid of the ash and stench." She pulled out a blue bandana and wrapped it around her head. "I just washed my hair, and I won't have it filled with ash." She secured her auburn hair beneath the scarf.

"I am glad I had a chance to know Grandmother," Judith continued, her voice taking on a mournful tone. "I would have liked to know her better. Now she's gone, along with so many others. Caleb said the numbers will probably climb into the thousands."

Kenzie tried not to think about that number, which perhaps included her mother's cousin, George Lake. Cousin George had given Kenzie, Judith, and Camri jobs at his chocolate factory when they'd first come to San Francisco in November. George was still unaccounted for, and Kenzie had encountered little luck getting anyone to let her go into his burned-out chocolate factory to search for him. She had sought the help of the army, only to be refused. "That area was completely destroyed," an officer had told her. "If your cousin was there when the earthquake hit, most likely he's dead. If not right away, then the fire got him."

It was terrible to imagine poor Cousin George pinned in the debris and burned alive. So many had died that way. Thankfully, the damage at the warehouse had been minimal, and the fires had been stopped before spreading this far.

". . . after that she was just fine," Judith said, looking expectantly at Kenzie for a response.

Kenzie shook her head. "I'm sorry. My mind wasn't on what you were saying."

Judith smiled. She had the sweetest disposition. "It's all right. It wasn't at all important." She patted Kenzie's arm. "I'm sure he's fine."

"Who?" Kenzie had said nothing of her worries about Cousin George, although everyone knew he was still unaccounted for.

"Micah. I'm sure he's safe."

Kenzie felt her mouth go dry. Even though she had discouraged him repeatedly, Dr. Micah Fisher had pursued her since her arrival in the city. At least it felt that way. Tall and handsome, Micah was a sought-after bachelor and Caleb's best friend. Truth be told, she *was* worried about him, despite her determination not to think about him. She wasn't sure how to react to Judith's comment without hurting her friend's feelings. Judith was in love, so naturally she thought the rest of the world should be too.

"I'm sure he is." Kenzie hoped her voice didn't sound too clipped. "You might let Camri know that we're going to need more firewood." She turned back to the kettle and began moving the clean sheets to the rinse water.

When she turned back around, Judith was gone. Kenzie let out a sigh of relief. She didn't want to discuss Micah and risk thoughts and feelings coming to the surface that she'd just have to explain away later. She cared about his well-being, of course. But nothing more. Nothing.

Kenzie glanced toward the warehouse. It wasn't much to look at. The exterior was in bad need of a paint job, but Patrick had made sure the structure was sound. He had also arranged to add a few more windows, for which Kenzie was very grateful. The small private rooms that they had arranged for themselves had been dark and cramped when she'd first been shown the warehouse.

Camri had insisted that each of the rooms have a window. "Even if we use them for nothing more than offices," she had told her brother and fiancé, "we're going to want the extra light."

Kenzie smiled at the memory. Camri was good at getting what she wanted, and the windows had served them well. Life would have been much worse if they'd all had to take up residence in one of the relief camps. Tent life was not at all appealing, and neither was the idea of living under the army's thumb. Although at the moment, it seemed the entire city was obliged to do the military's bidding.

Once she had transferred the clean sheets to the rinse water, Kenzie put new dirty sheets into the soapy water. Sheets were a small luxury that Camri had decided on when planning for the warehouse to become a home for women and children who were down on their luck. She had thought it would add a homey touch to the simple cots. Kenzie admitted that it did, but it also added extra work. Especially since Camri had decided that sheets needed to be washed once a week. She had no doubt read somewhere that this was the optimum schedule for the best hygiene. Camri was college educated and seemed to have a vast amount of knowledge about many things. Kenzie admired her genius, although at times she found Camri more than a little exasperating.

A shriek of laughter drew her attention as a group of children ran around the corner of the warehouse. Three little girls pursued a scruffy dog. The brown-and-white mongrel held a ball in its mouth and apparently was winning a game of keep-away. Kenzie couldn't help but smile. In the midst of disaster, it was nice to see such happiness.

With her work done, Kenzie decided to grab a quick bite to eat. She made her way to the opposite side of the warehouse, where their outdoor dining and kitchen had been arranged.

"Miss Gifford," a woman called from where she sat at one of the tables.

Kenzie went to her. "Yes, Mrs. Clark?"

The gray-haired woman held up a bowl of oatmeal and gave her a grandmotherly smile. "I know you haven't eaten yet."

Her kindness touched Kenzie. She took the bowl and smiled. "Thank you. I wanted to get the first batch of sheets washed."

"Well, you needn't worry with anything else." Mrs. Clark rose from the bench. "Gladys and I will take it in hand."

Kenzie put the bowl of cereal on the table, then reached out to help the old woman up. The long trestle tables and benches suited the feeding of a great many people but were difficult for the elderly to manage.

"Thank you, dear. Now you sit down and eat. You're far too skinny."

It was useless to argue. Kenzie gave a nod. "I just put the last of the sheets in the wash water. You may need to add some more soap."

Mrs. Clark cackled. "Now ain't that something? A sweet

young girl like you tellin' the likes of me how to wash clothes. Been washin' them since I was able to walk. My ma saw nothing good to be gained in idleness."

Mrs. Andrews appeared from inside the warehouse. She was a short, stocky woman whose piercing blue eyes missed nothing. "I'm ready to tend to the laundry with you, Minnie. I had to speak to Penelope. She has her little granddaughters with her today. It seems their mama and papa are working to clean bricks. Anyway, I told her it was probably best if she helped with something else and we managed the laundry."

"Good idea, Gladys. I wouldn't want those little ones around the fire." Mrs. Clark nodded her approval. They continued chatting about the matter as they left Kenzie to her breakfast.

The oatmeal tasted bland. At least it wasn't smoky. Kenzie sprinkled a bit of sugar onto the cereal and dug in. Milk and cream were luxuries they couldn't afford, even when they could be found, so Kenzie did her best to swallow the thick porridge without it. She fondly recalled breakfast at Caleb's house, where his housekeeper, Mrs. Wong, would fix bacon and eggs, biscuits and gravy, and even the occasional pot of oatmeal. The difference between her cereal and this, however, was like night and day. Mrs. Wong put cinnamon and other spices in her oatmeal, as well as a generous helping of raisins and cream.

"I've been going over the books since five, and they still prove only one thing," Camri said, joining Kenzie. She put a cup of coffee in front of Kenzie.

"What's that?" Kenzie continued eating.

Camri frowned. "Coffee, of course."

"No, I meant what do the books prove?"

"Oh, that. We need more supplies. We have fifty-seven people, not counting ourselves and Judith, and of course Caleb and Patrick." She shook her head, and her hastily pinned hair threatened to come undone. Camri began fussing with the hairpins.

"Caleb is going to speak with Judge Winters and see if he can get us some help from the army without them thinking they need to send someone here to run things. The judge is good friends with General Funston, and since he's in charge, Caleb is almost certain they can work something out."

"What if they can't?" Kenzie asked before she could stop herself. Camri tended to worry enough without her adding to the strain.

"That was my thought exactly. Caleb told me I shouldn't fret about it until we had an answer one way or the other. Patrick told me that no matter what happened, he was sure I'd find a way to manage. As if he thinks I can call down food from heaven."

Kenzie couldn't help chuckling. "Well, we have seen you do stranger things."

Camri straightened. "This took us all by surprise. No one expected such complete devastation. So many people have nothing to go back to. Providing a cot and blanket, a warm meal—even if it is watery soup—and a change of clothes means the world."

"It does, and you're managing it all very well, so stop worrying. As you once told me, the energy spent in worry is much more productively spent in prayer."

Camri sighed and finally finished with her hair. "I know you're right. I just want to do whatever I can to help these people."

"As do Judith and I. Thank the Lord she knows how to cook. We might have had to endure my cooking, which even in the best of circumstances is only fair in quality. I can't imagine trying to do it the way she has—with so little and for so many."

"She is a godsend to be sure, and she comforts Caleb."

"Comforts him?" Kenzie shook her head. "Judith's the one who lost her grandmother."

Camri's expression grew serious. "Caleb is worried about

Micah. He's heard nothing. Neither have the Fishers. I heard him speaking with Pastor Fisher last night. It would seem Micah's doing a great deal of work away from the hospitals."

"But he's alive?" Kenzie tried not to sound overly worried.

"He was, but there have been so many buildings collapsing and people killed. No one has seen Micah since the earthquake, and you know very well that the fires have been deadlier. Caleb's terribly worried. I am too. Caleb said that one of the newspapers mentioned a doctor being killed a couple of days ago—they had found an unconscious man pinned in one of the buildings that hadn't burned. Apparently the doctor went to help, and he and the others were killed when the building collapsed. It didn't mention his identity."

Kenzie knew it was senseless to pretend she didn't care. Micah was just the sort to rush into an unsafe building to save a life. "I've been praying for him and for Cousin George."

Camri nodded. "Poor Mr. Lake. I hope he managed to get to safety. Caleb was going to speak to the soldiers in charge of that area and see if they'd heard anything. They've started posting notes at the relief camps. Someone came up with the idea to create a board where people could tack up the names of those they're looking for. We should probably send someone to put up your cousin's name. Micah's too. Oh, and then check with the people handling . . . the dead."

Kenzie's throat constricted. She hated to think of her cousin dead, even though the odds were good that he was. But to consider Micah dead was almost more than she could bear. It wasn't because she had special feelings for him, but she hated to think of someone so talented being killed. At least, that was what she kept telling herself.

"I'll go. I'll write up notes that we're looking for George and Micah and post them on the relief camp boards."

Camri seemed to consider this for a moment. "I suppose

that would be good, but let's wait until Caleb and Patrick get back from their meeting. They should be back anytime, and they might have word."

Kenzie pushed her unfinished oatmeal aside. "I'll go write up the notes."

CHAPTER 2

Well, ladies, good news," Caleb Coulter said, shrugging out of his coat.

It was nearly ten o'clock, and Kenzie had begun to wonder if the men would ever return. The morning was nearly gone. She put aside some sewing she'd been doing and joined the others gathering around Caleb and Patrick.

"Do tell, brother." Camri stood beside her fiancé. Patrick Murdock looked down at her with a lopsided smile and slipped his arm around her waist. They were well-matched and clearly in love. Patrick was just the kind of man the willful Camri needed.

"I spoke with Judge Winters. General Funston has agreed to share some of the relief supplies with us. His boys will bring a load yet today." Caleb reached out to touch Judith's cheek. They, too, were very much in love.

Everyone is in love. Everyone but me.

Kenzie frowned as Micah came to mind. How easy it would be to give her heart to him. He said and did all the right things—well, when he wasn't being a pest or making a fool of himself. Kenzie pushed aside her memories. She was determined not to fall in love with him. She had lost her heart once. She wasn't going to be fool enough to do it again.

"I think we should make a place where we can receive and inventory the supplies," Caleb continued.

"I figure the dining tables are perfectly situated," Camri said, glancing toward their outdoor dining room.

"Generally I'd agree with you, but I saw Mrs. Wong, and she said it was going to rain this afternoon." Like the others, Kenzie marveled at Caleb's former housekeeper's ability to forecast the weather.

"How are the Wongs? I wish they could have stayed with us," Camri replied.

"They're well. They're helping their friends and family. Chinatown was completely burned to the ground. The Chinese have lost most everything, and now the Board of Supervisors wants to move Chinatown out south of Golden Gate Park, well away from the city. The land where Chinatown used to sit is being coveted, I'm afraid."

"That's completely against the law, isn't it?" Camri asked.

"It depends. The law these days is pretty much being interpreted as we go. The army acts as though they're in charge, although martial law hasn't been declared. I suppose we should be grateful for the order they helped bring, but they are also seen as the reason so much of the city burned. Most of the people handling dynamite for the backfires had no idea what they were doing. They caused more harm than good."

Judith looped her arm through his. "But they were doing their best. We have to remember that. I'm sure they feel terrible about it."

"For sure that's possible," Patrick jumped in with his Irish brogue. "But I'm thinkin' they enjoy bossin' folks around."

"Not to mention they've been given approval to shoot looters and miscreants on sight."

"That's terrible. Those poor people are probably just trying to find food and shelter," Judith murmured.

"Not all are bein' so selfless," Patrick said, shaking his head. "Not unless they're thinkin' to eat diamonds and pearls. I heard tell two men were shot siftin' through the remains of a jewelry counter."

"I'm sure most are just doing what they must to survive." Judith looked at Kenzie and smiled. "What of Micah? Were you able to find him or George Lake?"

Caleb looked at Kenzie, as did they all. She felt her cheeks grow hot. The trouble with being a fair-skinned redhead was that every bit of embarrassment showed up on her face in bright hues of crimson.

"I'm sorry. I asked around about Mr. Lake, but no one has heard a thing. The area around the factory and his home were both destroyed. As for Micah, the doctor in charge of the hospital where we last saw him told me he hadn't seen Micah since that first day. I can't imagine him not letting his parents know where he is, but what with the chaos and so many wounded, he probably doesn't feel he can leave his work."

"It seems rather selfish to let his loved ones worry," Camri interjected. "I can't imagine his poor mother has slept a wink."

"Well, at least we know he survived the quake," Caleb countered.

"But he might have been injured in the fires or some of the collapsing buildings. You showed me that article, and he could be—" Camri stopped and looked at Kenzie. "Never mind. I'm sure you're right and he's just busy."

"You haven't seen how the makeshift hospitals are operating. There's a lot of confusion. Doctors are even writing on patients themselves to note medications and circumstances. It's like nothing I've ever seen." Caleb's brows came together as he frowned. "And I hope to never see anything like this again."

Kenzie tried not to react in any obvious way. She couldn't help but feel a sense of fear where Micah was concerned. He thought he was invincible. He thought he had all the answers and could do most anything he put his mind to. His pride very well might see him dead, and where would that leave his poor family?

Caleb continued sharing information from his talk with Judge Winters, but Kenzie barely registered the words. She was determined for the sake of her own peace of mind and her parents' that she would steal away from the warehouse and go down to the remains of the chocolate factory. If Cousin George was still alive, he would no doubt be there, sifting through the debris, looking for anything he might salvage, just as other business owners were doing. She imagined he would see the earthquake and fire as yet another attempt to sabotage him. The poor man was suspicious of everything and everyone as a potential threat to his chocolate empire.

When she glanced up, she found that Patrick and Caleb were once again leaving. She had no idea where they were bound, but she was going to wash up and do what she must. Since she'd already told Camri she'd post the notes on the board at the relief camp, it would be the perfect cover for her additional activities. With Camri and Judith bidding their men good-bye, Kenzie hurried to her room and did what she could to tidy up her appearance. With her hair combed out and pinned and a clean blouse donned, Kenzie found her straw hat and positioned it in place. She secured it with a long ornate hatpin her mother had given her on her eighteenth birthday. The end of the metal pin was decorated with a white porcelain rose detailed in hues of pink.

She sighed. She missed her mother and father, missed so much about her old life in Missouri. "But I can't go back there. Arthur's there." The words were uttered before she realized it.

Kenzie glanced around to make sure no one had overheard her

whisper Arthur's name. Arthur Morgan—the man she might have married but for his failure to show up at the church.

Only a few weeks ago, she had written him at Camri's suggestion. It felt good to tell him all that she thought of him—what he'd done to her, how she hoped they might never cross paths again. There had been a sense of putting the entire matter behind her when she'd posted the letter, but from time to time little things would stir up memories of him.

"Go away, Arthur. You have no more power over me. I won't let you defeat me."

She marched to her cot, picked up her coat, and then headed out. She had no room in her heart or mind for Arthur, and she was determined to no longer be bound by the pain he'd caused. The notes she'd written awaited her on Caleb's office desk. She'd written several, in case each of the relief camps had a board. Her final stop was to take some tacks from Patrick's workbench. With these in hand, she made her way out the back door, hoping to avoid dealing with Camri and Judith. If they saw her leaving, they might try to stop her or suggest one of them accompany her, and then she'd have a difficult time with her secondary purpose of going to the chocolate factory.

She came around the side of the building only to find Judith and Camri. Several of the residents were with them, and all seemed to have one problem or another. Kenzie hoped Camri's attention would be so fixed on the issues at hand that she could slip past them. But it was too much to hope for.

"Where are you heading?" Camri asked.

Kenzie pulled on her coat. "I'm going to post our notes at the relief camps. I shouldn't be long."

"One of us should probably come with you," Camri said, looking at Judith.

"No, that's quite all right. You're needed here, especially since the army is bringing supplies."

"She's right," Judith said. "We'd nearly forgotten."

Kenzie gave a little wave. "I'll try not to be long. I'll help you get it all organized when I return." She hurried toward the street to avoid any further protest Camri might make.

She needed to find Cousin George.

Dr. Micah Fisher pulled the sheet over the deceased man's face. He was weary of death. Weary of life. He'd lost track of the days and knew only that he'd been working around the clock with just a few minutes of stolen sleep. The only thing that sustained him was thoughts of Kenzie Gifford. He needed to see her—to know that she was all right—to hold her in his arms. He knew she wouldn't welcome his attention, but right now that didn't matter. The world had gone mad, and Kenzie was his only sane thought.

Many of the hospitals had been destroyed, and doctors were performing treatments wherever they could set up a decent place to work. Micah had gone back and forth between several of the makeshift establishments, but mostly he went out on the streets and to the relief camps at the urgent pleading of people he saw along the way. There were so many injuries, so many hopeless situations. He spent nearly as much time praying with dying souls as he did patching up their wounded bodies.

"Doctor, here." A voice broke through his thoughts.

He glanced up to find a young woman cradling a babe in one arm and extending a sandwich to him with the other. "That soldier over there told me to bring you this."

Micah took the sandwich. When had he eaten last? "Give him my thanks, please." He looked only a moment at the unevenly sliced bread separated by a thick slab of ham, then devoured it. Nothing had ever tasted quite so good.

He gathered his bag and went to the pot of water he'd earlier instructed one of the soldiers to boil. Seeing the water was ready, Micah took out his instruments and dropped them into the pot. Cleaning anything was difficult, but he still did his best to keep some semblance of order and procedure. It was a well-known fact that proper sanitation was absolutely necessary, yet many doctors paid it little heed. Here, in a building that had once manufactured shoes, Micah was fairly certain sterilization was never a top concern.

"Doctor, we need you over here," a nurse called.

Micah quickly retrieved a clean towel and fished the tools of his trade from the water. He wrapped the cloth around the wet instruments and pushed the bundle into his bag.

"What's the situation?" he asked, joining the nurse, who stood over a man caked in blood, soot, and all manner of filth.

"They just brought him in. They found him buried in the rubble. He suffered a severe blow to the head. It crushed the back of his skull. There was a great deal of blood loss. His breathing is shallow, and his pulse very weak." She met Micah's gaze. "He's not responding to any stimulus."

Micah pried open one eyelid and then the other. The pupils were fixed and dilated. He took a pencil from his pocket and pressed it against the base of the man's index fingernail. There was no movement, no attempt to fight against his action. Micah did a few additional tests, looking for any kind of response whatsoever, but there was none.

"We can't help him. Have him moved to the waiting room."

The waiting room signaled the hopelessness of the man's condition. It wasn't a place where patients waited to be seen—it was where they waited to die. In the hours just after the earthquake, Micah had seen men and women lined up side by side with nothing more than the floor beneath them—all in various stages of dying. At least now they had the ability to give the poor soul a blanket to lie on.

He shook his head and gazed out across the large factory floor. Every inch of space was being utilized in some capacity, but it was such an inadequate arrangement.

"You look barely able to stand, Fisher," a gruff voice said behind him.

Micah turned to find one of the older surgeons. He had been called out of retirement to help treat the vast number of wounded.

"Better just prop me up against a wall and bring the patients to me, then," Micah replied with a grin. He rubbed his face, frowning at the thick growth of stubble. He'd given up the idea of growing a beard when his mother asked if it was possible for him to be clean-shaven for Easter. Had that only been a week ago last Sunday?

"Son, you'll do no one any good if you can't think clearly. I'm ordering you out of here. Don't make me get someone to remove you. Go home, or go wherever you can, so long as it's away from here. Take a hot bath and sleep for as long as you need and come back rested. After that, you can work another week without decent rest or meals."

Micah nodded. He knew the older man was right, but he hated to walk away from such urgent need. "It's just so hard to leave."

The gruff old surgeon touched Micah's shoulder. "Son, I know exactly how you feel, but if there's one thing I've learned, it's that rest and proper nourishment are vital to clear thinking. Many of these souls are going to die, which is despairing, but you'd feel a great degree worse if you were the cause of it. Now go."

"I will. I need to let my folks know I'm alive, anyway." Micah suppressed a yawn. "I'll be back here or elsewhere as soon as I have some sleep."

Walking from the factory, Micah felt his legs grow heavier

with each step. He wished he could hail a cab and be driven to his parents' house, but what few services were available were charging outrageous prices, and he'd given his last few dollars to a woman trying to buy milk for her children.

Focusing on putting one foot in front of the other, Micah barely registered the destruction around him. The blackened frames, mangled steel, and piles of stone and concrete melded together in strange formations. Ghostly reminders of the once glorious city.

Just ahead, a team of men and women were working to load some of the debris into the back of a large freight wagon.

"Halt! You there, halt!"

Micah yawned and blinked at the sight of an armed soldier, who leveled his rifle at Micah. "Is there a problem, son?" The soldier looked to be hardly more than a boy.

"You are to report for duty helping with cleanup. Every able-bodied man is commanded to report immediately," the private replied.

"Son, I'm a doctor. I just came from working at the hospital and various other locations. I've been working nonstop since the earthquake, and I'm going home for some sleep."

The boy looked momentarily confused, and the rifle lowered slightly. Micah took that as a sign the soldier understood and started again for home.

"I said halt, or I'll shoot!"

Micah stopped again and turned to face the young man. "You'd kill a much-needed doctor because he's tired?"

"I don't set the orders. You have to report for work." The boy's voice cracked and seemed to rise an octave as he added, "Right now."

Micah didn't know what to do. There was no way he could help remove debris. He could barely stand. Not only that, but he couldn't risk hurting his hands digging through the rubble.

"What's going on here, Private?" another soldier asked as he approached. Turning, Micah could see this man was older, an officer. The young private snapped to attention.

"The young private is only trying to follow orders," Micah offered. "However, he doesn't seem to understand that I am a physician. A surgeon. I've been working without much rest, and I'm heading home to sleep." He held up his black bag. "You can look at my medical instruments if you doubt the truth of it." He glanced down at his bloodstained clothes. "You can also see my attire."

The officer shook his head. "That won't be necessary. Go get some rest, Doctor."

Micah nodded. "Thank you." He resumed his journey.

As he moved away from the city's center, Micah saw areas that hadn't burned. He'd heard about citizens taking stands in various areas to fight for their homes. It seemed strange to see a seemingly undamaged house standing amidst the burned-out remains of other residences. What might have been the difference if each homeowner had taken a stand against the flames?

He crossed Van Ness Avenue. On one side of the street, the fire-damaged neighborhood looked much like downtown, but on the other side, it was as if nothing had happened. Almost as if a giant hand had put a barrier in place to keep the fire from going any farther.

After a few more blocks, Micah found himself in his childhood neighborhood. There were signs here and there that it had sustained damage from the earthquake, but except for the smell of smoke drifting from other parts of the city, the area had escaped the fires.

The church came into view first. The spire showed no signs of damage, which was good. Every time they had the slightest shaking, his father worried about the steeple falling down. The lawns of the church were lined with tents, and people milled about at various tasks. No doubt some of them were congregants who had been rendered homeless. Micah skirted the church grounds and made his way to the back, where he knew he'd find the parsonage. Even here there were signs of his father and mother's labors to lend aid. A second and third clothesline had been erected, and a half-dozen women were hanging laundry from the lines. On the far side of the yard was his mother's garden, and several young boys worked to weed and water it.

Micah stumbled up the back steps and through the open doorway. He could hear his mother giving commands like an army sergeant.

"Rose, you get someone to help you peel potatoes. We'll need some carrots too. Joseph, you help your mother with the firewood. Take the little wagon and fetch what you can."

Micah came up behind his mother. The top of her head didn't even reach his shoulder. He leaned over and rested his chin atop her hair. "And what would you have me do?"

She whirled around, nearly smacking him with the broomstick she held. "Micah! Oh, praise God! We were so afraid. Joseph! Joseph, come and see. Micah is home!" She embraced him without reservation. "Are you all right?"

"I'm exhausted. I've worked since the quake with very little sleep. I just wanted to stop here and rest a little before I go see if Caleb and the others are all right."

His father came into the room. He looked so tired. "Micah! Oh, son, it's good to have you home." He too embraced Micah. "The others are just fine. I speak to Caleb every day. They're all over at the warehouse he bought. They've set it up to help those who've no other place to go."

"And Kenzie?"

His father smiled. "She's fine, Micah. Just fine."

Micah felt relief wash over him. He swayed and shook his

head as his father reached out to steady him. "I'm all right. I just need to rest a bit."

Without a word, his father took him in hand as he had often done when Micah was a small boy. His father handed Micah's medical bag to his mother, then pulled him through the house and past all the chaos. At the end of the hall, he opened the door to Micah's room and ushered him inside. Micah sank onto the edge of his bed, and for a moment it escaped him as to what he should do next.

His father helped him from his coat, then pushed Micah back toward the pillow. "Lie down, son."

Micah nodded, eased back onto the bed, and closed his eyes. He could feel his father undoing the laces of his shoes and pulling them from his feet, but after that, nothing.

CHAPTER 3

Micah. Micah, wake up!"

Opening his eyes just a fraction of an inch, Micah saw his mother's worried expression. "What's wrong?" His tongue felt like it was coated with ash.

"I'm so sorry. I know you haven't had but a few hours of sleep, but we have an emergency."

The word *emergency* brought Micah fully awake. He sat up and glanced around for his shoes. "What is it?"

"The Walters boy. He was working with his father today over at their burned-out house. He went through one of the floorboards and has a bad gash on his leg. He's bleeding. A lot."

Micah found his shoes at the end of the bed and quickly stepped into them. "Did you put on a tourniquet?"

"Yes. But then I came for you."

"Good." He bent to tie his shoes. "I'll need a clean, clear space to work."

"I've already got him on the kitchen table."

Micah smiled up at his mother. "You'd make an excellent nurse. Care to assist me?"

She smiled. "You know I would never expect you to manage alone."

He straightened. "Where's my coat?"

She looked around. "Oh, there." She went to the dresser. "Your father must have left it here. Goodness, it's filthy."

"I know. I haven't time to worry about it, but it seems wrong to put on my Sunday coat without a bath." He shrugged into the jacket.

"No one will care. Come on." His mother exited the room, motioning for him to follow.

Micah made his way to the kitchen, where Mr. and Mrs. Walters stood beside their son. Mrs. Walters' face was ashen, and she bit her lower lip as if to keep herself from crying out. Mr. Walters didn't look much better, but he kept his jaw clenched in a stalwart manner.

"Tell me what happened," Micah said, looking down at the boy. "It appears you had quite an adventure." He loosened the tourniquet. The wound oozed blood but didn't gush like he'd feared it might.

The twelve-year-old was pale and doing his best not to cry. "We were trying to clear out . . . ah . . ." He writhed in pain and looked at his dad.

Mr. Walters put his hand on his son's shoulder. "It's all right, Frank."

Micah assessed the wound on the boy's calf. The eight-inch cut wasn't all that deep. He smiled at Frank. "This could have been a whole lot worse. I think you'll be fine. We'll just wash it out and sew it up. I've got some medicine with me that will help with the pain. You'll probably sleep, in fact."

Frank's eyes were wide. Perspiration lined his upper lip. He gave a little nod, but Micah could see the pain was more than the child or his mother could bear. Mrs. Walters was equally pale and in tears.

"Mrs. Walters, why don't you wait outside? It's sometimes easier for young men if they don't have to worry about upsetting their mothers." Micah smiled at the harried woman. "Mr. Walters, if you want to stay, I could probably use your help to keep Frank steady. At least until the medicine takes hold."

Mr. Walters nodded and looked at his wife. "You go on outside, Essie. No since worryin' the boy. Frank's gonna be just fine."

Mrs. Walters looked as though she was torn between escaping the misery of her child and staying to help.

Micah tried to reassure her. "My mother will stay here and assist me. I'll send her out to you as soon as we're finished."

Finally, Mrs. Walters gave a slight nod. She leaned down and kissed her son on the head, then left the room. She paused only a moment at the back door and then was gone.

Micah found his black bag and took out a bottle of strong medication. His mother brought a spoon and helped him administer the thick syrup to the boy. While he waited for the medicine to take effect, Micah instructed his mother to bring soap, water, and bandages. He knew she'd have everything he needed. Ever since Micah had finished his surgical training, people would drop by the house for help with one injury or another. Mother had started keeping basic medical materials around the house for just such occasions. It wasn't at all unusual to come home and find her tearing up old sheets to make bandages.

The exhaustion he'd felt earlier seemed to disappear as Micah focused on the injury. He loved what he did—treating the wounded, healing the sick. He was born to be a doctor. Even as a child, he had taken to treating injured pets. Blood had never bothered him. Blood was life. His father had often preached about the saving blood of Jesus, after all. Micah supposed it was things like that which made it seem a wondrous thing rather than a fearful one.

Once Frank was dozing, the work went quickly. Making small

stitches, Micah couldn't help but remember repairing Kenzie's fingers not so long ago. She had been so frightened—so vulnerable. She always worked so hard to hide her emotional wounds, but when the glass had sliced her fingers, she hadn't been able to hide that. She hadn't wanted Micah's help, but at the same time, he'd known that he was the only one she truly needed. Not just for his medical expertise. It was something more. He knew Kenzie had feelings for him, but they were buried under layers of betrayal and pain.

I'll help her see that we belong together.

It was a promise he'd made himself more than once that week. Seeing so much death and destruction, Micah needed to believe there was hope for beauty and life.

"There," he said, putting in the final stitch. He felt a deep sense of satisfaction when he stepped back to consider his work. "Mother, please wrap it snug, but not too tight." He looked to Mr. Walters. "You'll need to keep him off that leg. We need to give the skin a chance to knit."

"We still have that pair of crutches we could loan," his mother offered as she wrapped bandages around a thick padding of bleached cotton.

Micah nodded and washed his hands in the basin of soapy water his mother had provided. "Good. Frank's a tall boy, so they should be just fine."

"Son, why don't you go back to bed?" His mother's expression was tender and proud.

"No, I'll rest later. Right now, I need to go see someone."

He began to gather his things. "Just leave those," Mother told him. "I'll clean them and have them ready for you when you return." She smiled and returned her attention to the boy's leg. "Tell Kenzie we said hello."

He chuckled and leaned over to kiss her cheek. "You know me too well."

"Well enough that I won't even bother suggesting you take a bath and put on clean clothes."

Micah was already heading for the door. "That would take too much time."

Kenzie's frustration and anger at failing to get through the barricaded lines left her feeling out of sorts with everyone. Her mood was as gray as the rain-laden clouds. Why could no one understand her need to find George? She just wanted to see him—to know he was all right. He could be hurt and in need of help.

"I need to find him," she muttered under her breath, but for just a moment, it wasn't Cousin George's face she saw. It was Micah's. Her heart was betraying her again.

She marched into the warehouse, thoroughly annoyed with herself. Kenzie knew if she didn't get a hold on her feelings, Camri and Judith would never leave her be.

"Oh, Kenzie! Come and hear the good news!" Judith exclaimed. She hurried across the room to take Kenzie's arm. "Caleb and Patrick have come from speaking with the mayor. You won't believe what's happened."

Joining the happy foursome was the last thing Kenzie wanted to do. However, she knew if she refused or tried to avoid the situation, it would only stir up more attention. She let Judith pull her toward the others.

"Tell Kenzie what you just said," Judith encouraged.

Patrick's smile stretched from ear to ear, but it was Camri who spoke. "The mayor has agreed to reinstate Patrick's business license. He's going to be allowed to help with the rebuilding."

"Not only that," Caleb interjected, "but he agreed to issue Patrick a voucher in order to repurchase the things taken from him. We might even be able to get back his family home. Mayor Schmitz said he would check into it."

Kenzie knew without being told what was coming next.

"With everything in order, we told the girls to set the wedding date," Caleb finished, putting his arm around Judith.

Camri leaned into Patrick's hold. "Isn't it wonderful?"

"It is." Kenzie forced a smile. "It truly is. I'll be glad to help you with the plans."

Camri gave Kenzie's hand a squeeze. "And one day we'll do the same for you."

Kenzie didn't want to tell her friend that she didn't believe that day would ever come. Instead she gave a little nod. Before Camri could say anything else and cause more unintended pain, Kenzie spoke up. "I posted the notes about Cousin George and Dr. Fisher."

"What's that?" Caleb asked.

Camri nodded and let go of Kenzie's hand. "We heard about the board being put up at the relief camp so people could post notes about their missing loved ones. We thought we'd put up notices that we're trying to find George Lake and Micah."

"That was a good idea, but I wish you hadn't gone by yourself," Caleb said, fixing Kenzie with a stern look. "It's not safe out there."

Kenzie knew the dangers well enough. "We felt we had to do what we could. And now I'm back." She shrugged. "And no worse for the trip."

"Well, next time you want to do something like that, let me or Patrick know, and we'll go with you or arrange for someone else to do so."

Kenzie nodded, knowing it was senseless to argue. To her relief, a young soldier entered the warehouse.

"Who's in charge here?" he called out.

Caleb immediately went to him. "I am. Have you brought us supplies?"

"Yes, sir. Where do you want them?"

"Just bring them in here. We don't want them getting wet. It hasn't started to rain yet, has it?"

"No, sir, but it looks to pour any minute. If you can lend a hand, we can get everything inside faster."

"Of course." Caleb gave Patrick a nod. "How about it?"

"I'd be insulted if ye didn't ask me," Patrick said with a grin.

"We'll all help," Camri said. "I'll get some of the residents to help as well. Good thing we finished clearing out the corner. We'll just stack it all over there." She pointed to the far side of the warehouse room.

Kenzie followed the others and picked up a twenty-five-pound bag of beans. She thought back to the days she'd helped her father in the mercantile. Her great-uncle had owned the store, but her father managed it. He did such a good job that eventually his uncle left him not only the store, but also a tidy sum of money. It had taken her father from a position of workingman to owner, and eventually into a relaxed retirement. Of course, even that hadn't been good enough to put her on equal ground with the likes of Arthur Morgan's family. She knew they had never approved of her. They'd made their feelings well known.

She tried not to let the pain of those memories fuel her anger at failing to find George. It wouldn't help matters for her to get lost in times gone by. Nothing positive could be gained by remembering her mistakes.

Kenzie made trip after trip with the others, going back and forth and carrying whatever she could until her arms ached. The hard work helped clear her mind. The army had been generous with the amount of food they'd sent. The folks at Solid Rock wouldn't eat high on the hog, as folks might have said back in Missouri, but at least they would eat.

Once the wagon was unloaded, the work to inventory and put everything away began. Camri organized the residents, and Kenzie decided to catch up on some cleaning. With the kitchen area void of people for the time being, she could get the floor scrubbed. She discarded her hat and coat and pulled on an apron to protect her dress. A pail awaited her at the back door. She picked it up, grimacing. She'd worn a blister on her hand from all the toting and fetching she'd been doing.

Better not let Micah see it, she mused. *He'll no doubt think he needs to render medical attention.* Of course, he'd need to be there in order to do so. She frowned. *Please, God, let him be all right.*

Outside, the caldrons were bubbling with fresh hot water. Sprinkles of rain had begun to fall, causing Kenzie to hurry as she filled the bucket, but it was no use. The rain was pouring steadily by the time she made her way back into the warehouse. She bent to place the pail of water on the kitchen floor, and a strand of wet hair fell across her forehead. With a sigh, Kenzie straightened and pushed it back into place. It was impossible these days to worry about keeping up appearances. To think she had been worried about keeping ash out of her hair. Thankfully everyone else was in the same position, and no one really cared. Fighting to stay alive had taken precedence over every other earthly concern.

Kenzie added soap to the water and picked up her scrub brush. She got on her hands and knees and began the rhythmic motions of cleaning. There was something calming in the mundane washing of the floor, although she'd gladly give up the job should someone else want it.

Camri's raised voice caused Kenzie to look up. Her friend was in a heated discussion with Patrick regarding something. Her arms flailed in different directions as she pointed and tried to explain her desires. Kenzie couldn't help but smile as Patrick moved closer and bent until they were almost nose to nose. He countered her commands with a few of his own. They were a feisty couple, to be sure. Kenzie had never once argued like that with Arthur. Of course, she fought like that with Micah all the time. Micah Fisher was possibly the most obstinate man she'd ever known.

How she longed to see him—just to know he was all right.

And then, as if he knew what she were thinking, Micah appeared at the door of the warehouse. He was drenched from the rain and filthy from what had no doubt been hours of tending patients. His dark blue eyes narrowed as he scanned the room. The look on his face was determined.

Kenzie's gaze locked on him. She was unable to look away. Her heart beat faster, and she dropped her brush. Caleb and Camri spied Micah and rushed to his side. Judith gave a squeal of delight and came from where she'd been helping make up the cots. They all crowded around him, everyone talking at the same time. Micah nodded and even commented, but still he searched until his eyes met Kenzie's. She watched as his stern expression changed. The corners of his mouth lifted in that smile he often got when dealing with her. Without warning, he stepped past his friends and marched across the warehouse like a man on a mission.

What was he doing? Kenzie thought about standing but wasn't sure her legs would support her. No matter how hard she tried, she couldn't look away. She watched Micah move toward her and then felt her breath catch in her throat as he reached down to take hold of her. He drew her to her feet without so much as a word and then pulled her tightly to him. Kenzie could only look up in wonder, which made it easy for Micah to complete his next move. With one hand still holding her fast, he put his other hand to the back of her head and lowered his mouth to hers.

The kiss was unlike anything Kenzie had ever experienced.

There was a hunger, a desperation in the way he kissed her. Almost without realizing what she was doing, Kenzie's arms went around his neck, and she began to kiss him in return.

She lost track of time altogether. They might have been that way for mere seconds or days. It didn't matter. The effect was overwhelming and rendered her completely speechless as he pulled away.

"The thought of doing that is all that got me through the week," Micah said, grinning like a mischievous child. "I'm so glad to see you're all right."

Kenzie just stared at him in dumbstruck silence. Caleb and the others were coming toward them, and the looks on their faces left little doubt that they were just as stunned as she was.

Micah released her and turned to face the others. "Sorry. I didn't mean to ignore you, but I had business to take care of."

Caleb laughed. "Seems your business is similar to our own." He looked at Camri and Judith with raised brows. "Maybe you girls should be planning a triple wedding instead of a double."

CHAPTER 4

Micah had never been happier. He knew by the way Kenzie had responded to his kiss that she had wanted it as much as he did. As he released her, he could see the confusion coursing through her. Her eyes—those incredible big blue eyes—were wide with wonder, and her lips were slightly parted as if she were about to speak but couldn't find the words. He wanted very much to kiss her again but knew they'd do better to talk instead. However, Caleb and the others weren't about to let that happen.

"Micah, where have you been? We've been so worried," Camri said first.

He forced his gaze away from Kenzie and smiled. "Working. There was this earthquake and then a fire, and lots of people were caught up in it. Maybe you read about it in the paper?" He grinned as Camri rolled her eyes.

"We knew you were working, but we hadn't heard anything from you. We were worried, and I know your poor parents were half sick, wondering if you were still alive." Her tone was more chastising now.

Micah shrugged. "I couldn't leave. There was too much to do. Even earlier today, they brought me a man who'd just been dug out of the rubble. People had to focus on putting out the fires, but there are so many places untouched by the fire that the earthquake put in ruins. Unfortunately, rescuers are still finding people who were trapped."

"Can they be saved after such a long time?" Judith asked.

"Some, but it's becoming less and less of a possibility." Micah remembered the young man from that morning. "I've seen far too many die, however, and the camps are filled with injured people." He glanced around the warehouse. "I see you've got things in order here. God certainly knew what He was doing in getting you to buy this place, Caleb."

"We've said as much ourselves," Caleb agreed. "Although the army was quick to set up the relief camps and at least get folks the shelter of a tent and hot food."

Micah nodded. "They're forcing people to work at gunpoint. I got stopped myself. The poor boy couldn't have been much more than eighteen or nineteen. Pointed a rifle at me and told me to get to work. I tried to explain I'd just come from working an entire week with very little rest."

"What did you do?" Judith asked.

"I wasn't sure what I was going to do. I tried to show him my medical bag, but he wasn't interested. But then one of his officers came and realized the situation. He sent me on my way, which was good, because I probably would have collapsed from fatigue had I not kept moving for home."

Caleb smiled and put a hand on Micah's shoulder. "You saw your parents?"

"Yes. I even managed to sleep a couple of hours and then stitched up a leg wound. Then I had to come here." He grinned and looked back toward where Kenzie had been.

But she was gone.

"We heard many of the hospitals were destroyed. What are they doing to replace them?" Camri asked.

Micah frowned. He wanted to know where Kenzie had gone. He wanted to speak with her and tell her how he felt. No doubt the kiss explained that in part, but he needed to tell her.

"Micah?"

He looked at Camri, who, by her expression, seemed to understand. "She slipped out the back door."

He nodded. "We can talk more about the hospitals, but first I need to speak with Kenzie."

Camri gave a slight huff. "I think you said plenty."

He grinned and looked at his best friend and then Patrick. "Gentlemen, I'm sure you understand."

"Of course they do," Camri interjected. "We all do. Go find her." She pointed the way.

Micah didn't need to be encouraged further. He headed out the back door of the warehouse and glanced around. The rain was no deterrent to a man in love. He went to one side of the warehouse, but she wasn't there. He went quickly to the other side and saw her standing by one of two large kettles. It looked like she was stirring something.

She was soaked. Her auburn hair had been braided and twisted together, but pieces had pulled loose and hung limp and wet around her face. Never had Micah thought her more beautiful.

"Kenzie." He said her name with a soft reverence. She didn't seem to hear him.

He stepped to her side and glanced down at the water in the kettle. It was empty. She kept stirring with her paddle even though there was nothing there to stir.

"Kenzie."

She looked up, almost startled to find him there. He grinned as her expression again took on a look that suggested wonder—awe.

"Don't ever tell me again that you don't have feelings for me." He chuckled. "I think we both know now that it isn't true."

Her eyes narrowed as she seemed to regain her wits. "I was . . . worried about you, just like the others. I'm glad you're safe. That's all."

"That's all? You kissed me like that because you were glad I'm safe?" His right brow arched up.

She bit her lower lip and looked back at the water. After a long pause, she said, "Yes."

He leaned closer. "Have you been kissing all of the survivors like that?"

She dropped the paddle and moved away from the kettle. "I didn't kiss you. You kissed me."

He laughed. "I may have initiated the kiss, but you, my dear, most assuredly returned it."

"It didn't mean a thing."

He laughed even more and reached for her. "Shall I do it again and prove my point?"

She whirled on her heel and put several steps between them before crossing her arms. "What do you want, Micah?"

"You, of course. I want you to stop denying your feelings for me. I want you to admit you love me, because I love you. You do know that, don't you?" He closed the distance between them. "I love you, Kenzie."

Her porcelain skin seemed to pale even more. "Don't. Don't love me. I don't want you to love me, and I most certainly do not want to love you."

He felt almost sorry for her. There was fear in her eyes. "Kenzie, you don't need to be afraid. I'm not Arthur Morgan. I would never treat you as he did."

"You can't promise that."

"Yes, I can." He reached for her again, but she quickly sidestepped him and put out her hand.

"Don't. Please." Tears slid down her cheeks and mingled with the rain. "I can't bear it."

Micah studied her for a moment. He wanted to punch Arthur Morgan square in the jaw for how he'd wounded this beautiful woman. "All right. I won't touch you. Not right now, anyway. But I won't stop trying to prove that you can trust me."

She shook her head and lowered her hand. "Please just go."

Micah didn't want to upset her any further. She needed time to consider all that had happened. He could at least give her that. "All right. I'll go. But I will be back. We will talk about all of this. I love you, Kenzie, and I want to marry you." He started to leave, then stopped and gave her an enormous grin. "I rather like the idea of a triple wedding."

Kenzie shook from head to toe as she watched Micah walk away. She could hardly comprehend what had just happened. He had declared not only his love for her, but his desire that they marry. What in the world was she going to do?

For a few minutes, she paced back and forth by the laundry kettles. The rain had stopped, and she knew it wouldn't be long before someone showed up to feed the fires or start a load of wash. If she stayed here, she'd only have to answer a lot of questions. Questions she wasn't at all sure she could answer for herself, much less anyone else.

"I want you to admit you love me, because I love you." Micah's words rang over and over in her head.

The feelings she had suspected he had for her were now openly declared. They couldn't be taken back. Worse still, Micah had pried open the place where she kept her own feelings safely hidden away.

"I want you to admit you love me. . . ."

She stopped pacing and closed her eyes as if she could undo

the last half hour. She tried her best to make an argument for why he was wrong.

I'm only reacting to the trauma we've all been through. Difficult times make people do and say things they might otherwise never do. That's all that happened. I kissed him back because I was relieved he was alive and well. Nothing more.

She opened her eyes again and squared her shoulders. "I don't love him. I don't."

The earth began to shake under her feet. It was nothing more than a tremor, one of the many they'd had after the large destructive quake, but this time it seemed different. It was almost as if the earth were mocking her.

When the shaking stopped a moment later, Kenzie glanced heavenward. "Lord, I don't know what to do. Help me, please."

Caleb, Patrick, and Micah walked to Mayor Schmitz's temporary office. Micah had plans for getting back to work, but Caleb couldn't help teasing him about his encounter with Kenzie.

"So, did you win her over at last?"

Micah laughed. "I did my best. She's not going to let herself love me easily. She's much too stubborn."

"Well, for sure ye got her attention," Patrick threw in.

"I'll say," Caleb agreed. "She all but melted into the floor from that kiss. You were quite the brazen paramour. I don't think I've ever seen anything quite like that."

Micah sobered and shook his head. "She was all I could think about. All week long, when I thought exhaustion or discouragement would overtake me, Kenzie kept me going. Kenzie and thoughts of that kiss."

"I can see how that would keep a man going." Caleb nodded as they reached their destination. "Here we are. Are you sure you won't join us? This will be an important meeting. We're supposed to get an update on the sewers and water pipes."

"I can give you the same information without sitting through hours of boring conversation," Micah replied. "They're busted all to pieces. At least that was the report I heard yesterday from one of the firefighters I worked on."

"I'm sure you're right, but given we're already looking at plans for rebuilding, things like pipes have to come first. They'd be smart if they redesigned the entire city, but water is the most important. I suppose we'll hear from Phelan about his ideas for pulling water from the Tuolumne River. No matter how many times he proposes them, Schmitz and Ruef find ways to ignore him and promote their own belief that the Spring Valley Water Company can provide for all our needs. Never mind that they failed us miserably."

"Well, good luck accomplishing anything," Micah answered. "Now that the shock is wearing off, business as usual will be everyone's goal. Especially where Schmitz and Ruef are concerned."

"There are a great many men who intend to see it done otherwise." Caleb slapped Micah's back. "Don't be a stranger, and try not to take on responsibility for all the injured and sick. They've brought in doctors from around the area, as well as shipped out a great many of the worst cases to Oakland. At least that's what the mayor told us in the last meeting."

"It's true, but they're still finding people in the rubble, and there are still plenty who need my help." Micah smiled. "But believe me, it won't be long before I come visiting."

The meeting was already underway when Caleb and Patrick slipped into the back of the room. The men at the front of the room were arguing loudly.

"Mayor, you know as well as the rest of us that Ruef did it so no one but his beloved Home Company would be able to bid. No one else even knew the bid was out for telephone service."

Another man jumped in. "Ruef posted that notice in the ruins of City Hall, demanding bids be received by three that afternoon. No one even knew where to bring the bids."

Caleb leaned over to Patrick. "It seems our hopes of being rid of Ruef were short-lived."

Patrick nodded and crossed his arms. No doubt he was worried about whether Ruef's actions would also bring an end to Schmitz's promised reinstatement of Patrick's business. Caleb looked around the room but saw no sign of Ruef. He was probably too much of a coward to show his face. He had to know Schmitz would be dealing with an angry group of men.

"I need everyone to calm down," Schmitz said, motioning with his hands as if he were trying to stuff everyone's rage into a box. "Right now we have a city to rebuild, and that cannot happen until we clear away the debris. United Railroads has agreed to put up a bunker at First and Mission. Wagons loaded with the rubble that is not reusable will be brought to the bunker. From there it will be hauled away and dumped into the bay. This will create additional acreage to build on. However, before that can happen, we will need every available man, woman, and child helping with the cleanup. We intend to salvage what we can."

An elderly man got to his feet. "The army shot my son-in-law." The statement rendered everyone else silent. "He was doing nothing more than going through the rubble of our business. They didn't even ask him who he was." The old man's eyes dampened. "My daughter is now a widow with five young ones to raise."

Schmitz ran a hand through his wavy hair. "That is unfortunate, sir. However, you must understand that looters and thieves are everywhere. The soldier responsible no doubt made a mistake, but you see the problem with our situation. People need to be obedient to the law officers."

"Which brings up a good point." Another man stood. "Who's in charge?"

Caleb listened as the arguments began to build again. The army believed they were in charge and had probably kept crime down in the midst of the chaos. However, the National Guard felt they were equally in charge, as did the city law officials.

"Folks," the mayor said over the crowd, "you need to calm down. The army is only helping temporarily. They are maintaining order while your city officials coordinate relief and recovery."

A young clerk came up to Caleb and Patrick. "I wonder if you would both step outside with me."

Caleb frowned but nodded. He and Patrick followed the young man into the hall.

"Right this way," the clerk said, looking over his shoulder. He led them to an office down the long, dimly lit hall. Opening the door, the young man stepped back. "Mr. Ruef would like to speak with you."

Caleb stiffened, as did Patrick. A quick glance into the room revealed Ruef sitting at a desk, its surface cluttered with stacks of books and papers.

"Yes, gentlemen, do come in."

"What do you want?" Caleb asked, moving to stand in front of the desk. He didn't look back to see if Patrick had followed.

Ruef craned his neck to look past Caleb. "Mr. Murdock, I want to speak to you as well. If you would allow for bygones to be bygones in the spirit of our sad city."

Caleb looked toward the door, where Patrick's large frame filled the opening. He could see apprehension and anger in Patrick's eyes. For a moment, Caleb feared Patrick would walk away, but finally the big Irishman came into the room.

Patrick's eyes narrowed. "And what would ye be wantin' to speak to me about?"

Ruef smoothed his mustache. "As I said, in the spirit of our sad city, we must put aside our past differences and make changes. Mayor Schmitz advised me to do whatever it took to see you were compensated and your business restored. I'm happy to say I have arranged everything."

Caleb could feel Patrick's tension. He was like a cat ready to spring. He put his hand on Patrick's shoulder, but he looked at Ruef. "That is good news. I hope it also means that Mr. Murdock's family home will be returned as well."

"It does. I cannot vouch for how much damage it might have sustained from the quake, but it was not at risk from the fire."

"And what of his business inventory and all necessary licenses?" Caleb asked.

Patrick remained silent, although Caleb knew it would take nothing more than a single snide comment or negative word from Ruef to throw him into action.

"It's all been arranged. I have vouchers here that will allow you to pull money from the mint, as well as clearinghouse certificates established by the mayor's office. Area merchants have all agreed to honor them. I've also had some of my men round up a large inventory of tools and supplies that you might have had prior to . . . well, that's unimportant at this point in time." Ruef gave a nervous smile. "Suffice it to say, we have been more than generous, hoping to go beyond the loss and compensate you for monies you might have made. Outside you'll find a large freight wagon loaded with various tools of your trade, as well as a fine team of Belgians that are also yours to keep. What we haven't been able to provide, you will be able to purchase with the vouchers."

He held out a sheet of paper, and Caleb took it.

"As you will see in this letter, we took you at your word—that is, we agreed with the amount you listed on the ledgers you submitted from your previous business. The monies you claimed were taken from your bank accounts and business assets have been approved, and all that we have provided will compensate for that."

"But it won't bring back my father."

Ruef looked at Patrick for a moment. Caleb hoped he wouldn't foolishly suggest that Patrick's father got what he deserved. Right now, Caleb wanted nothing more than to see Patrick secure what was rightfully his. Their battle with Ruef could wait for another day.

Ruef cleared his throat. "No, I'm afraid it won't. You have my utmost regret for that. However, I hope you will see that we are all doing our best to put aside the past in order to build for the future."

"So that's the way it's to be, then?" Patrick asked. The undercurrent of anger was clear in his voice. "In the spirit of rebuilding our broken city, we'll just sweep aside the wrongs done in the past?" His Irish brogue was thickening with emotion.

Ruef had the good sense not to react in anger. "We can hardly change what's happened, but a good man looks to the future and how to make things better. Isn't that true?"

"And yer a good man, looking to the future?"

Ruef shrugged. "I'm doing what I can, Mr. Murdock. Hundreds, nay, thousands are dead, and millions in damages have all but shut this city down. It seems the petty differences of old squabbles—even the major ordeals of our encounters—pale in comparison to seeing these poor folks get the relief they deserve. I believe even God himself would agree with that."

Caleb wanted to ask Ruef what he knew about God but held his tongue. He pushed the letter Ruef had given him toward Patrick. "Are these figures agreeable?"

Patrick did nothing but stare at Ruef for several seconds, then finally he glanced down at the paper. If he was as surprised as Caleb had been, he didn't show it.

"Here are all the papers you need to prove your business

and home ownership. The previous tenants have already left the city, so the house and attached shop have been abandoned. You'll be able to start business immediately, and I know that Mayor Schmitz is anxious for you to help with the downtown restoration. Your prior experience with commercial construction is invaluable to us at this time. There will be a meeting in three days with other contractors and business owners. All the details are in the folder. Plans need to be drawn up to decide what will be rebuilt and what will be abandoned. We'll expect you to be there, Mr. Murdock." Ruef held out a thick folder. "The vouchers are on top."

Patrick took the folder but didn't bother to look inside. Ruef seemed about to say something else, then seemed to think better of it.

"I'm sure Mr. Murdock will be available for the meeting," Caleb said.

"If you would be good enough to sign this, acknowledging receipt of compensation," Ruef said, holding out another piece of paper.

Caleb took it and looked at it. It was simple and to the point. He handed it to Patrick. "It's safe to sign."

Patrick looked up from the letter. "I'll be needin' a pen."

"Of course." Ruef quickly complied.

Patrick signed the receipt and tossed it atop the mess on Ruef's desk. He followed that with the pen. "Now, if that's all . . ." He looked at Ruef as if challenging him.

Ruef gave a cool smile. "It is. If you take the door to the left of my office, it will lead you downstairs and out into the alley. You'll find the horses and freight wagon awaiting you there. My man is expecting you."

Patrick fixed Ruef with a hard gaze. "In the spirit of rebuildin', I'll keep my peace, but there is bad blood between us, and an Irishman can't be easily settin' that aside—even if he is a man of God."

He didn't wait for Ruef to reply but strode from the room. Caleb looked back at Ruef and shook his head. He wanted Ruef to account for so much, but now wasn't the time.

"Good day, Mr. Ruef."

Walking away was the hardest thing Caleb had ever done, but he kept going. The day would come, he promised himself, when Ruef would account for all the wrong he'd committed. It might be a long way off, given the current situation, but it would come.

CHAPTER 5

Twenty?" Micah looked at the tables set up for surgical procedures. "Twenty gunshot victims?" Most of the patients were conscious and in pain. The man nearest to Micah begged to be put out of his misery.

"They were shot by soldiers," the nurse told him. "Some of them more than once." She sounded as disgusted as he felt.

"It's bad enough we have thousands of earthquake and fire injuries to contend with, but the army has to make it worse by sending us gunshot wounds as well?"

"I'm afraid so." Micah turned to find one of his associates, Dr. Nystrom. The older man shook his head. "And it's not just the army. Any ninny who has declared himself a law official is out there abusing his power to shoot and kill."

"It's out-and-out murder for those who die."

"And additional work for us if we want them to live," Nystrom replied. "I'll take this side, you take the other. Nurse, get me someone to assist."

She nodded and went to do just that.

Nystrom motioned to Micah. "Come on, let's get scrubbed up."

Micah could see there was nothing else to be done. He certainly wasn't going to convince the army to stop shooting people. San Francisco was in a state of madness. He would have thought lives would be considered dearer after losing so many to the earthquake, but if anything, it had created an insanity that seemed to discount that precious commodity.

"Have new supplies come in?" Micah asked, shedding his outer coat.

"Yes, thankfully," Nystrom said. "A ship came from Oakland, loaded with everything we needed. God bless those people and so many others across the country. From what I've heard, money and supplies are pouring in."

"That is definitely something to thank God for." Micah rolled up his shirt sleeves.

They washed and prepared for a day of surgery. As repulsed as Micah was by the army's casual attitude toward life, he couldn't keep his thoughts from drifting to Kenzie. He prayed God would show him how to win her. He knew he would have to move slowly, and that wouldn't be easy. He loved her and wanted very much for her to be his wife, and he didn't want to wait. Maybe it was the earthquake and seeing life easily lost on a day-to-day basis that made him feel so urgent, but he was desperate for her to see that they belonged together.

By nightfall, another dozen patients had been brought in—all with gunshot wounds. Over the course of the day, Micah had repaired more than fifteen such injuries and assisted in two cranial surgeries. Neither of the latter two patients survived. They simply needed more than this facility could give.

Rather than go home, Micah collapsed on a cot in a storage closet. The room was used exclusively by the doctors to catch up on rest. Dr. Nystrom had brought Micah here and commanded him to sleep, then given the nurse strict orders that Micah wasn't to be disturbed for at least six hours. Given his state of exhaustion, Micah didn't argue.

He also didn't bother to take off his shoes. He simply pulled a blanket across his body and closed his eyes. His last thoughts were of kissing Kenzie.

"Patrick has done such a good job repairing things," Caleb said, looking around his house. He went to the fireplace and knelt to look up inside. "He said everything, including the chimney, is in good working order, and we can move back in anytime."

Judith looked toward a long section of fresh plaster. "Camri will have to have the walls repapered."

"Or you can arrange it, since this will be our home, at least for a time."

Judith shook her head. "I'm no good at things like that. Your sister, on the other hand, has a wonderful way with it. I think the job should be hers, if it doesn't add too much to her schedule."

"She won't mind that. My sister is always happiest when she has a stack of projects requiring her attention." Caleb stood. "Except for a few knickknacks breaking, we fared pretty well."

"We were very blessed." Judith went to the piano. Something had fallen on it and gouged the beautiful wood. She ran her hand over the damage.

Caleb came up behind her and wrapped his arms around her. His hand covered hers. "It will still sound beautiful. Why don't you play us something?"

Judith would have much rather remained there in Caleb's arms, but she nodded and took her place at the keys. She began to play a Beethoven piece and glanced up with a smile. "You were right. It sounds perfect."

"Your playing always sounds perfect," Caleb replied.

"I didn't mean it that way, and you know it." She looked down.

"Well, it's not the most expensive piano in the city, and certainly not as fine as the one your grandmother owned."

"Perhaps not, but that piano was destroyed." Judith let her fingers dance over the keys. She was never quite so happy as when she was playing the piano. "I'll never forget the first time I played Grandmother's piano, however. It was the finest instrument I'd ever touched. Even Cousin Victoria's poor playing had a ring of beauty." She stopped abruptly. "Victoria!" She looked at Caleb. "I never even thought to contact her. She must have heard about the earthquake by now. She must wonder about her family. Oh, I feel terrible." She stood up and moved to Caleb's side. "What can we do? We must get word to her and let her know about her father and brother. Grandmother too."

"Do you know the name of the finishing school she's attending?"

"No. Only that it's in Switzerland." Judith frowned. "I wish I'd paid closer attention, but I was terribly sick when she left." She couldn't help remembering that only a short time ago, she had nearly died from poison her cousin Bill had given her. He had resented her for claiming her rightful inheritance, and hated their grandmother for giving it to her.

Caleb seemed to consider this a moment. "We could go to her fiancé. What was his name?"

"Piedmont Rosedale. I heard Grandmother say his house was in a peculiar location for a man of his great wealth. Apparently, he built some monstrosity overlooking the ocean."

"I know exactly where it is. Rosedale's oddities are known to one and all. I think we should pay him a call. Let him know about the other family members and see how we can go about contacting Victoria."

"Can we go now?" She touched his arm and looked up into his chocolate brown eyes. She had fallen in love with him at first sight, and being so near to him caused her breath to catch in her throat. "Please?"

He touched her cheek. "Of course, my darling. For you, I would set San Francisco back to rights—turn back time—whatever it took to make you happy."

"You make me happy." Judith smiled. "I've never been happier. I suppose that sounds strange, given all that's happened, but I mean it. I don't mind living at the warehouse and working in the kitchen. So long as you are there—or I know you soon will be—I find I can face anything."

He leaned over and kissed her gently on the mouth. Judith was still in awe of how such a simple action could send her heart racing. When he straightened, she smiled again.

He grinned back, then took hold of her arm. "Come along, Miss Whitley. We have business to attend to, and I won't have your flirtations distracting me. It's scandalous enough that we've been in the house alone for at least fifteen minutes. What will the neighbors say?"

She giggled and let him lead her out to the horse and wagon. His car had been confiscated by the army, but Judith didn't mind. She'd always loved horses, and the wagon, albeit uncomfortable, was just a minor inconvenience. Besides, the horse could get them through areas that a car could never pass.

They made their way out past Golden Gate Park, where thousands of tents had been erected in precise order. People were everywhere, and the army was clearly present. Judith saw long lines formed where various goods were being distributed. There were also lines of able-bodied men and women registering to work.

"They're keeping folks fed, clothed, and busy," Caleb commented, snapping the reins lightly. The horse picked up its pace a bit. "That's always key to keeping people happy. Without it, they'd have open rebellion, even riots on their hands."

The tents had been set up in military fashion with only a small amount of space between each one. People, however, were doing what they could to make their allotted space a home. One tent had a framed piece of embroidery hanging from the outside tent wall. It read, "God Bless Our Home." On another, someone had pinned lacy curtain panels along the entry flap.

People had also brought what possessions they could and arranged them to create some semblance of normalcy. Judith saw a man in a full suit and top hat sitting on a ladderback chair outside his tent. He was reading the newspaper as if nothing were amiss. Here and there children played, and mothers cooked over stoves of expedient design. One woman had even set up her treadle sewing machine and was busy making something.

"They are trying their best to go on," Judith murmured.

"The alternative would be to give in to hopelessness," Caleb countered.

"Yes, and that would be worse by far." Judith thought of all the money she'd been left by her grandmother. "Caleb, is there anything I can do? I mean, I have my inheritance."

He turned to her, his expression admiring. "You are such a generous soul. What we need to do is figure out what industries you now own. Perhaps with the shipping company, for instance, we can bring in supplies free of charge. I recall the Whitleys owned several lumber mills in Oregon. You could probably arrange to ship lumber down here for rebuilding."

She clapped her hands in excitement. "That would be wonderful! I never even thought of things like that. Oh, Caleb, I want to do whatever I can to help. I didn't earn that money. It was given to me, and I want to give in return."

Caleb kissed her cheek. "That's only a small part of why I love you."

They finally arrived at the Rosedale estate. The house looked like nothing Judith had ever seen. She gaped at it.

"Rosedale is known for his eccentric taste," Caleb said, amused at her reaction.

"What a strange house!"

The mansion was constructed of white marble in some places and brown stone in others. It had a sort of castle-like look to it with four corner turrets. But these were crowned with domes that gave the place a more exotic feel.

"It would seem he's mixed Romanesque with Italianate and Queen Anne," Caleb said, chuckling. "In fact, he's probably utilized every form of architecture to create this behemoth."

"I'm sure it must suit him. Grandmother said he was older than Victoria."

"Older is putting it mildly. He is at least as old as Victoria's father."

"How awful for her." Judith shuddered. "I can't abide that Grandmother would force Victoria into a loveless marriage with an old man."

Caleb brought the horse to a halt. He tied off the reins and set the brake. "Not everyone is as fortunate as we are."

"No, I'm sure that's true." Judith waited for him to help her down from the wagon. He took her arm and led her up the stone walkway to the massive oak doors.

It wasn't but a moment before a butler appeared. He looked at Caleb and Judith as if they were stray animals.

Caleb extended his card. "Would you please let Mr. Piedmont know that Miss Judith Whitley, cousin of his fiancé, Victoria Whitley, and Caleb Coulter have come to speak with him?"

The butler hesitated, then took the card. He studied Judith for a moment, then stepped back to allow them to enter. Once they were inside, he closed the door. "Please wait here."

He left them in a strange circular foyer. The white marble floors were spotless and polished to perfection. The walls were papered in gold-patterned material, and overhead a large gold and crystal chandelier hung but offered no light.

It wasn't long before the butler reappeared. "Come this way, please."

He led them through a maze of rooms. Judith found it all dark yet rather fascinating. Paintings of stern-faced men and women dotted the brief corridors. It was as if they kept watch on anyone who passed by and judged whether or not they were worthy of being there. They seemed very disapproving.

Finally, Judith and Caleb were shown into a library. This room was lighter and quite large. It was open to the third floor, with rows of books lining the walls from floor to ceiling on each level. There were two sets of stairs at either end of the room, and large windows let in light as well as gave a beautiful vista of the ocean.

Judith looked around but saw nothing of Mr. Rosedale. She started to question the butler, but he had already gone and closed the door behind him.

"This is quite the room," Caleb said, moving to the windows that looked out over the water. "Come see."

Judith joined him. "It's breathtaking."

"Maybe we should buy some coastal land and build our house there." He looked at her and winked. "Maybe just not this big."

"Or this fashionable." Judith couldn't help but giggle. "I'm afraid I'd get lost in this house. I thought Grandmother's was bad enough."

The door opened behind them, and Caleb and Judith turned to find themselves face-to-face with a rotund man. He had long sideburns whose purpose might have been to compensate for his balding head. He was perspiring, and it gave his ruddy complexion a fiery glow.

"Mr. Coulter. Miss Whitley. I must say, I had no idea of meeting either of you today."

"I realize that," Caleb said, stepping forward to offer his

hand, "but we felt, under the circumstances, that formalities could be set aside."

Rosedale's eyes narrowed. He looked a moment at Caleb's hand, then turned away, dabbing a handkerchief to his lips. "What circumstances?"

Judith didn't care for the way he'd snubbed Caleb. "You're engaged to my cousin, Victoria." She stepped past Caleb and went to stand in front of Rosedale, who had plopped his obese frame into a large overstuffed chair.

"You are the woman who stole her inheritance," the large man said matter-of-factly.

Judith was surprised by his comment. "I did no such thing. I didn't even know there was a fortune to be had. My grandmother arranged for my share to be given to me."

"Your share and everyone else's. I have knowledgeable friends who assure me that you now hold the family purse strings." He paused a moment and gave her a once-over. "You are without a husband, I believe?"

"She's engaged to marry me," Caleb interjected. "However, her marital status isn't the reason we've come. We wanted to know if you knew about the death of Victoria's family. Obviously you do, so we'll move on. Have you informed Victoria?"

"Why should I? It's hardly my job to be a messenger."

"I would think you'd want to offer her comfort in her time of loss." Judith could hardly believe his callous attitude. "She no doubt has heard about the earthquake and fire and must long for news of her family."

"I seriously doubt Victoria has worried overmuch about anything of the sort. She's not given to sentimentality. However, there is something I will address with you regarding that young woman. Since I have become aware that she has been left practically penniless, I find that I must reevaluate the nature of our relationship."

"But Victoria isn't—"

Judith was about to set him straight and explain that Victoria was far from penniless, but Caleb squeezed her arm. She looked at him and saw something in his expression that suggested she remain silent.

"You would abandon your fiancée because of her inheritance?" Caleb questioned.

"More like her *lack* of inheritance," the man said, dabbing at his mouth again. "The arrangement was made purely for financial reasons . . . and the unfortunate necessity to produce an heir."

Judith shuddered. The thought of marriage to this pompous toad was something she wouldn't force on anyone—not even her mean-spirited cousin.

"I'm afraid the loss of her family and wealth has left me with no choice but to discharge our agreement. In fact, I've already attended to the matter legally. My lawyer has tendered the papers to the Whitleys' law firm. Any further concerns you have, I suggest you take to them."

"Very well," Caleb said evenly. "Would you, however, be so gracious as to give us the name and location of the school in Switzerland where Miss Whitley can be reached?"

"I have no idea where it is, nor its title. I'm sure you can learn that from the law firm as well. Now, I bid you good day." He stared at Judith and Caleb with blank indifference.

Caleb didn't even bother to reply. He pulled Judith toward the door so quickly that she almost lost one of her shoes. He didn't wait for the butler or anyone else to show them back through the labyrinth of rooms, but made his way through the house as if he'd lived there all his life. It wasn't until they were well down the road that he let out what could only be described as a growl.

"That man was abominable."

"He was indeed." Judith shook her head. "I've never met anyone quite so terrible, and that includes my cousins—one of whom tried to kill me. I'm glad you kept me from setting him straight about Victoria's inheritance."

"I felt fairly confident the arrangement was purely for the purpose of marrying money to money. He doesn't need to know that your grandmother set aside money for Victoria. He doesn't need anything but a good swift kick to the backside."

"Or a fist to the mouth."

Caleb turned at Judith's comment. The scowl left his face, and he began to laugh. She was glad to see the darkness pass from him. She looped her arm through his.

"I'm so glad we're together because of love. If you were marrying me for my fortune, I would be devastated," she said.

Caleb sobered. "There are some who will say I'm doing just that. After all, we didn't become engaged until after I learned your true identity and that you were an heiress."

"Do you really think I care about that?"

He shrugged. "People can be cruel. I've seen all manner of suspicion created where money was concerned."

"I don't care what others might say." Judith met his gaze. "I only care about what you say. I know the truth, and so do you. Most importantly, God knows our hearts."

His expression grew tender. "I do love you, Miss Whitley. I would love you even if you were just Judith Gladstone, a poor girl from Colorado. Your money doesn't matter to me. I'll even sign papers to relinquish all rights to any say over your fortune."

She smiled. "That isn't necessary. What I have, I want to share with you. I've been so alone all of my life, and now I have a chance for real love and a family. I love you, Mr. Coulter. I've loved you since I first laid eyes on you, and I will never stop."

CHAPTER 6

Kenzie finished with her duties at the warehouse, then decided once again to try to get through the restricted areas to find her cousin. She'd heard there were parts of town where a person could slip through relatively unnoticed, and she intended to find one of those.

At ten o'clock every morning, Camri had taken to giving a reading class. Quite a few of the elderly people staying with them couldn't read, and with Camri's deep commitment to education, she felt it her duty to rectify the problem. Judith, meanwhile, was busy with preparations for lunch. She and some of the other women were laughing and sharing stories about their childhood days while they made noodles from the newly furnished flour and eggs. It was the perfect opportunity for Kenzie.

She slipped out the back of the warehouse, unnoticed by anyone but the collection of old men playing checkers on the outside tables.

"Miss Kenzie, you're sure purdy today," a man named Bartimaeus declared.

"She's purdy every day, you old codger," another man

declared. He grinned up at her, revealing that he was missing most of his teeth.

"You're very kind, Mr. Lawrence." Kenzie returned his smile and kept moving. If stopped to engage in conversation, she risked Judith or one of the other women coming outside.

She made her way toward the city, crossing Market near the Ferry Building. People were plentiful here, and with the general confusion and activity, it was easy for one woman to move through the crowd without drawing attention to herself. She decided to keep close to the bay and moved along the collection of piers. It was busy there as well. The piers that had been damaged were being inspected and repaired, while the ones that had remained safe were being used to bring in much-needed commodities. Normally, Kenzie would have avoided this area due to the sailors and rowdy stevedores, but like the repairmen, they were much too busy to pay her any heed.

Proof of the fire was everywhere. Some buildings had suffered complete destruction, while others were only partially destroyed. In some areas, there was even a building or two that had escaped the fire entirely.

"I want this first group of ten to start on the corner of Sansome and Green Street."

Kenzie paused at the sound of a man barking out orders. She couldn't tell exactly where he was, but she ducked behind a collection of charred framing and concrete to avoid being seen.

A moment later, a man appeared with a long line of tent city workers in two columns following him. He was explaining what he expected of them and where he would leave each group to start working. From her hiding place, Kenzie heard him announce that he would have three trucks positioned at various places for the loading of rubble. He told the men they would be fed at noon and dismissed at six, but only if they were steadfast in their work.

Once they had moved on, Kenzie hurried off in a different direction, hoping to avoid any possible encounter and the risk of getting pulled onto a work crew.

She made her way as best she could, thankful that many parts of the city were deserted. As she neared the industrial area where Lake Boxed Candies had been manufactured, it was clear that conditions were much worse. Here the fires had been all-consuming, and the earthquake had left indelible marks. For a long moment, all Kenzie could do was stare. It brought tears to her eyes. So many lives lost. So much property destroyed.

"Say there, ain't you a sight."

She stiffened at the words. She didn't see anyone nearby at first, but then a scraggly blond man, hardly more than a boy, stepped out from the shadows. On his heels was another boy who looked to be the same age, but his hair was coal black. Both were tall and muscular but filthy and clearly up to no good.

Kenzie moved away, only to have the men close the distance.

"You ain't gonna be all uppity now, are you?" the blond asked.

The other boy grinned. "We ain't had any decent female companionship since the fire."

"I'm neither uppity nor companionship for you," Kenzie replied. "I'm meeting my cousin. Perhaps you know him. George Lake."

The grinning boy shook his head. "Nope, don't know him and don't want to." He took hold of Kenzie's arm. "But you, lady, I do wanna know. I wanna know you real bad."

Kenzie pulled back, but he held her fast. The blond, not to be outdone, grabbed her other arm. "Unhand me. If you're looking to rob me, I have nothing. I brought neither purse nor coin." She struggled to free herself, but the duo were much stronger than she was.

"We ain't lookin' to rob you, darlin'. We just want a little friendly fun. We got a nice, quiet spot where we can have a real good time," the black-haired boy said, leaning down. He tilted his head to avoid the wide brim of her hat and pressed his lips against her cheek.

Kenzie fought to put distance between them, but it was no use. The hoodlums only laughed and held her all the tighter.

"You need to learn how to have fun," the blond said. "Come on, let's show her how to have a good time."

They moved toward the darkened abyss from which they'd emerged. Kenzie had no other choice but to scream, so she did. This startled the boys so much that they momentarily halted.

The blond looked at her and shook his head. "That weren't very nice."

"I'm not trying to be nice. Let me go." She screamed again, and the black-haired boy clamped a filthy hand over her mouth.

"If that's the way you want to be," he said, "then this ain't gonna be nearly as much fun."

Kenzie felt sickened by the young man's stench and the thoughts of what he had in mind. She found herself wishing she'd listened to everyone's advice and stayed home where she would be safe from such people.

"Halt! Unhand that lady!"

She felt a rush of relief at the authoritative voice. The young men loosened their grip, then let go of her in order to face their new opponent.

"What's the matter with you? We're just having a little fun with our friend," the blond declared.

Kenzie hurried away from the duo toward the two men who wore uniforms and badges. "I am not their friend. They accosted me."

"Is that right?"

The black-haired man shrugged and grinned. "Didn't mean no harm." He hit his buddy in the chest, and the two started to run down the alley.

The men at her side drew their side arms and fired, dropping both men with a single shot each.

She looked at the officers, stunned by their reaction. "You didn't have to shoot them."

"Riffraff. They won't learn any other way," the man nearest her replied. "It sets an example for the rest."

His partner moved to where the young men lay facedown in the street.

Kenzie's stomach clenched. "They were just boys."

"Foolish boys," the older officer declared. "Ma'am, this isn't a safe place for you. You need to get on home." He went to join his partner while Kenzie stared after them in dumbfounded silence.

"Let's put 'em with the others," the older man instructed, holstering his gun. He bent and hoisted the black-haired man over his shoulder while his partner did likewise with the blond. Neither officer seemed to feel even the slightest remorse for their action.

Kenzie watched as they moved off down the street, still struggling to believe what had just happened. While she was grateful for the rescue, she had never thought it would result in the death of her attackers. It was hard to understand. Surely the officers could have just taken the men into custody.

They were just boys. No more than seventeen or eighteen at the most.

Kenzie forced herself to move. It wasn't safe to stay here. She knew the situation could easily repeat itself if she wasn't careful.

She hurried to the chocolate factory and found a burned-out shell of brick and steel. She knew it was probably dangerous to go inside, but if Cousin George was here, she needed to know. If he were trapped or buried in the rubble, then maybe she could lend aid. It was doubtful, but it gave her the courage to go inside.

"Cousin George? Are you here?" she called, entering the area that had once been the office.

She saw the ashen remains of what had been a desk and chairs, as well as metal filing cabinets that had melted in the fierce heat. Had Kenzie not known what the office looked like prior to the fire, she certainly wouldn't have been able to make it out now. No doubt this was the scene throughout the city. It was hard to imagine a lifetime of work up in flames—yet here was proof.

Kenzie continued down the hall to the assembly room where she had once worked with Camri and Judith. The collapse of much of the roof allowed the sun to shine down on the devastation. There was nothing left.

"Cousin George?" she called again as she moved toward the machine rooms where the chocolate had been made. "It's Kenzie! Are you here, Cousin George?" She heard noise coming from the far side of the room. "Cousin George?" She strained to see around an impassable pile of debris.

"Kenzie, what are you doing here?" George Lake emerged from beneath a mangle of iron and steel. He appeared to be in one piece.

Kenzie rushed toward him. "I've been so worried about you. I didn't know if you'd survived the earthquake or the fires."

The short, balding man pushed up his wire-rimmed glasses. "There wasn't time to look for you. I figured you were safe, since you weren't downtown when the earthquake hit." He looked her over and nodded. "I see you're fine."

"Yes. We sustained some damage, but the fires didn't make it as far as our neighborhood."

"That's good," he replied. "That's very good."

"We're staying at the warehouse—the one you looked at when you were thinking about moving the factory. We opened a shelter there for some of the homeless." She looked around at the hopeless mess. "What are you doing here? None of this can be salvaged, can it?"

George shrugged. "Who can say until I go through it? I've been down here since things cooled off enough to get into it."

"Were you here when the earthquake hit?"

He nodded. "Me and a few of the boys had arrived. We sought shelter under one of the machines as it rained down brick and glass. We thought for sure we would die."

"I'm so sorry. I've been trying to find a way to get down here since it happened, but they have all sorts of roadblocks and sentries. Did the fire consume the factory that day?"

"No. It wasn't until the next day. A fireman came to tell us that we had to leave. The fires were spreading fast and were out of control. I had managed to pack up the important records, and we hauled off as much of the boxed chocolate as we could. I donated it to the relief camps."

Kenzie smiled. "That was an admirable thing to do."

"Wasn't much else to be done with it. It could hardly be sold in such conditions." He shook his head. "It's all gone now."

"You had insurance, however, so you can rebuild." She knew this because she'd handled the payments for his premiums.

"Yes, I had insurance, but apparently you haven't heard. Most of the companies are refusing to pay out."

"What? But how can they do that?"

George Lake pulled off his glasses and rubbed his eyes. "They can't afford to pay the claims. No one figured on something like this happening. The insurance companies weren't required to keep collateral equal to their policies, so there simply isn't enough to go around."

"I had no idea." She felt an overwhelming sadness for this man who had been so kind to her and her friends. "I'm so sorry, Cousin George."

"Well, what sabotage from my enemies couldn't manage, God did in one swift stroke."

She shook her head. "What are you talking about?"

"We both know Ghirardelli and Guittard wanted to see an end to my chocolate. They tried to see me ruined, but what they couldn't accomplish, God did through the earthquake."

"I don't think God wanted to ruin you, Cousin George." Kenzie was used to his fears of sabotage, but she'd never heard him bring God into the matter.

"Well, it seems to me that He did. Ghirardelli was unharmed. They've continued to work the entire time."

"You think God would allow San Francisco to be destroyed in order to ruin you as chocolatier?" She shook her head. "Even you have more sense than to believe that."

He frowned at her. "Then what? Why all of this?" He waved his arm at the destruction.

"Perhaps if this is to be blamed on God, then He did it to get the attention of all who live here. I mean, think of Sodom and Gomorrah. They had plunged into all sorts of decadence and sin just as San Francisco had. Maybe God felt total destruction was all that could be done to get our attention and bring about change."

"Then He is a cruel and heartless God, punishing the innocent for the sins of the guilty."

Kenzie shook her head. "I'm no theologian, cousin. I merely pose the suggestion that if God is the one responsible, then perhaps we should take heed. After all, are we truly innocent when we see evil happening and do nothing to stop it?"

He considered this for a moment. "I suppose I don't have an answer for you on that."

"Neither do I, but I think that instead of railing at God or blaming Him, we should be bowing before Him, praying to Him for guidance and direction. I believe God is good and that He has a plan in all that happens. Even when bad things happen, I feel confident that He will make something good out of it.

Perhaps He will open a door for you to have something even better—greater than before."

George's shoulders slumped. "I'm an old man, Kenzie. I don't have that many more years ahead of me anyway. Maybe it's best I just forget about making chocolate."

Gently, she said, "Perhaps you should. It's possible that this is the right time to walk away. But it's equally possible that it's not. You know, sometimes bad things happen and they're no fault or punishment to that person, but rather the circumstances of the moment. We live in a flawed world. The important thing is that we learn to trust God no matter the situation. There will always be evil men who plot against us and do us wrong."

She paused for a moment, thinking of Arthur. She wouldn't call him evil, but he had done her wrong. "There will also be people who simply seek to have their own way and aren't really striving against us but hurt us nonetheless. There are even people who cause us pain in perfectly innocent ways. It's a part of life, Cousin George. God allows us to make our choices, including how we will stand up to evil and wrongdoing."

The boys who'd attacked her on the way to the factory came to mind. Their choices had gotten them killed. Or maybe it was her choice that had caused their deaths. If that were true, how could she live with the guilt? She sighed.

"Cousin George, why don't you come to the warehouse with me? You can have a good lunch, and if you've nowhere else to stay, you'll be welcome to make it your temporary home."

He put his glasses back on. "I'd like that. My house was utterly destroyed in the fires, and I've been sharing a tent at the relief camp with an annoying group of young men. A little peace and quiet would calm my nerves."

She smiled. "I won't lie and suggest we have peace and quiet all the time, but we are fairly calm. Most of the folks staying with us are elderly and didn't feel they would be cared for properly at the relief camps. We have three good meals a day and clean cots and bedding to sleep on. I think it should suit well enough."

He nodded. "Well, let us be about it then. There's nothing here for me."

CHAPTER 7

"It's amazing," Caleb said as he drove Judith in the wagon to find her grandmother's lawyer. "Many men are setting up offices in the middle of their destroyed buildings so that people know where to find them. I doubt that will last once the reconstruction begins, but it does offer some semblance of normalcy. Not to mention that the restrictions are easing up and people are able to move around the city a little more."

"Is it safe?"

Caleb looked at Judith. "I would never put you in danger, so that should answer your question."

"I know you wouldn't." Judith gazed around them. "I've just heard such horrible stories."

"There have been some very bad situations, to be sure, but also some exaggeration. I promise we'll be just fine. We needn't even worry about being forced into the cleanup because we have papers to show we are busy with other ways of lending aid. But if you find yourself frightened, you can always scoot closer to me."

Judith noted a group of men handing pieces of concrete

down the line until the last man was able to toss the rubble into the bed of a wagon. "I have to admit, they've done a good job getting the streets cleared. Even if they've only managed to open a few. It's still progress."

"Now that things are calmer, we should see more and more progress. Mayor Schmitz is determined to put this city back together before the end of summer. That doesn't mean everything will be rebuilt, but he believes the debris will be cleared. They're dumping it into the bay to create the foundation for additional acreage. Of course, it won't make for a solid foundation, and everyone knows very well how that would be, should another big earthquake hit."

"Then why do it? It seems foolhardy."

"It is, just as the Bible warns about building your house on sand. But these are men of industry and commerce, and they are used to gambling on the future. Some are even confident that there will never be another earthquake like the one of April eighteenth."

"How can they suppose that?" Judith considered that kind of thinking very naïve.

"Some people say events like this come only once every one hundred years. However, others are confident that it could happen again tomorrow. It has to do with the earth having a lot going on under the surface that we can't begin to comprehend. Scientists are working to better understand earthquakes, but they have no way to predict them."

Caleb drew the horse to a stop in front of a small open tent that had been erected outside the building that once housed the Whitleys' law firm. The sign outside read, *Pettyjohn, Bridgestone, and Davis*.

"This looks to be it," Caleb said. "I'll go speak to the clerk."

Judith folded her gloved hands and whispered a prayer. She hoped it wouldn't be difficult to get information regarding her cousin. She watched as Caleb and the clerk spoke. She couldn't hear what was being said, but the clerk pointed off behind where she sat. It wasn't long before Caleb climbed back up into the wagon and took the reins. He didn't look happy.

"Well there's good news and bad. Obviously, the building was burned completely, but there was also a loss of life. Mr. Pettyjohn was killed in the earthquake."

"How awful. I'm sorry to hear that."

"As was I." Caleb put the wagon in motion. "However, the good news is that the clerks and other lawyers were able to move the office records to Mr. Bridgestone's residence ahead of the fire. They have set up business there temporarily. He gave me directions, so if you're up to it, we might as well make our way there now."

"I'm perfectly fine. All of my cooking duties have been given over to the other ladies, and I have the rest of the day completely free of responsibilities."

He chuckled. "Perhaps I should take you out for dinner and a concert."

"If such things still existed, I would let you."

"Oh, but they do. There's a band concert at Golden Gate Park tonight, and if you haven't noticed, there are a multitude of tent restaurants all over this area. We can sit on wooden kegs at plankboard tables and enjoy sandwiches and coffee for outrageous prices."

"I think I'd prefer our little warehouse. Maybe we could take a walk later." She offered him a sweet smile. "I might even be persuaded to share a kiss."

Caleb raised a brow. "Are you flirting with me, Miss Whitley?"

"Trying to. I suppose I'm very bad at it. I haven't had much experience."

He chuckled. "Well, with practice you'll become quite good, and I believe I'll take you up on your offer."

They drove in contented silence for several blocks. Both seemed too occupied by the destruction around them to do more than take it all in. On one street, Judith saw an entire row of houses all tilted to the right. They looked like dominos about to be knocked over. On the opposite side of the street, most of the houses looked to have collapsed, one floor on top of the other. Had people been inside them when it happened? Since the earthquake had taken place just after five in the morning, Judith imagined many had been crushed to death.

"I don't see how it can ever be made right," she murmured. "There's so much to do."

"True," Caleb agreed, "but human beings are a resilient bunch, and when they are driven to accomplishment, they do great things. I think you'll be surprised."

"I suppose, but so many are dealing with sorrow on top of the loss of property. Their loved ones have died. I know very well how that can discourage a soul."

He reached over and squeezed her hand. "You're missing your grandmother, aren't you?"

Judith hadn't really considered it, but now that Caleb had put it into words, she had to agree that she did long for the woman's return. "I knew her for such a short time. I wish she could have been with me longer."

"You made the most of that time. You went to live with her even though she was a complete stranger."

"Yes, and how glad I am now that I did, even with all of the trouble I faced there. I might never have learned as much as I did about my family." Judith was still trying to understand her past, which included being raised by a man and woman who weren't really her parents, but rather her aunt and uncle. She couldn't imagine the desperation of a woman stealing one of her sister's twin daughters to raise as her own.

"It's good that you know about the past, Judith," Caleb said, "but you mustn't dwell on it. You have a future ahead of you, and we will create our own family and memories. I presume you do want a family?"

She turned to him and saw his questioning look. "Of course I do. I hope we have a dozen children."

His expression changed to concern. "A dozen? Well, I hadn't thought of that many, but I suppose if that's what you desire, I will do my best to comply."

She felt her cheeks warm. "Oh, Caleb, I honestly don't care how many children we have, so long as we're together."

He nodded. "I feel the same way, and it isn't ours to decide anyway. Only God can create a life, and if He chooses to bless us with a dozen or just one child, I will be a happy man."

They arrived at the address Caleb had mentioned. Here the houses showed some signs of damage but overall looked to be in decent condition. Caleb helped Judith down from the wagon, and together they made their way up the stone walkway.

The door was quickly answered by a housekeeper who ushered them inside without question. "The front rooms have been converted to offices," she explained. "Just sit here, and I'm sure Mr. Bridgestone's secretary will be with you directly."

She left them in a small room that had once no doubt been a family parlor. It wasn't long before the pocket door across the room slid back and a man emerged. He took one look at Caleb and smiled.

"Caleb Coulter, as I live and breathe."

Caleb stood, smiling. "Samuel Deter. I haven't seen you since last year's Bar Association charity dance." The two men shook hands. "I didn't realize you worked for this firm."

"I was just hired on. Mr. Bridgestone is a good friend of my father's, and after Mr. Pettyjohn's death, he was looking to add to the firm."

"Then he chose well." Caleb turned and drew Judith to her feet. "This is my fiancée, Miss Judith Whitley. Judith, this is Sam, an old friend."

Judith smiled. "I'm pleased to meet you."

"Likewise. I've heard all about you. Goodness, you were all the firm could talk about until the earthquake. Quite an amazing story you have."

"It is," Caleb said, "and it's the reason we're here today."

Sam looked at Caleb. "Regarding the will?"

"Regarding Victoria Whitley. We've realized we have no way of knowing whether she's been informed of her father and brother's death."

"Grandmother's as well," Judith added. "Although she knew Grandmother was most likely going to pass."

"Of course. Let me explain the situation to Mr. Bridgestone. I'm sure he will want to discuss the particulars with you. Would you care for something to drink?" Sam glanced around. "I think the secretary is sorting records, but I don't mind getting it for you. We have coffee and tea."

Caleb looked at Judith, who shook her head. "No, we're fine."

Sam disappeared back down the hall for a moment, then returned just as quickly. "Mr. Bridgestone will see you. Follow me."

They were taken to a large office at the back of the house. Mr. Bridgestone was a man in his late fifties with salt-and-pepper hair and a mustache. He rose from the chair behind his desk and extended his hand as Caleb and Judith entered the room.

"I'm glad to be of service to you, Miss Whitley," he said, coming to stand directly in front of her. "Mr. Coulter." He gave a nod.

Judith took his hand. "Thank you for seeing us. We're concerned about my cousin Victoria."

Bridgestone nodded. "Yes, Sam mentioned that. Won't you have a seat? Sam has gone to find my secretary and have him retrieve the files related to your estate. Mr. Pettyjohn was in the process of readying them to be given over to Mr. Coulter when the earthquake struck."

"Has my cousin been notified of her father and brother's death?" Judith asked as she sat.

"No. We hoped to speak to you first. We felt that such news should come from you."

"We have no idea how to reach her," Caleb said, taking the seat beside Judith. "I'm sure you must have the name of her finishing school in Switzerland."

Bridgestone reclaimed the chair behind his desk. "Of course. We are the ones who issue the checks for the school. I have all of that information and can make sure you have it as well. Especially now."

"Why especially now?" Judith asked.

"Well, given the situation and your responsibility for Miss Whitley."

"My responsibility?" Judith looked at Caleb. "What is he talking about?"

Caleb shook his head. "I'm not sure." He looked at Bridgestone. "Maybe you should explain."

"Well, the matter is very simple. Miss Victoria Whitley has not yet reached her majority. She is nineteen and unmarried. You, Miss Whitley, are her only living relative, and as such, and because you are of age, you have become her guardian and she your ward."

Judith had never imagined that such a thing could happen. Victoria already hated her, and now that hatred would be fueled by the realization that Judith was in charge of her estate.

"But I don't want that responsibility. My cousin hates me." She hadn't meant to blurt it out, but now that she had, Judith felt it important to continue. "She resented my arrival and that our grandmother arranged for my father's money to come to me."

"You don't really have a choice in the matter," Bridgestone declared. "Although you could appoint someone in your stead. A trustee could be put in charge, but he would still need your approval on matters of wealth distribution."

Judith sank back in her chair. This news was not what she wanted to hear. She couldn't imagine what Victoria would do or say when she found out.

"First things first," Caleb said. "We need to let the school know what has happened and have someone there break the news to Victoria. Judith could write a letter, but as she said, Victoria hates her, and it might be better if your firm were the ones to get in touch with the school."

"We're happy to do so," Bridgestone assured them.

Sam returned with several thick folders. Judith felt her eyes widen at the sight of the papers. Sam only chuckled. "This is only a portion."

"My goodness, I'm glad you're a lawyer, Caleb. I should never be able to understand it all without your help," she said.

"That is the purpose of lawyers," Bridgestone said. He took the folders from Sam and dismissed him. Once Caleb's friend had gone, Bridgestone opened the top folder. "Mr. Coulter, I think you'll find everything in order. The files will show a complete accounting of each business and industry owned by your fiancée. The companies will all be notified that you are managing the legal affairs of Miss Whitley in the future."

"Thank you."

Caleb's assured tone helped Judith relax a bit. She was still overwhelmed by the thought that she was Victoria's guardian. That was a matter that needed to be changed immediately.

"Can Caleb be appointed guardian—I mean, trustee for Victoria? We are soon to marry anyway, and I will gladly let him manage all of my affairs. Could we go ahead and appoint him to be in charge of her now?"

"If that's what you want, Mr. Coulter can arrange it."

Caleb looked at Judith. "Are you sure that's how you'd like to set things up?"

"Do you mind?"

"No. Not at all." He smiled. "If it puts your mind at ease. However, I'm very busy at present, so would you allow Mr. Bridgestone to arrange it?"

Judith looked at the older man. "Would you?"

"Of course. I can get my staff on it immediately. I will also have a letter sent to the school. I presume you wish for us to continue payments for her needs there?"

"Yes. Absolutely. Give her whatever she needs."

"Within reason, of course," Mr. Bridgestone replied. "Payment for the school and her clothing allowance and personal needs as set up by your grandmother should be sufficient."

"That sounds fine for now." Judith couldn't imagine that her grandmother had been overly generous, but that could all be figured out later. "As long as Caleb is the one to handle Victoria, I believe I'll rest better."

Kenzie sat down beside Mr. Lawrence and began to unwrap the bandage around his lower leg.

"I never 'spected to have somebody like you takin' care of me," the old man said, chuckling.

"Well, we all do what we must," Kenzie replied. "I'm not very good at tending to my own wounds, but I have little trouble when it comes to other people."

She pulled back the dressing and surveyed the damage. The old man had been injured during the earthquake when he'd been struck by falling debris.

"How is it feeling?"

"Good," he answered. "Ain't givin' me no trouble."

She nodded and began to gently clean the wound. "Well, Dr. Fisher says that keeping it clean is the most important thing."

"And Dr. Fisher is happy to learn that you've heeded his advice."

Kenzie turned abruptly to find Micah watching her. She swallowed hard and turned back to Mr. Lawrence. "He's occasionally right in his thinking."

Micah laughed and joined her. He examined the wound and nodded. "You've done a good job with it, Mr. Lawrence. You should be right as rain in another week or so."

"I ain't done nothin' but let this purdy gal take care of me."

"She is very pretty, I agree," Micah said in a conspiratorial manner. "I would very much like having her take care of me."

Mr. Lawrence roared with laughter. He elbowed Micah. "You ought to marry her before she gets away."

Micah took the cleaning cloth from Kenzie and finished what she had started. "I have plans to do just that, but she's kind of strong-willed."

Kenzie rolled her eyes and started to leave.

"Miss Kenzie," Mr. Lawrence called out.

She turned back. "What is it, Mr. Lawrence?"

"You could just marry me instead."

Kenzie couldn't help but smile. "I'll keep that in mind." She hurried to get away before Micah could say or do anything to stop her. Let him rebandage the old man.

She thought maybe she'd escaped Micah's attention when he still hadn't found her fifteen minutes later. She felt an odd sense of disappointment and chided herself.

You know he only confuses you. Stay away from him, and you'll be much happier.

She told herself this over and over as she checked to see if the laundry was dry. She needed to keep herself safe and free of emotional entanglements.

She jumped at the sound of someone behind her but relaxed when she saw that it was only Cousin George with the widowed Mrs. Andrews. Ever since Kenzie had brought George to the warehouse with her, Mrs. Andrews had made him her pet project. Surprisingly enough, Cousin George didn't seem to mind her attention. Perhaps they would court and marry. Kenzie smiled. But at the thought of courtship and marriage, Micah wormed into her mind once again.

"You are positively radiant when you smile," Micah said. "Were you thinking of me?"

She turned to find him at her side. A hint of a smile played on his lips. "Yes. I was just thinking of you going away—back to wherever you came from."

"Ah, but you *were* thinking about me." His grin broadened.

"You are impossible." She hurried down the laundry line to put distance between them.

Micah didn't seem to mind, however. He followed her at a leisurely pace. "You did very nicely with Mr. Lawrence's wound. It gave me an idea."

Kenzie refused to let him draw her into conversation. She continued to check the clothes, and when she found the third line was dry, she began to remove the pieces.

"I could use a nurse to accompany me when I visit the relief camps this week," Micah said. "We doctors are rotating responsibilities there, and it's my turn. You could come with me. We're very shorthanded."

"I'm not a nurse." Kenzie bit her lip. She hadn't meant to speak.

"No, but with a little training, you will be quite competent." He stepped up behind her and leaned close to her ear. "And I'm very good at training."

She couldn't keep from shivering at his breath on her face.

Why didn't he just go away and leave her alone? Couldn't he see how hard he was making this for her? Of course, he could. That was why he kept doing it. She frowned and tried again to set her resolve against him.

"I need help, Kenzie, and you need to see that we could be good together. If you come and work with me, you'll be able to get to know me, and then you won't be so afraid of me."

Kenzie turned to face him, which was a mistake. It put them almost nose to nose, much too close for comfort. "You don't frighten me."

"Then what?"

She shook her head. "You . . . you confuse me, and I don't want to be confused."

His blue eyes seemed to search the very depths of her soul. Kenzie wanted to turn away, but she couldn't. She was completely under his spell.

Micah reached up to cup her chin. "I would love to help you not be confused." He stroked her cheek with his thumb. "Help me out at the camp, Kenzie. We can get to know each other in a completely nonthreatening way. You can assist me with the wounded and sick and get to know me better."

He leaned forward as if to kiss her, and Kenzie closed her eyes. When his kiss didn't follow, she quickly opened them again to find Micah looking at her with a serious expression on his face. Kenzie couldn't quite swallow the lump in her throat. Why did he have to have this kind of effect on her?

"I need you, Kenzie."

She knew he meant something more than his request for nursing help, but she wasn't about to acknowledge it. Instead she gave him a curt nod and pulled away from his touch. "I'll help you with the relief camps, but only if Camri thinks she can spare me from my other duties."

He smiled. "I'll go talk to her right now."

CHAPTER 8

By the middle of May, city officials deemed it safe for banks to open their vaults and safes. Most people had adhered to the recommendation that the vaults be allowed time to cool, especially after seeing the explosive results when some immediately tried to retrieve their funds. However, the delay created a sense of panic, and in a city where panic was already far too prevalent, people's patience ran thin.

The cleanup of debris was another source of irritation to the public. The army's attitude was that people who didn't work didn't qualify for their accommodations and help. This brought protests from some and begrudging acceptance from others. But even with all the problems, the work continued, and headway was being made.

Donations flooded in from all around the world to fund the rebuilding and see people adequately cared for. Liberal gifts of food, clothes, and other supplies were sent from as far away as Europe, and San Franciscans were grateful. Many citizens left the city and had no intention of returning, but those who stayed were determined to do what they could to make their town the beautiful gem it had once been.

Kenzie found her work with Micah extremely satisfying. She had never considered nursing as a profession but the thought regularly crossed her mind these days. The more she learned about the body and the care involved, the more intrigued she was. She had to admit Micah was a good teacher. He was patient and deliberate in his methods, and it was easy to get caught up in his passion for healing. Their time together also helped her see him as something other than the man who was in love with her.

"You're a fast learner, Kenzie. I couldn't ask for a better nurse," he told her as they walked back to the warehouse.

"Your training and instructions are easy to follow." She hadn't meant to say as much, but his comment caught her off guard.

Micah chuckled. "Would that you'd listen to me regarding our relationship as easily."

Kenzie pretended to ignore him. The day was warm with clear skies, and for the first time in a long while, the burnt scent seemed to be gone. "It's really a lovely day."

"Indeed it is. One of these days I'm going to take you sailing."

She looked at him. She hated to admit that she was more and more attracted to him. Micah was a handsome man. His black hair had just a hint of wave to it, and the way he combed it back from his face always seemed to allow for one or two strands to fall back over his brow. Those strands begged her touch, though Kenzie would never give in to that urge.

"If you keep looking at me that way," he said, "I'm going to kiss you right here on the street."

Kenzie frowned and turned her attention to the sidewalk. It only served to make Micah laugh. He seemed amused by her unwillingness to give in to his flirtations. Other men might have given up long ago, but not Micah Fisher.

"So will you do it?"

She didn't even glance his way. "Do what?"

"Go sailing with me."

"I know nothing about it and therefore would make a poor companion. I'm certain, however, that there must be any number of young ladies who would cherish such an outing."

For a moment he said nothing. Kenzie wondered if he was offended. If he was, then perhaps it was for the best.

"I'm certain you'll enjoy it. There's nothing quite like it."

She decided it would be safer to change the subject. "I've been thinking that I might want to attend nursing school after things get back to normal. I enjoy helping people."

"I think you enjoy helping me even more."

She sighed. "You are probably your greatest fan, Dr. Fisher, but I am honestly intrigued more by the intricacies of medicine. Hmm, maybe I should become a doctor instead of a nurse."

"You'd make an excellent doctor. We could team up and open an office together. How easy that would be for a husband and wife. We could get a large house and turn part of it into examination rooms."

Her heart skipped a beat at the thought. Kenzie shook her head to regain control of herself. "Why did you become a doctor?"

He shrugged. "I wanted to help the sick. From my youth, it was all I wanted to do."

"I'm sure your parents are proud."

"Mother and Father wanted only the best for their children, as most parents do. However, I think my father thought I might follow in his footsteps and become a preacher. We used to sit up late sometimes and talk about the Bible. He taught me Latin and Greek, which served me well in my medical training. We would discuss the Bible and the meaning of words. Words are very important, I came to learn. Sometimes things get misinterpreted."

"Your father's preaching is easy to understand. I was never enthusiastic about church before coming here. It seemed more of a gathering place for complaining and gossiping."

Micah nodded. "Every church has a bit of that, because the congregation is made up of fallible human beings. We all have our bad sides."

"Even you, Dr. Fisher?" She looked at him. "Surely not. I thought you were practically perfect—that is, I thought *you* think you are practically perfect."

He laughed. "No, I think you had it right the first time. You think I'm practically perfect, and I am . . . for you. But that's because you love me."

"You're impossible. I've never made such a declaration." She picked up her pace, hoping to leave him behind, but he only lengthened his strides.

I don't love him. Kenzie bit her lower lip. *He's very nice—sometimes—and a good doctor. No, he's an excellent doctor. I admire his abilities. Nothing more.*

She repeated these things over and over in her head. They were nearly back to the warehouse, and she needed to take her thoughts captive. If she didn't, it wouldn't bode well for her. Camri and Judith were merciless in demanding to know all the details of her time with Micah. They were constantly reminding her of how much he cared for her, and if Kenzie gave them the slightest reason to believe she returned his feelings, she would never hear the end of it.

She was about to bid Micah good-bye when she spied Cousin George sitting at one of the tables outside the warehouse by himself.

"I wonder what's going on," she murmured.

"What?" Micah asked.

"My cousin. I thought he was going to be tied up with business today." She made her way to the table. "Cousin George is something wrong? Are you ill?"

He looked up at her and seemed almost lost. "I am perplexed."

Kenzie sat down opposite him. "About what?"

"Well, you know that I had meetings today regarding the business?"

"Yes. You were going to speak with the insurance people and the bank."

George nodded. "But there was something more. Something I didn't mention because I wasn't even sure I would go."

She wasn't sure if she should press him for more. "I see."

"No," George said, shaking his head, "I don't think you do. I was invited to come for a meeting at Ghirardelli."

This was surprising news. "And did you go?"

For a moment, George Lake just sat silently, contemplating his hands. Finally, he looked up and nodded. "I did. Although even as I approached the building, I was arguing with myself to turn back."

"What happened?" She couldn't believe her cousin would go to the men he deemed his enemy.

"They were very gracious. They told me they were heartily sorry for my loss and commended me for my excellent candy."

Kenzie smiled. "So they weren't seeking to destroy you after all?"

George shook his head once again. "No. In fact they offered me a position."

"A position? At Ghirardelli? Doing what?"

"They want my help developing new recipes. They want to buy some of my recipes while I develop additional ones. They will give me a contract for the next ten years with an option to renew if I desire."

Kenzie considered this news for a moment. "But if you work for them and sell them your recipes, then you wouldn't be able to continue with Lake Boxed Candies."

"But I wouldn't be able to anyway." He looked at the table. "My insurance company isn't going to pay anything. They've been completely ruined by this earthquake and fire. My meager savings isn't enough to entice a bank to give me a loan to rebuild, so I am unable to move forward."

"I'm sorry, Cousin George. This must be a terrible blow."

"The worst of it is that I would actually consider their proposal if I thought it was trustworthy."

"Why do you suppose it's not?" Micah asked. "The Ghirardellis are good people. They are known to be generous to their employees and customers."

"But I know they wanted me out of business. They must have. There were far too many incidents that had to come at the hands of a saboteur."

"Cousin George, isn't it possible that those incidents were just the normal things that happen in business dealings?" Kenzie gently asked. "Machinery breaks down. Parts wear out. People leave employment without warning. It doesn't mean that anyone is seeking to harm you. Don't you think maybe it's time to put the past to rest? If these people are offering you a legitimate contract and you would like to take them up on it, then I think you should. And even if someone did try to hurt you in the past and ruin your business, that doesn't mean you should mistrust everyone."

"Kenzie is quite right," Micah said. "Sometimes people hurt us, but that's no reason to believe everyone will do likewise. Sometimes you have to let go of your fears and step out in faith that something good can come of your trust."

Micah's words cut Kenzie to the heart. Against her will, she met his gaze. His expression was void of emotion, but his eyes bore into hers. He was talking to her—she knew that full well. She also knew he was right. When was she going to heed her own advice?

Victoria Whitley stared in silence as the schoolmistress explained the details of her situation. Her grandmother, father, and brother were dead. Well, good riddance. Equally good—wonderful, in fact—was the news that her engagement had ended. Piedmont Rosedale had dissolved their agreement due to his certainty that Victoria's grief would be overwhelming and the time needed for mourning would interfere with his plans for marriage.

Fool. She knew very well that he was concerned about whether or not she would inherit the Whitley fortune. Frankly, it was something she'd like to know the answer to herself.

"I am sorry, my dear. This is difficult news to bear. However, you should not worry about your future. Your solicitor has assured us that your expenses will continue to be covered."

"I want to go home." Victoria met the schoolmistress's surprised expression. "I *must* go home." She knew if she wanted to get anywhere, she would have to play up her devastation.

"But, child, there's nothing you can do there. Your home was destroyed. You wouldn't even have a place to go to."

"I must see my papa's grave. I must kiss his headstone." Victoria squeezed a tear from her eye. "And my dear brother—oh, my heart is filled with grief. My sorrow is too great. Bill was my dearest friend in all the world."

"My poor child." The headmistress touched a lacy handkerchief to her own eyes. "Of course you must return home, if that is your desire."

Victoria nodded. "I will never find comfort until I am there."

"I'll prepare things immediately. You will need someone to accompany you. I'll see if I can arrange that as well."

Victoria didn't want to argue with the old woman that she was more than capable of traveling without a nursemaid. Better to remain silent and endure whatever the schoolmistress deemed necessary. Victoria knew very well she could finagle things to her liking later.

"Why don't you go ahead to your room? I'll have your dinner

brought there and speak to your roommates about what has happened."

"Thank you." Victoria put her hand to her eyes and walked slowly from the office.

It was difficult to keep her steps slow when she felt like running and shouting for joy. Ever since her engagement was announced, she had been plotting ways to rid herself of that fat toad, Piedmont Rosedale. Bill had suggested she could always kill him after they wed, and then she'd inherit his wealth and be set for life. Bill never had trouble considering the option of murder, but such things left a bad taste in Victoria's mouth. She didn't mind people dying. In fact, it was welcome news when the dead included those who had made her life miserable. However, she didn't want to be the one responsible.

Now, thanks to the earthquake, she didn't have to worry about it. Her ridiculous father was dead, and her evil brother could no longer harm her with his schemes and nonsense. Better still, her overbearing grandmother was gone too. No longer could she order Victoria to wear obnoxiously childish fashions or dictate how she spent her days.

Reaching the confines of her room, Victoria closed the door behind her and leaned back against it. A smile curved her lips, and she fought back the laughter that threatened to bubble over. She was free. Truly free. She would return to San Francisco, lay claim to her inheritance, and leave that cursed town and all her memories behind. She was young and beautiful, and although she wouldn't inherit as much money as she might have prior to Judith Whitley's appearance, she would still have a decent amount to live on. More than enough to entice a handsome man to make her his wife.

"A handsome *rich* man. A man of my choosing."

CHAPTER 9

Micah sat in his father's study, waiting to speak to him alone. With the arrival of summer, the parsonage was a private home again, but there were always people about, and today was no exception, given his mother was hosting a tea.

The door finally opened, and his father stepped into the room. "Sorry. You know how hard it is to get away from your mother and the church ladies."

"I do." Micah laughed. "I don't know how you do it. They always seem to want your attention."

His father closed the door, then plopped down in the chair beside Micah. "I listen to their complaints and worries—something a great many husbands refuse to do. It's important to a woman to listen to her, not merely talk to her. Sometimes we must put ourselves in their place but not be overtaken by their complaints or concerns. It's the same for men, although their manner of complaining isn't usually accompanied by tears."

Micah nodded. "It's the same for my patients. I have to have compassion for what they're feeling without getting overwhelmed by it. If I let myself get carried away, then I'm of no use to them as a doctor."

His father steepled his fingers and nodded. "It's a fine line to walk. Pastors and doctors can easily become like mythological heroes of old, and that too is dangerous. If we allow praise and gratitude to turn our heads, we also become useless."

Micah leaned forward. "I've always admired the way you handle yourself with the congregation."

"It's sometimes hard, especially with certain people. . . ." He grinned. "Those who are irritatingly sure they know more than anyone else and those who simply want to argue no matter the topic."

Many was the time Micah had seen his father deal with those people as well. "God's definitely given you more self-control than He has me. I would no doubt tell them exactly what I thought."

"Which is why it's best you aren't a preacher," his father said, laughing. "So why do you want to talk to me?"

A sigh escaped Micah. "I'm in love."

"I know." His father sobered. "Kenzie Gifford."

"She's been hurt so badly, and she's terrified to let herself fall in love again." Micah eased back in his chair. "The thing is, I know she loves me."

"I was surprised when she agreed to work with you."

"As was I," Micah admitted. "However, I think she did it more for herself than for me. I think she wanted to prove that working with me would have little or no effect on her. Maybe there was also the desire to learn. She's found working with the sick and injured appeals to her, and she's good at it."

"But telling me this isn't why you're here today." His father gave him a sympathetic smile.

"No. I suppose I'm hoping for wisdom. I want to ask her to

marry me. I've told her I want to marry her, but I haven't made a formal proposal."

"And you think now is the time?"

Micah considered the question. "I don't know. I would have married her six months ago. I fell for her almost the first time I laid eyes on her." He shook his head. "Of course, she'd have nothing to do with me then, but now, well . . . I'm certain of her feelings as well as mine."

"Still, time is important for healing. As a doctor, you know that full well. If you try to rush using a broken bone, the results are disastrous."

"True, but if a patient refuses to even try to use the injured limb after a proper time of healing, they create an entirely different problem. They can render themselves crippled for life."

His father smiled in a knowing way. "Of course, each patient heals differently."

Micah sighed. "Yes."

After a long pause, his father spoke again. "Have you prayed about this?"

It was a question Micah had anticipated. "I pray about it all the time. I pray for her healing and for her to see the truth of her heart and mine. I pray for wisdom to do the right thing and for patience."

"The book of James says that if we lack wisdom, we may ask and God will give liberally. He won't scorn or find fault for the request. But it also says that we must ask without doubt of His giving it."

"I remember you making me memorize those verses when I was young." Micah had memorized a good portion of Scripture, but those verses in James held a special place in his heart. "They've guided me in all of my decisions."

"Then trust that God will give you wisdom in this one. He never fails, as you well know. He won't suddenly start now because it's a matter of the heart and not the head." His father put his hand on Micah's shoulder. "Why don't we pray about it together?"

"I think we should all move back to the house," Camri said, looking at Judith. "Now that we're down to just ten residents, I think we can put someone in charge for the evening and nighttime hours." They had just finished cleaning the entire warehouse top to bottom, and it was only eight o'clock in the morning.

"I wouldn't mind living here permanently if we could add some rooms for privacy," Judith said. "There's still so much to be done in the city, however, and I don't know what we might do to help or if we can do it here."

"I know," Camri agreed. "But frankly, I'm desperate to sleep in a real bed and have the comforts of home. I want to move forward with our original plan of this being a shelter for the women and children who have need, but right now the relief camps are seeing to that. The time will come, once things return to normal and the relief camps are gone, that something like this will be needed."

"The relief camps are doing such a good job," Caleb said, joining them, "that they're having trouble getting people to return to their homes."

Kenzie shrugged. "Perhaps they have it better there. Food, clothes, even medical needs are all met in one form or another. They're required to help with debris removal and such, but given that many of them didn't have work before, perhaps this is a better way."

"It's possible." Caleb looked at his sister. "I'm in complete agreement about getting you ladies back to the house. We'll have to keep taking care of ourselves until new help can be hired though. Mr. and Mrs. Wong have informed me that they're going to stay on, helping their friends and family. It seems the city is trying to force the Chinese to relocate, but the Chinese are adamant about remaining where they were."

"What will happen to them?" Camri asked.

"I can't say for certain, but I've heard they appealed to the empress of China to speak to President Roosevelt. They believe it is entirely racially motivated, and I'm inclined to agree. The defense by the Board of Supervisors is that the Chinese were the ones who had the highest number of plague cases and thus they are dangerous to the rest of society. Chinatown is in the heart of the city, and if its residents become ill, they could potentially spread diseases to the rest of San Francisco."

"Never mind that cases of the plague have appeared elsewhere."

Everyone turned at the new voice to find Micah walking in through the open warehouse door.

"Sorry to jump into the conversation uninvited, but I couldn't help it. I was just listening to a tirade of this very thing yesterday," he said.

"I suppose the medical officials believe the Chinese are responsible for the plague," Camri said more than asked.

"Not the wise ones. They understand that it's filth and rodents that cause the spread of that disease. Unfortunately, you find filth and rodents in poorer neighborhoods, and the Chinese are among the poorest. But the Irish and Mexican communities suffer poverty as well and have also known plague."

Caleb nodded. "Well, as I see it, the Board of Supervisors and Mayor Schmitz think they can use the earthquake as an excuse to snap up the most valuable pieces of property for themselves. I can't say I mind that they're refusing to rebuild the Barbary Coast, but I hardly think it right to push out thousands of people who own businesses and homes and have done nothing but contribute to society."

"Be careful, Caleb. Some people would challenge you and say that the owners of those houses of vice and libations were also contributing to society," Micah said with a grin.

"They contributed, all right," Camri countered, "but it wasn't to the good of society."

"Granted."

"What brings you here today?" Caleb asked Micah. "I suppose you've come for your nurse."

Micah nodded. "I have. I'm making my way to one of the relief camps and need her assistance."

Kenzie nodded. "Let me get my apron." She had taken to using a pinafore apron to keep her clothes clean. Camri had suggested the use of a red cross, as well, so Kenzie had sewn one onto the bodice. She rather liked the distinction.

She went to the peg and took down her apron while Micah continued talking to the others. Donning it, she straightened the bodice, then tied the sashes in a bow at the back. She made her way back to the others, pushing down her anxiety. Lately she'd been thinking about her future, and thoughts of Micah and medicine were ever present.

"What about your hat?" Camri asked.

"I'm not going to bother. It only gets in the way."

"I feel the same," Micah agreed. "That's why I seldom wear one." He smiled at the others. "We shouldn't be long. Come, Nurse Gifford."

Kenzie rolled her eyes and followed. The day was threatening rain but warm. She thought about making small talk, but that seemed silly. Micah would want to talk about their relationship and the future, no matter what topic she chose. However, to her surprise, he said nothing. Nothing at all.

At the relief camp, Kenzie made the rounds with Micah,

doing as he instructed. From time to time, she took the initiative before he could instruct. It seemed to please him that she knew what to do. Then again, she knew Micah was pleased with her no matter her actions.

She'd been thinking a lot about his comment regarding trust and letting go of the past. It was the right thing to do. Arthur was no longer part of her life, and she couldn't impose his poor judgment and hurtful actions on Micah. At least she shouldn't. She should accept that Arthur had done what he felt best and move on with her life.

But I'm afraid.

Fear was the major reason she couldn't allow herself to love Micah. She was certain of that now but had no idea how to stop being afraid. When she thought of admitting her feelings for him—of letting him love her—she felt almost sick with fear. What if he turned out to be just like Arthur? So many of the things Micah said were the same words Arthur had spoken to her.

"Doctor, come quick! My mama's havin' a baby!"

The boy's frantic declaration brought Kenzie out of her thoughts. Micah squatted down to the young boy's level. He whispered something to the boy, who nodded enthusiastically. Micah handed him some coins.

"Show us the way." He gathered his bag and looked at Kenzie. "You're in for an amazing part of medicine."

Kenzie couldn't even imagine. She followed him as he hurried after the boy down rows and rows of tents. All at once, the boy came to an abrupt halt.

"She's in there." He pointed.

"All right. Now you go do as I told you and be quick," Micah instructed.

The boy raced off.

"What did you tell him to do?" Kenzie asked.

Micah smiled over his shoulder. "I told him to gather his friends, go to the man selling shaved ice, and buy them all a treat. That'll keep him busy and happy." He didn't wait for Kenzie's response, just pushed back the tent flap. "I'm the doctor."

Inside the tent, a young woman moaned in pain. An older woman sat by her cot, wiping her forehead. "I'm Miss Snyder. This is my niece Mary," the older woman said. "The baby is coming fast. I don't know anything about delivering it, so when I heard you were in the camp, I sent the boy to find you. We don't have any money to pay you."

Shaking his head, Micah unbuttoned his coat. "I didn't become a doctor in order to get rich. I'm happy to help you for the mere satisfaction of bringing a new life safely into the world." He handed Kenzie his coat. She set it aside, awaiting his instructions. He rolled up his sleeves. "Miss Snyder, would you be good enough to get some hot water so that I can wash up?"

The older woman turned to the expectant mother. "Mary, I won't be far. You just listen to the doctor."

The girl nodded and tried her best not to cry out.

"We'll need some towels, as well," Micah said as Miss Snyder headed out of the tent.

Kenzie felt sorry for the frightened girl and knelt by her cot. "Dr. Fisher is the best doctor around, so you don't need to worry."

"Besides," Micah said, "you've done this before."

"No," Mary moaned. "This is my first."

Kenzie was just as confused as Micah. "What about the little boy who came to get us?"

"That's my husband's son. He was just a babe when I married his pa." Mary buried her face in the pillow and cried out.

"Well, there are surprises around every corner," Micah said, not sounding the least bit concerned.

Miss Snyder returned with a basin of water. "I brought some soap too."

"Thank you." Micah took the offered bar of soap and washed his hands thoroughly. He nodded to Kenzie. "You too."

She got up and did as he said. When that was finished, Miss Snyder gave them a clean towel to dry off on.

Micah quickly got down to business and checked the baby's progress. He looked up in surprise. "This won't take long. Come see, Kenzie. The head has crowned."

Kenzie moved to stand beside him. She looked at the exposed woman, not feeling the slightest bit of embarrassment or shock as she had thought she might.

The woman cried and writhed in pain. "Ohhhhh, please. Please make it stop."

Micah turned to Miss Snyder. "I'll need those towels now and some clean water."

Kenzie watched in awe as the baby came into the world only moments later. Micah's procedures were unknown to her, but she found it all fascinating as he tied off and cut the cord. The infant gave a weak mewing cry that grew in volume as Micah quickly examined him before wrapping him in a towel.

"You have a healthy boy, Mary."

The young woman began to cry. "A boy? Dan will be so happy. He wanted another boy so Timmy would have a brother."

Micah handed the baby to Kenzie. "Clean him up."

She froze. She'd never held a baby, much less a newborn. How in the world was she supposed to manage this?

If Micah noticed her apprehension, he said nothing. He was already busy tending to the mother. Miss Snyder stood bawling in the corner and offered no help. Kenzie whispered a prayer and looked down at the baby. The boy had calmed and now looked up at her with dark blue eyes. There was something in his expression that reached deep into Kenzie's heart.

She went to the small table where Miss Snyder had put the towels and basin. With great care, Kenzie placed the baby beside the towels and unwrapped him. He was so incredibly tiny. She felt completely inadequate to manage what needed to be done, but she was equally determined that she wouldn't let Micah down.

The basin of water seemed the perfect size to bathe the baby, but Kenzie wasn't sure if the water would be too warm. She felt it. It seemed cool enough.

But what if I drop him? He's already so slippery, and the water will only make him more so. She looked at the baby and then back to the water. She bit her lower lip and put her hand around the back of the infant's neck and head. With her free hand, she gripped the child's legs and lifted. It seemed manageable. She dipped the baby into the water and did her best to wash him thoroughly. He seemed at ease with her actions, giving Kenzie more confidence.

Feeling she'd done all she could, Kenzie carefully lifted the baby back out and dried him with a clean towel. She smiled in amazement. A new life had come into the world, and she'd been a part of it.

"I have diapers and pins in the trunk, Auntie. A gown too," Mary said from her bed.

Kenzie frowned as Miss Snyder brought her the items. She'd never diapered a baby. She wasn't even sure how to go about it. She looked at Miss Snyder, who shook her head. Kenzie turned to Micah. To her surprise, he was watching her.

"I . . . I don't know what to do. I've never been around babies."

Micah chuckled. "Well, there's a first time for everything." He pulled the sheet over Mary, then joined Kenzie and Miss Snyder. "Let me demonstrate."

Kenzie moved aside as he picked up a square of white flannel and folded it over several times, making a small triangle.

"With boys you put extra padding up front. With girls you put it in the back. Works best that way," he said. He positioned the flannel triangle under the infant, picked up one of the pins, and drew the edges of the diaper together. "See, you just pin it snug, but not so tight that it cuts off circulation. Oh, and you always put your hand inside the fabric where the pin comes through. Better to stick yourself than the baby."

Kenzie was amazed at how easily he handled the situation. Once the baby was diapered, Micah dressed him. "If you have a blanket, I'll show you how to swaddle him. Babies prefer to be wrapped snug."

Miss Snyder pulled a baby blanket out of the trunk and handed it to Micah. Kenzie watched carefully as he tucked the blanket across the baby, drew up the bottom, then pulled the other side across. The baby was soon wrapped up like a mummy with only his head visible. Micah smiled down at the infant, then took him to his mother.

"Here you are, Mary. He'll want to eat, and the sooner you put him to suckle, the better."

The young woman nodded, not at all embarrassed by Micah's intimate references. Kenzie watched in surprise as the woman opened her bodice and put the baby to her breast. The newborn rooted a moment, seeming uncertain what to do, but Mary gently guided his mouth, and soon he had the right idea.

The tender scene brought tears to Kenzie's eyes. It was too much. Micah was talking to Mary and Miss Snyder, so Kenzie took the opportunity to step outside.

Once there, she didn't stop walking—or crying. She felt so confused. She was delighted at what she'd just participated in. Happy that she could be of use in something so wonderful. But also overwhelmed by a surge of emotions she couldn't even name.

She hurried back to the warehouse but didn't bother going inside. Instead she walked behind it so she could look out at the bay and regain control of her feelings. She wiped her eyes with the edge of her apron, then hugged her arms to her body.

"God, I don't know what to do. I don't know why I feel so . . . so . . ." She had no words and stood there in silence for some time.

"Kenzie?" She turned at the sound of Micah's voice. His expression was full of concern. "Are you all right?"

"I hardly know. That was such an amazing thing to witness, but . . . I feel . . . I don't know what I feel." Her tears flowed anew.

Micah's expression softened. He came to her, and for just a moment, Kenzie thought he might embrace her. And in truth, she wanted nothing more.

Instead, he reached up and touched her wet cheek. "You did really well. I wasn't sure if you'd had any experience with babies, but for someone who hadn't, you managed it perfectly."

"It was unlike anything else. It was like seeing the hand of God right there—giving life after so much destruction and death." She sniffed and shook her head. "It's like telling me there's hope for the future."

He smiled. "There's always hope, Kenzie. God is hope itself. Our sorrows may reign in the past, but God alone controls the future. We can put our hope in Him and know that no matter what happens, He will never leave us nor forsake us."

She nodded. "I know you're right."

"Good. Then maybe you'll also accept that I'm right when I say I think we belong together. I'm asking you to be my wife, Kenzie."

"I barely know you." Her words were just a whisper.

"You know me better than most." His voice became low and husky. "You're afraid."

"Yes."

"Of me?" he asked with a look of doubt.

"Of everything. I'm afraid of you—of us. I'm afraid to feel and be hurt again. I'm afraid of making foolish mistakes. I'm afraid we'll have another earthquake. Sometimes I wake up at night thinking I smell smoke." She knew she was rambling.

Micah put his hands on her shoulders. "Kenzie, you don't have to be afraid of me. I love you. No one will ever love you as much as I do."

"Arthur once said the same thing to me."

Micah pulled her into his arms and kissed her. Kenzie stood stiff, unwilling to give in to the desires that coursed through her. Seeming to understand what she was doing, Micah pulled back just enough to speak.

"I'm not Arthur. I'm Micah Fisher, and I want to share my life with you. I love you, and I want to marry you, and I'm pretty sure you feel the same way."

"I . . . don't know what I feel. I want to believe you. I want to . . ."

"Just tell me you'll give me a chance. Agree to court me—to consider marriage. Don't make me pay for Arthur's mistakes."

She nodded, knowing that more than anything, she wanted this chance for herself.

Micah gazed at her in surprise. "Are you saying yes? Yes, that you'll give me a chance—give us a chance?"

Kenzie nodded again. "Yes."

She saw the elation in his expression before he kissed her with the same enthusiasm he had the very first time.

"Unhand my wife!"

At first Kenzie thought she had imagined the command, but when Micah straightened and turned toward the voice, she knew she hadn't.

"Excuse me?" Micah said.

The handsome blond man stepped forward. "I said, unhand my wife."

Micah looked back at Kenzie, who was certain she might faint. She whispered the name of the man she'd hoped never to see again.

"Arthur."

CHAPTER 10

"I'm here to see Mr. Bridgestone," Caleb said to the young man who served as the law firm's secretary.

"Yes, he's expecting you." The young man motioned Caleb to follow him.

Caleb looked around, hoping he might spy Sam and learn what the trouble was before he had to be surprised by Mr. Bridgestone. The letter Caleb had received that morning said the matter was of the utmost urgency and requested he come as soon as possible.

Rather than go to Bridgestone's office, the secretary took him to another part of the house. "This is one of the family's sitting rooms," he explained. "Mr. Bridgestone asked for you to join him here." He opened the pocket door to reveal a large, well-appointed room with a fire burning in the hearth despite the warmth of the day.

Caleb stepped inside to be greeted by Bridgestone, who sat at the far end of the room with a woman. The woman, obviously in mourning, wore black, and a heavy veil hung from her stylish hat. Bridgestone got to his feet and greeted Caleb.

"I appreciate you coming so quickly. I wouldn't have bothered you, but given you are rather critical to this situation, I felt it best to start with you."

How in the world was he critical to this situation? Caleb nodded at Bridgestone. "How can I help?"

The young woman pushed back her veil and fixed Caleb with a frown. "You can tell me why I am not allowed access to my inheritance, and furthermore, why you think you have the right to be my guardian."

Caleb stared at the young woman, hardly more than a girl. "Victoria Whitley, I presume."

"Yes."

"Please sit, Mr. Coulter," Bridgestone instructed. "I believe this will take a bit of time to discuss."

"I don't know why," Victoria said, her gaze never leaving Caleb. "Mr. Coulter doesn't even know me. He has no right to tell me what I must do or how I can spend my money."

"I'm afraid he does have that right, Miss Whitley. He is the trustee of your estate. You have yet to reach your majority, and until you are twenty-one, your cousin Judith Whitley is your guardian. She has appointed those responsibilities to her fiancé, Mr. Coulter."

Victoria gave a harsh laugh. "I should have figured you would make such a move. Grandmother said you were probably nothing more than a money grubber. Now you've engaged yourself to my cousin—who I understand holds most of the fortune my dear family left behind."

Caleb smiled despite her snide tone. "Miss Whitley, we presumed you were at school in Switzerland. Might I ask how you managed to return to San Francisco?"

Victoria gave an exasperated sigh. "I told the headmistress I wished to return home to mourn my family, and she arranged it. Now, what I want to know is when you intend to release my inheritance so I can make my own decisions. I do not intend to remain in this repugnant town."

Caleb looked at Bridgestone, who wore a look of weary consternation. He returned his gaze to Victoria. She was clearly furious. No doubt she'd thought she merely had to show up and demand her own way, and when that hadn't worked, she had taken it out on Bridgestone.

Knowing this would take some time, Caleb sat in the leather wingback chair beside her and turned it so that he faced her directly. Once seated, he addressed her in the professional manner he might use with any other client, rather than as a family member.

"Miss Whitley, you are nineteen years of age. The legal age that entitles you to access your inheritance is twenty-one. Therefore, until such time, your money will remain in trust for you. Your housing, clothing, and other needs will be provided for by an allowance paid directly to those providers. Should other needs arise, you have but to come to me with your requests, at which time I will judge whether they are acceptable expenditures. Judith wants you to be comfortable, but obviously you will not be returning to the family home, as it was destroyed by fire. You will instead be housed with your cousin."

"This is utter nonsense." Victoria slammed her gloved hands down on the arms of her chair. "I will not be treated like a child."

Caleb smiled. "Then don't act like one."

This only served to infuriate her even more. Victoria jumped to her feet and shook her fist at Caleb. "I spent a lifetime under my grandmother's thumb, and I will not allow some ridiculous, two-bit lawyer to tell me what to do."

"Miss Whitley, please calm down and retake your seat," Bridgestone begged. "I'm sure that your loss is making this harder than it needs to be."

"My loss was a blessing. I wear black only because it serves my purpose," Victoria declared, refusing to sit. She began to pace around the room, always watching Caleb as though he were a wild animal about to attack.

He thought her an interesting character, to be sure. Had he not known about Bill's confession to Judith's attempted murder, he would easily have assumed Victoria was the culprit. Her entire demeanor suggested she would rid herself of all obstacles no matter the cost.

"I have no money and no place to live," Victoria stated, looking back and forth between the men. "What do you expect me to do?"

"Mr. Coulter and your cousin will arrange your lodging," Mr. Bridgestone said in carefully chosen words. "You must give them a chance to do so."

"I don't want their arrangements. I have friends with whom I can stay in New York City, and that is where I wish to be. I want my money released to me so that I can arrange passage on the next ship."

"I'm afraid that isn't going to happen." Caleb knew she would fly into another tirade, but he felt he had to speak firmly with her. "What *is* going to happen is that you will accompany me to where your cousin is, and we will discuss the matter like civilized adults."

Victoria's eyes narrowed. "I'm not going anywhere with you."

"I'm afraid you must," Bridgestone interjected. "He has a legal right to direct you."

"He probably plans to take liberties with me," Victoria said, turning to Bridgestone. "Will you allow him to take advantage of an innocent woman?"

Caleb picked a piece of lint off his trousers. There was no doubt about it—dealing with Victoria Whitley was not going to be a simple matter.

"Miss Whitley, I have no interest in a child such as yourself, except to see you safely protected." Caleb got to his feet. "As you've no doubt noticed, a good portion of the city was destroyed by fire and earthquake. My own residence was damaged but has recently been repaired, and it is my intention that we will return to live there. However, for the time being, your cousin and the others who were residents of my house are living at a warehouse that we converted to offer shelter to some of the homeless. You will have plenty of female companionship. But if need be, I can hire a nurse to watch over you."

She scowled.

He looked at Mr. Bridgestone. "If there's nothing further to discuss with you, sir, then I will take Miss Whitley and return to the warehouse. You can reach me there if need be, but in a day or so, I'm sure we will be reinstated at my home."

"I'm not living with riffraff," Victoria declared. "I was raised with the best of society."

"Yes, well, the best of society are currently living in the relief camps in tents," Caleb countered. "Now, if you're through stomping about like a child, I have other things to tend to."

Victoria went to Bridgestone's side. "You aren't going to just let him take me away, are you?"

"I must. He has the legal right to do so, and I will not interfere." Bridgestone's tone was relieved. "I'm sure in the coming days you'll reach an amicable solution."

Victoria straightened, and for a moment Caleb wasn't sure what she would do. She seemed to consider the matter for several silent moments, then lifted her chin and reached up to pull down her veil.

"You are sending a lamb to the slaughter, Mr. Bridgestone. I hope that weighs heavily on your conscience when I turn up injured or dead."

Caleb shook his head and turned for the door. It was going to be a long, long day.

"What are you doing here, Arthur?" Kenzie asked. Her knees felt like jelly, and she wondered if it would be best to move to the tables for this conversation. She had no chance, however.

Arthur came to her and grasped her hands before she could so much as protest. "My love, I thought I might never see you again."

"I wish you hadn't." She yanked her hands away and freed herself from his touch.

His expression turned hurt. "Don't say such things. I've tried to find you since receiving your letter."

"Letter?" Micah asked.

Kenzie sighed. "Camri insisted I write him a letter to tell him how much he hurt me and how glad I am to be rid of him."

Arthur shook his head. "I don't mean that letter. I mean the one I got on our wedding day."

"I sent you no letter. The only letter I know of is the one you sent to me, telling me you'd changed your mind and didn't plan to go through with the wedding."

"But I didn't send that," Arthur began in a pleading tone. "That wasn't penned by me. I believe my father is responsible for it."

Kenzie began to feel sick. "What are you saying?"

"I'm saying that I never intended to stand you up. I thought *you* called off the wedding. I was dressing for the ceremony when the letter came. It said that you had changed your mind, that you didn't feel we were right for each other."

"You weren't," Micah muttered.

Kenzie could hardly believe what Arthur was telling her. "So all of this time, you thought I canceled our wedding?"

"Yes." Arthur's eyes pleaded with her. "You must believe me. I would have never left you. You know how I feel—how hard I worked to win you. You always believed me above your station, but I never felt that way."

"But your family certainly did." Kenzie studied him. He was just as handsome as when she'd last seen him. His blue eyes sparkled in that old familiar way. He was dressed impeccably, as always, and he looked at her with that same expression of adoration. Only this time it was mixed with a beseeching countenance that she'd never known him to use.

"Kenzie, you are the love of my life. When you refused me—when I got the letter—I went to see you, but your father wouldn't admit me. I'm afraid at that point I gave myself over to my brother's suggestion and remained in a drunken state for days afterward. When I finally sobered up, my father convinced me to go abroad with him. When I returned in January, I went again to your father, but he told me you had gone. He wouldn't reveal where."

Kenzie thought it strange that her mother had said nothing of this in her letters. Then again, maybe her father had said nothing to her.

"I was so happy when I got your second letter. Well, happy and sad. But at last I knew why you had gone and where." Arthur knelt on one knee and again took her hands. "Kenzie, I wept bitterly when I read that letter. To think that you thought I had deserted you—left you at the altar to face utter humiliation. It was almost more than I could bear. I caught the first train west, but then the earthquake hit. Despite my best attempts, they wouldn't allow people into the city. I went nearly mad trying to figure out if you were alive, and when I went to the address from your letter and saw the note that you were safe, it was all I could do to keep from shouting. I was so relieved—so happy."

Kenzie tried again to pull away, but Arthur held her tight.

"Please, please come away with me and marry me tonight. Before my family can interfere again."

"That's quite enough of your blathering," Micah said, grabbing Arthur's arm. He dragged the other man to his feet. "Kenzie is no longer interested in you, Morgan. She's going to marry me."

Kenzie felt her face flush. She felt more confused than ever before. The thought that Arthur was just as duped as she had been was too much to fathom. She knew his parents—especially his father—to be hateful people who thought themselves better than everyone else. But to imagine they would do something so betraying to their own son was almost unthinkable.

"Is that true, Kenzie? Are you going to marry this man instead of me?" Arthur's voice was full of pain. "Please tell me the truth."

"What in the world is going on out here?" Camri asked as she and Judith joined the trio. "I could hear you all the way inside the warehouse."

"Micah, are you all right?" Judith asked.

"I assure you, my dear woman, this man is hardly the one to concern yourself with," Arthur replied. "He's threatening me, not the other way around."

Micah still held Arthur's arm and looked as if he would pummel him at any moment. Kenzie didn't know what to say or do. As Micah and Arthur began to talk over each other in explanation, Kenzie wanted only to get away from them all. So, with everyone clearly occupied, she did exactly that.

CHAPTER 11

Camri had little tolerance for ranting. "Silence, both of you!"

Micah looked at her in surprise, while Arthur straightened and freed himself from Micah's hold.

"Honestly, the two of you shouting over each other is hardly the way to explain yourselves."

"Then ask Kenzie," Micah said. He turned to question the redhead, but she was gone.

"I can't say I blame her for leaving," Camri declared. She looked at Arthur. "Who are you?"

"I'm Arthur Morgan, the man Kenzie was supposed to marry."

Camri couldn't hide her surprise. Her mouth dropped open, and she wanted to speak, but the words stuck in her throat.

"He says he never deserted Kenzie. That the letter you encouraged her to write proved to him that his family were the ones to blame," Micah interjected.

Camri regained her composure. "I think maybe we should go inside and sit down. Judith, would you get us some coffee and maybe something to eat? I have a feeling this is going to take a while." She started into the warehouse and called over her shoulder. "Don't just stand there, gentlemen. Come along and let me hear what you have to say."

Once they were inside, she waited until Judith brought coffee and cookies before she posed the first question. She fixed Arthur Morgan with the look she gave students who failed to turn in an examination.

"Are you saying that you had nothing to do with leaving Kenzie at the altar?"

"I swear I didn't. I received a letter on the day of our wedding. It was supposedly from Kenzie, and she said she was canceling the wedding. She refused me. Or so I thought," Arthur declared. He straightened his suit coat and brushed off the sleeves. "I was just as deceived as she."

"Where is she?" Judith asked.

Camri glanced down the warehouse toward the private quarters. "I imagine she's gone off to be alone. We can talk to her in a bit. Right now, I want to know why Mr. Morgan is here."

"But I've already explained. It was all a mistake, and I've come to rectify it. I want Kenzie to come away with me and marry me."

"Well, we don't always get what we want," Micah said, his eyes narrowing.

"I do," Arthur countered with equal hostility.

"Look, you two. This isn't helping." Camri poured them each a cup of coffee. "Drink this and calm down."

Micah ignored his coffee. "This buffoon thinks he can show up months after the fact with a story of how he didn't leave Kenzie at the altar and just expects us to believe him. I'm telling you it's a bald-faced lie."

"How can you be so sure?" Judith asked.

"Because what man in his right mind wouldn't fight for that woman? He just accepted the notion that she was rejecting him." Micah grinned. "That would never have stopped me, as you both well know. I find it hard to believe any man who was truly in love with her would have let it stop him."

"I tried to go to her. Her father refused me." Arthur put down his cup. "I did my best to see her."

"I find that hard to believe."

"I do too," Camri replied. "Kenzie said you never came to explain or offer her any kind of understanding. You simply went abroad."

"I was drunk when I agreed to go. My father, the same man who is surely to blame for this misunderstanding, took advantage of my state and all but forced me out of the country. When I returned, I tried again to find Kenzie, but her father told me she had gone."

"And you did nothing to find her? You, with all the money and resources in the world at your fingertips, you did nothing?" Micah asked.

Camri gave Arthur a questioning look. "He makes a good point, Mr. Morgan."

"I was . . . well, I was devastated at the loss," Arthur answered in a hesitant voice. "When I returned, I was determined to forget my sorrow and move ahead with my life. I had no idea that Kenzie thought I no longer loved her."

"Again, that would never have stopped me. I would have gone out of my way to woo her back—to convince her that we belonged together." Micah shook his head. "I don't believe you, Mr. Morgan."

Camri got to her feet. "I want to speak to Kenzie. I expect you two to conduct yourselves in a gentlemanly manner and refrain from fisticuffs. Judith, would you mind staying here to help these two remember who they are?"

"Of course." Judith smiled. "I'm sure we can just sit and talk about the weather or the rebuilding."

Camri was equally certain they wouldn't, but said nothing.

She made her way to the room she shared with Kenzie and Judith and knocked on the door. She tried the handle, but it was locked.

"Kenzie, it's Camri. Please let me in."

She wasn't sure if Kenzie had heard her and was about to knock again when the key scraped in the lock and the door opened.

Kenzie's eyes were red from crying and her face blotchy and tearstained. "I don't know what in the world God has in mind for me, but this seems to be a cruel joke."

Camri shook her head. "Let's sit and talk."

"Is he still here?"

"Yes. Judith is sitting with him and Micah. She'll keep them out of trouble. At least momentarily. Please tell me what's going on. Mr. Morgan says he's here because of the letter I had you write. I feel horrible for it and want to make things right if I can."

"It's not your fault." Kenzie sat on her cot.

Camri lowered herself to her own cot opposite Kenzie. "If I hadn't encouraged you to speak your mind in that letter, you might never have had to deal with him again."

"Yes, but if what he's saying is true, then he believes I'm the one who left him." Kenzie wiped her face with a handkerchief. "Oh, Camri, I never in my life imagined something like this could happen. I truly never thought that his family would have deceived us both."

"Do you believe that's what happened?"

"Why should I not? If Arthur truly deserted me as I thought, then why would he come here now? He knows I have no great fortune to settle upon him like Judith. I'm still the same woman he left at the altar. There would be no reason to come here unless he really did love me."

"I suppose that's true. But, Kenzie, even if his family did

deceive you both, what's done is done. You have feelings for Micah now."

"That's what makes this so impossible." Kenzie buried her face in her hands and cried in earnest.

Camri slipped from her cot to Kenzie's and put her arm around her friend's shoulders. "It's all right. You aren't to blame for any of this."

Kenzie looked up. "But I'm so confused. I never wanted to hurt Arthur. I was prepared to spend the rest of my life with him. I honestly thought we could be happy together."

"It isn't your fault."

"But that doesn't change the facts. What has happened has ruined everything. I just want to disappear. I can't bear the idea of hurting either Arthur or Micah. All the pain that I went through, I . . . I can't willingly do that to someone else." She slumped against Camri. "I don't know what to do."

"Well, for now you should simply rest. I'll send Arthur away and tell him to come back tomorrow. Or better still, I'll find out where he's staying, and when you're ready, we'll go to him."

Kenzie said nothing, and Camri decided it was best not to press her.

"You rest now," Camri said, getting up. She gave Kenzie's shoulder a pat. "It'll be all right. I promise you. We'll sort through it, and above all, we'll pray. None of this has taken God by surprise. He'll have answers for us."

Camri made her way from the room and rejoined the others. Micah looked furious while Mr. Morgan spoke with Judith. Camri had never known a greater predicament where the human heart was involved. This wouldn't be easily resolved.

Stopping beside Arthur, she offered him a smile. "Kenzie is quite upset, as I'm sure you realize. I told her I would send you away. You can tell us where you'll be, and when she's up to it, we'll come to see you."

He jumped to his feet, nearly knocking her over. "I will not leave without her. She's my wife."

"She's not!" Micah said, getting to his feet. "Nor does she want to be."

Camri touched Arthur's sleeve. "Mr. Morgan, it really is for the best that you go."

"And I said no." He turned on her in a rage, grabbing her shoulders and shaking her hard. "I won't go!"

"You'd better be lettin' her go," Patrick said, appearing at Camri's side. He towered over Arthur and gripped his shoulder. Micah came to her assistance as well.

Camri had expected Patrick to come home soon but hadn't anticipated him being here quite this early. If Arthur didn't mind his manners, she knew there would be a fight.

"Now, ye'd be wise to back away," Patrick said, giving Arthur a push. At the same time, he all but pulled Camri behind him.

Arthur nodded. "I'm sorry for my conduct. It's just that I've been half mad trying to find Kenzie. I love her, and I don't want to lose her again."

Patrick did nothing but eye the man with suspicion.

Micah let go of Arthur's arm and stepped back. "You've already lost her," he said in a way that suggested there was absolutely nothing more to be discussed.

Arthur's head lowered. "Please just let me see her. Talk to her."

Camri felt sorry for him. He seemed sincere. She stepped around Patrick. "As I said, Mr. Morgan, she's not able to see you now and wishes for you to go. Let us know where we can reach you, and we'll make arrangements for a meeting in a few days."

Micah didn't wait for Camri to say more, just started dragging Arthur toward the door.

When they were outside, Camri turned to Patrick and smiled. "Hello, sweetheart. I'm so glad you could join us."

"And for sure I'm glad I could as well. What in the world would that be about?"

"That is Mr. Arthur Morgan, the man who left Kenzie at the altar. The man who says, however, that he didn't desert her, but rather his family deceived them both. The man who wants her to marry him as soon as possible."

Patrick gazed toward the ceiling. "Heaven help us."

Judith was about to clear the table of coffee cups and uneaten cookies when Caleb arrived. She was so happy to see he'd returned. Given all the excitement, she wanted nothing more than to sit quietly beside him and listen to him read to her, as he often did.

She had left the dishes and started toward him when she caught sight of a woman dressed head to toe in black. The woman's veil concealed her face, but the cut of her clothes and manner of walking left little doubt that she was wealthy.

"Judith, I have a bit of a surprise for you," Caleb said. His tone and expression were almost apologetic.

The woman lifted her veil, and Judith couldn't suppress her gasp. "Victoria!"

Her cousin sneered. "Yes. I've come for my inheritance, but I'm told you've stolen that away as well as the rest of my family's money."

Judith looked at Caleb. "How?"

"Apparently she convinced the headmistress of the school to arrange her return. She arrived in town this morning, making her demands at Mr. Bridgestone's office."

"Her demands?"

"Yes, my demands. I want my inheritance," Victoria said, stepping closer. "I don't care about the rest of it—although it does sicken me to see you take what is rightfully mine."

"I don't want your money, Victoria," Judith said, finally gathering her wits. "And I had nothing to do with the arrangements Grandmother decided."

"*Grandmother*." Victoria's voice dripped with sarcasm. "You hardly knew her well enough to call her that. I suppose, however, knowing there was money to be had, you could call her whatever she desired."

"I'm sorry I had to bring her here," Caleb said to Judith. "We are in charge of her, however."

"No one is in charge of me," Victoria countered. Her face reddened in anger. "I won't have it."

"I'd rather not have it either," Judith admitted.

"As I tried to explain to Miss Whitley," Caleb began, "the city is in shambles, and none of her old friends are in a position to take her in. Otherwise, believe me, I would happily deliver her to them."

"I can stay at a hotel," Victoria shouted. "I won't stay here."

"I also tried to explain to her that she is underage and no respectable establishment would have her without a chaperone. She doesn't seem to understand the dangers of being on her own."

"I am perfectly able to take care of myself."

By now Camri and Patrick had joined them. Judith looked at her friends and shook her head. The situation was more than she could begin to understand. What in the world was Caleb thinking, bringing Victoria here?

"We can set up a cot for her in our room," Camri offered. "It'll be tight, but I don't see what else we can manage, other than putting her out here with the others. Once we move back to the house, she can share Judith's room."

"I will not!" Victoria said, shaking her head.

Camri gave her a patient smile. "Well, then you can have my room, and I'll share with Judith."

"I don't know why you all refuse to listen to me," Victoria said, stamping her foot. "I don't want to be associated with you. I will not be forced to stay with any of you."

Caleb spoke up at this. "You will, as I told you on the way over here, unless you want me to have you locked up in an institution where you can be dealt with until you calm down and become more reasonable."

This caused Victoria to take a step back. "You're all monsters. You would put me in prison for no other reason than to suit your own desires."

"No one wants to lock you up, Victoria." Judith smiled and tried to reach out to her. "I want to be your friend. We all do. You've suffered a great loss. You aren't yourself."

"Oh, I think you know exactly how much those people meant to me," Victoria said. She was calmer, but her voice was filled with hate. "I could not possibly care less about what happened to them. My father was a fool, my brother conniving, and my grandmother was an overbearing tyrant. I don't care that they're gone. I'm neither in mourning nor shock. I simply want my money and to be left to go my own way."

Victoria's acrid words left Judith's stomach on edge. If she hadn't known better, she might have believed the girl was simply distraught. But Victoria was telling the truth. She didn't care about her family dying. She was ruthless and heartless, and Judith could see the hate in the girl's blue eyes. They would all have to watch their backs until she could figure out how to manage the situation.

She looked to Caleb. "Whatever are we to do?"

CHAPTER 12

At his sister's insistence, Caleb went to Arthur Morgan's hotel to meet him and speak to him about his claim on Kenzie. The lobby of the hotel was crowded as Caleb made his way to the grand staircase. He walked up to the second floor, then sought out Morgan's room number. He wasn't sure what his insertion into the matter could do, but Camri had begged him to at least go and meet the man.

Morgan answered the door after Caleb's first knock. He was a tall, well-groomed man of thirty or more years, and his demeanor exuded confidence.

"Mr. Arthur Morgan, I presume?" Caleb held his homburg in his hand.

Morgan nodded. "And you are Caleb Coulter."

Caleb handed him his card. "I am. Thank you for receiving me on such short notice and at such an early hour."

"It's no problem. I want to do whatever I can to convince everyone that I am innocent of wrongdoing in this matter. I want very much for Kenzie and I to be married at the first possible opportunity." Morgan motioned to the sitting area. "Please have a seat. Would you like me to arrange to have coffee served?"

"No, that isn't necessary." Caleb chose a gilded-frame throne chair and sat. "I'd rather just get to the heart of the matter."

Arthur Morgan smiled, and a look of relief crossed his face. "I would like that as well." He sat and crossed his legs. "What would you like to know?"

Caleb smiled. He was glad to see the other man let down his guard. "I suppose you realize your arrival here has caused quite an upset."

"I do, but I couldn't leave things as they were. Kenzie thought I had abandoned her—that I no longer loved her. That simply isn't true."

"Then tell me your side of the matter."

Morgan nodded and began to explain the details of what had happened the previous September. "I worked so hard to win her over. My parents were appalled that I would marry beneath our social standing, but I told them that Kenzie is perfect the way she is. She is graceful, charming, and kind—even my parents had to admit that much. I love that Kenzie treats everyone with respect and the deepest sincerity. It doesn't matter if they have money or are begging on the streets."

"She is very considerate of others. It's amazing that you would risk your family's ire to court and marry someone of whom they disapproved."

Morgan shrugged. "I couldn't allow them to dictate my future. I thought I had convinced them that my choice was a good one and that they would come to love Kenzie as I do. However, that apparently wasn't what happened at all. When I received Kenzie's letter, I was mortified. I confronted my father, who admitted to interfering in the matter. I soon learned that my entire family had some part in it. I told them they had betrayed me and that I intended to come here, tell Kenzie everything, and marry her immediately."

"And what was their response?" Caleb watched Morgan carefully. If he was lying about the situation, he would surely give himself away at some point.

"My father threatened to disinherit me, but it didn't matter. I told them that I would go no matter what."

"And you wish to take Kenzie back to live in that atmosphere?"

"Of course not. I have a house of my own in Missouri—Kansas City. I have my own investments and business dealings, and while being disinherited would rob me of a vast fortune, I would gladly give it up for Kenzie."

"Mr. Morgan—"

"Call me Arthur, please. I feel we can become good friends."

Caleb smiled. "I doubt that. You see, the other man who intends to marry Kenzie is my best friend, Dr. Micah Fisher. And I won't betray his trust in me. I won't even pretend to be on your side in this matter. I believe Micah and Kenzie love each other very much."

"I'm sorry, but I have first claim to her. Your friend must recognize that."

Caleb shook his head. "I doubt where matters of the heart are concerned that either of you will listen to reason. However, my sister asked me to come here today and speak to you about the situation."

"To what purpose? Are you supposed to convince me to give Kenzie up? Are you here to threaten me and tell me to leave town and never darken her doorstep again?"

Caleb noted the sarcasm in his tone. "Hardly that. I wanted to hear your side of the story and judge for myself the truthfulness of your statements. You see, I'm a lawyer, and as such, I've learned to assess people rather well. I'm also a Christian with a gift for discernment that has yet to fail me."

A look of concern flashed in Morgan's expression and was quickly replaced with a smile. "Then you know I'm speaking the truth. I would never lie about something so vital to my own happiness. You must believe me."

Caleb returned the smile. "I find that generally when people demand I believe they are speaking the truth, they aren't. However, I will reserve judgment for the moment. Kenzie has been greatly upset by this turn of events. I believe you would do well to give her some time. We know how to reach you when she deems the time is right."

"But that's not fair. I'm sure Dr. Fisher will come and go as he pleases. I will not sit by idly while he steals her away. She belongs with me."

Caleb didn't like Morgan's tone but didn't react. There was something about Arthur Morgan he didn't entirely trust. Perhaps it was his privileged upbringing that gave him an air of entitlement and the belief that he could demand his way and people would heed it. It might even be that his love for Kenzie was blinding him to everything else. Whatever it was, Caleb discerned a problem, and he had learned to heed that feeling.

Caleb turned his hat in his hands, but his gaze never left Arthur Morgan's face. "Mr. Morgan, I am of the firm belief that Kenzie is capable of making up her own mind in matters of the heart. She's lived under my roof and care for these last months, and I've come to know her quite well."

"I suppose you fancy yourself in love with her too?" Morgan sneered. "It hardly seems appropriate that a single woman should live in the same house with a single man."

Caleb raised a brow. "I owe you no explanations, Mr. Morgan. I will say that I have no interest in Kenzie other than that of a concerned friend. However, you would do well to guard your thoughts and speech. I am an honorable, Christian man and do my best to overlook mistakes, but once warned, I believe that should suffice."

Morgan looked at him for a moment, then gave another

shrug. "Surely if you've ever been in love, you know what it is to want to protect that person. I don't want Kenzie hurt."

"She's already been hurt, and now she's dealing with a very confusing situation. If you love her, you will give her time to sort through her thoughts and feelings. If the love she once held for you is real, then she will realize that and come back to you." Caleb got to his feet. "I do hope you will be considerate in this matter."

Morgan followed him to the door. "I won't stand idle and let someone else take her away from me. I doubt any man worth his mettle would. I hope you will convey that message to your dear friend Dr. Fisher."

Caleb turned and met Morgan's gaze. There was something hard, almost cold in his eyes. He was a man of power and wealth who was used to getting what he wanted. "I will let him know how you feel, and I will also relate what happened here today to Kenzie. I think it only right that she knows you care more about having your own way than about her feelings."

"I didn't say that," Morgan protested.

"But that is what you've implied." Caleb looked at him, daring him to dispute it.

Morgan's shoulders slumped a bit. "I can't stay here forever, waiting for you and the others to decide whether or not I can see her. Kenzie knows me, and I believe she still loves me. No one would write such an impassioned letter without having deep feelings."

"She has deep feelings, of that I can vouch. But whether any of those remain as love for you, I cannot say." Caleb donned his hat. "Good day, Mr. Morgan."

Victoria looked at the others seated around the table and found it difficult to hold her tongue. Her situation was completely impossible, but she was reliant upon these people for her very existence. Unless, of course, she could find some of her old friends. Her family had long been associated with other powerful families. Surely with their help she would be able to battle the likes of Caleb Coulter and her cousin.

"I must be getting to work," George Lake announced, standing. "However, let me say that my time spent here with you has given me a new perspective on life." He looked at the old woman he'd been sitting beside and smiled. "I am grateful for new friendships."

"Cousin George, we are very glad you could stay with us, even for a short time," Kenzie said, smiling at him. "I am happy, however, that you've been able to purchase another house. Especially now that you and Mrs. Andrews are planning to marry."

Mrs. Andrews smiled up at George Lake. "I never figured to have a whirlwind romance and marry again, but George and I are well-suited. I think we'll be quite happy together."

"As do I, my dear." George gave her a smile and a bow. "But for now, I must attend to business. I have meetings with the Ghirardelli people prior to my regular working hours."

Once he'd gone, Mrs. Andrews got to her feet and began collecting their breakfast dishes. "I'm going to bake a cake for our dinner tonight. George told me he has a fondness for carrot cake. Apparently his mother used to make it."

"Might I help you, Mrs. Andrews?" Victoria's cousin asked in her sweet, charming way.

Victoria hated Judith more than she could say. It wasn't just for appearing and upsetting the normalcy of Victoria's life. Judith's very demeanor irritated her. Judith was capable and strong, yet everyone loved her and befriended her. Victoria's strength and abilities did exactly the opposite and always seemed to offend. It didn't matter, however. She wasn't going to change to suit the likes of Judith and her friends.

"I'd love to have your company, Judith," Mrs. Andrews said.

"Just give me a few minutes to deal with these dishes, and we'll get it all planned out."

Judith smiled and turned to Camri and Kenzie. "I hope Caleb had no trouble with Mr. Morgan. Caleb cares so much about you, Kenzie. I'm certain he will be able to help Arthur understand your feelings."

"Maybe he can help me understand them too," Kenzie said, getting to her feet. "I'm going to work on that inventory, Camri."

"I'll help you." Caleb's sister rose and gave Victoria a nod. "You can join us, if you like."

"I'm not a laborer." Victoria picked up her cup and sipped the tepid contents.

Camri merely shrugged and followed Kenzie from the room. That left Judith and Victoria to deal with one another. Victoria narrowed her eyes as she scrutinized her cousin. Judith was like a beautiful china doll, just as her twin sister Cora had been. Victoria had hated Cora too. Everyone always fussed over her and spoiled her. She had been Grandmother's pet because of her circumstances. Victoria could still remember Grandmother explaining that someone had stolen away Cora's twin sister when they were babies, so they needed to give Cora extra attention and care.

"Is there something you wish to say?" Judith asked.

Victoria considered her reply for a moment. "I don't imagine anything I have to say will be of importance to you."

Judith frowned. "I think it is. I've wanted to be your friend from the start, Victoria. I know you think I'm to blame for all your loss, but I'm not. I never desired to interfere in your life at all."

"And yet you did, and now, when you have the chance to make things right, you won't."

"I'm sorry you feel that way. Grandmother told me you and the others would be unhappy with her decision, but she had her reasons. I think it's important that you know them. Your father was apparently not a very good businessman, and while I do not like to speak ill of the dead, Grandmother said he wasted or lost most of the inheritance left to him by his father."

Victoria shrugged. "That was no secret. Oh, I'm sure Grandmother and Father thought it was, but Bill told me the truth of it. Our father was a fool, and Grandmother had to rein him in and impose her way of doing things in order to assure that Bill and I had something to inherit. And before you tell me that she didn't leave more to Bill because of his manipulation and conniving, I already know that as well. Bill took matters into his own hands."

"Even to the point of murder," Judith interjected.

"Yes, even so. Would that he had been better at it." Victoria hoped her comment would get a rise out of Judith, but when it didn't, she continued. "Grandmother was demanding and imposing. You have no idea what we went through, having to live under her rule. You only knew her a short time, and like Cora, you instantly became her pet."

"She tried to impose her will on me, but I stood my ground," Judith countered. "Maybe that's the real reason you hate me. I didn't care about the money, so her threats of disinheritance didn't work on me."

"That's because you grew up without money. You had a miserable, impoverished existence, so losing what you never had wasn't important to you. I, on the other hand, have never known want. Even though Grandmother was harsh, she was meticulous about seeing that proprieties were met. I had the finest—although rather childish—clothes, the best horses and carriages, the nicest furnishings. Now you intend to strip that away from me."

"I have no such intentions," Judith replied. "I have only the desire to see you properly protected and your reputation upheld. I was so relieved for you when Mr. Rosedale dissolved the engagement. However, if you go off and live a life of wanton pleasure, your reputation will be ruined, and you'll never find a decent husband."

Victoria laughed. "You know nothing. With my inheritance, I can buy any husband I like."

"Wouldn't you rather have one who loves you? I can speak from experience—the love of a good man is worth everything."

"Ah yes, your 'good man' Caleb Coulter. Did it never dawn on you that he only wants you for what he can get? You weren't engaged when I went away in April, yet just two months later, you are. Funny how that worked out. You became an heiress and then found yourself engaged almost in the same breath."

Judith frowned. "Caleb and I love each other, and that is why we decided to marry. It has nothing to do with my inheritance."

Victoria shook her head. "There's no way to prove that. No way at all." She got to her feet. "If you'll excuse me, I'm going for a walk. And before you chide me to be careful of my surroundings, I assure you that I won't venture far. I wouldn't be caught dead in the company of the ruffians who inhabit this neighborhood."

She left Judith and made her way outside into the fresh salty air. There had to be a way to best Judith and Caleb Coulter. Victoria wasn't used to people refusing her demands. Even Grandmother's denials had often been sidestepped by Victoria appealing to her father.

"If only I could take everything away from her," she murmured.

A thought came to mind. At first it was just a thread of an idea, but within a moment of its inception, Victoria had the answer to all her troubles.

"I'll take Caleb from her." Victoria smiled. "I'm prettier and know far more about men than she does." She glanced down at her black dress. "I'll rid myself of this ugly thing and get out one of my prettier gowns. I'll do up my hair and appeal to his masculine nature."

The sound of a wagon approaching caught her attention. Victoria turned and found Caleb driving the wagon toward the warehouse, an automobile following directly behind him. She decided there was no time like the present to put her plan into play. She hardly waited for him to stop the wagon and climb down before she went to him.

"Caleb, would you help me?" She made her voice soft and sweet.

He looked at her in surprise. "If I can."

The car came to a stop beside the wagon. "Is this where you want it, Caleb?"

"That's fine, Micah. I'm just glad to have it back." He looked at Victoria. "The army confiscated my car just after the earthquake to help with their transportation needs."

Micah gave them a wave. "I'm going to speak to Kenzie."

Caleb nodded, then turned back to Victoria. "What is it you need from me?"

She put on her most sorrowful expression. "I'd like to see my family's house. I know it's been burned, but I need to see it. Their graves too."

"I can arrange that."

"Would you go with me? I'm afraid, with all the time I've had to think about things, that I'm feeling a bit overwhelmed."

He smiled. "Of course. I'd be happy to take you. Let me take care of few matters, and we can leave directly."

"Thank you, Caleb. I know I haven't been very cooperative, but . . . well, I'm trying to face this the best I can."

"I understand. I just want you to know that we truly have your best interests at heart. No one wants to see you unhappy."

She sniffed as if about to break into tears. "Thank you. I see that now."

"I'll see if Judith wants to join us."

"I'd rather you didn't. I'd like a few private moments with my grief." Victoria hurried to explain. "I don't like public displays of tears and such. They make me uncomfortable."

Caleb nodded. "Very well. I'll let Judith know what's going on and tend to a couple of other things, and then we can go."

An hour later, Victoria stood at Caleb's side, looking at the blackened remains of her once-stately home. Seeing it like this and knowing this was where her father and brother had met their demise struck a chord deep inside her. She wasn't sad as much as displaced. Her entire life had been lived here, and now it was gone.

All that she'd known here, all that she'd enjoyed, was like a veiled memory. She couldn't pull anything good from those thoughts, with the exception of distant memories of her mother. Thoughts of Mother always made her melancholy. Mother was the last person Victoria had ever loved, and when she died, Victoria had been determined never to love anyone else. She had put up a shield of indifference around her heart, and it remained firmly in place.

Mother had loved her. She had perhaps been the only person who truly did. Everyone else had been far too concerned about Cora and Aunt Edith. The kidnapping of Judith had ruined any hope that Victoria might become the favorite. But Mother had assured Victoria that she was her pride and joy and that no one else would ever mean as much to her. Not even Bill.

Mother's death had been harder than anything else in Victoria's life, and even now, the loss of the house and remaining family hurt only because it severed her final connection to the woman who had loved her most. Tears came to Victoria's eyes, and she used them to her advantage.

"It's just too terrible." She buried her face in her gloved hands.

As she had hoped, Caleb put his arm around her shoulders. "I'm sorry, Victoria. I'm sure it must be very hard for you."

She raised her face, lifting her eyes in a way that she knew would be appealing. "I thought I didn't care. I thought I could avoid the pain."

He gave her a sympathetic smile. "We all do our best to avoid pain, but rarely are we successful. I know your family wasn't overly interested in God, but He is my mainstay and the one I turn to at times like this. He gives me peace and comfort when no one else can."

Tears slipped down her cheek. "I'd like to know more about God. Would you be willing to tell me about Him? I would like to have that peace and comfort."

"Of course." He gave her shoulders a squeeze. "Come on. Let's leave this place, and I'll share a little with you about God's love."

He led her back to the car, and Victoria did her best to hide her delight. Things were going better than she could have hoped. It had never occurred to her that winning Caleb would be easier if she appealed to his religious nature. He was devout in his beliefs and would never deny an opportunity to share them with another. She could easily manipulate this for her benefit.

CHAPTER 13

"I knew you'd want to hear this news right away," Judge Winters told Caleb.

Kenzie didn't mean to eavesdrop, but she was mending some clothes at the opposite end of the table from where Caleb and the judge sat. If they had meant for their conversation to remain private, she presumed they would have gone to Caleb's office in the warehouse.

"So nearly all of the work we did was for naught?" Caleb asked.

"We can't look at it that way. Just because so much of the physical record was burned in the fires, it doesn't mean we can't still see Ruef behind bars."

Caleb shook his head. Kenzie had never seen him look so defeated. "But now we'll have to start over."

"Not exactly. Some records remain, and there is still the driving force of Spreckels and others who want to see Ruef pay for what he's done. President Roosevelt has appointed Special Prosecutor Francis Heney to help us. That, along with Spreckels' pledge of a hundred thousand dollars, will put strength behind our mission."

"It just seems like we've been pushed back so far that we'll never be able to overcome. Especially now. Schmitz and Ruef want to play benefactor to the city. They're doing whatever they can to come out on top, and unfortunately, people are buying into their act."

"Caleb, it doesn't change the fact that Ruef has taken money to the tune of hundreds of thousands of dollars, maybe even a million or more, to turn a blind eye to unsafe building practices. A great many buildings crumbled to rubble in the earthquake and fires due to substandard building materials. That isn't just going to fade away unnoticed. It's the talk of every anti-Ruef committee." He patted Caleb's shoulder. "Have faith. That's what you'd tell me."

"You're right, of course. It's just not going to be easy. I thought we were close to seeing something accomplished."

Judge Winters got to his feet. "I have a feeling we're closer than you think. But now I must be on my way. I have some court business to deal with this afternoon."

"Let me walk you out," Caleb said, standing.

"No, don't bother. I know you've got plenty to tend to, as I recall you plan to move today."

Caleb nodded. "Temporarily, at least. I'm not sure what the future holds. Judith and I have discussed living here once we get it set up properly. With the earthquake, things were rather hectic, and now we're back to this political nonsense."

"Don't let this business with Ruef rob you of joy in your young lady. The future holds good things, son. Of that I'm convinced. Keep your faith in God rather than the people of this world. You won't be disappointed in Him. And never fear, I'll be praying."

Caleb squared his shoulders. "I know you're right. Thank you for everything." He shook the judge's hand. "I appreciate your mentoring and prayers."

The judge bid him farewell and left. It wasn't long, however, before a loud knock sounded on the warehouse door. Kenzie watched as Caleb went to answer it. She stiffened at the arrival of yet another bouquet of flowers from Arthur.

"Kenzie?" Caleb said her name as more of a question. "Do you want to receive these?"

She shook her head and joined the men. She reached for the card and read it. *Please let me come to you. My heart isn't whole without you. Love, Arthur.*

She shook her head again. "Take them away. Give them to one of the hospitals, or better yet, the makeshift orphanages. Children need to see pretty flowers too."

The delivery man frowned, but when Caleb handed him a dollar, his countenance perked up. "Yes, ma'am." He turned without another word and departed, taking the ostentatious arrangement with him.

"You have to speak to him sooner or later," Caleb said.

Kenzie nodded. "I know. I just don't know what to say to him."

"Tell him the truth. Tell him you aren't in love with him anymore."

She looked at him, her eyes narrowing slightly as she frowned. "How do you know that?"

Caleb's black mood seemed to fade. "It isn't that hard to see. I know you love Micah. You might have loved Arthur at one time, but I don't think that's the case anymore."

"But did I kill that love based on what happened? If so, and it was all lies and deception on the part of Arthur's family, then maybe I was wrong to do so. I just don't know." She felt the same confusion rise up again.

Caleb took her arm. His touch was light as a feather. "Kenzie, do you really think it's possible to kill true love? Think about it for a minute."

"I've done nothing but think about it." She shrugged. "I was so overwhelmed with grief after Arthur deserted me—or I thought he had. I wanted to die because I couldn't believe he no longer loved me. It tainted everything in my life."

"I don't doubt that you cared for him, Kenzie. You're a good woman with a kind heart and loving nature. I'm just suggesting that if it were true love—love strong enough to overcome any and all obstacles—you'd still be sure of it. When Arthur showed up here, you would have left everything to be at his side when he declared himself innocent. The pain, the perceived wrongs—they would all have passed away in forgiveness and joy."

"Just like that?" She doubted that was even possible.

"First Corinthians thirteen talks about love. It uses the word *charity*, but the original Greek was *agape* which means *love*. But not just any love—it's a deep, abiding, overcoming love that isn't based on anything the recipient deserves or earns. The best example is God's love for us, but Paul writes about us having it for each other. The chapter says that this kind of charity—love—beareth all things, believeth all things, hopeth all things, endureth all things. Do you feel that kind of love for Arthur Morgan? Did you ever?"

Kenzie felt a glimmer of understanding. "If I had, then I wouldn't have believed in his abandonment." She looked at Caleb and smiled. "I would have gone to him and demanded an explanation. I wouldn't have hidden from him and believed the worst." She began to nod as the mist seemed to clear from her mind. "I would have stayed and fought for him . . . for us."

"Maybe you have your answers now." Caleb looked past her and out the warehouse door. "And it would appear you have them just in time. Mr. Morgan is here."

Kenzie looked out the door to see Arthur stepping out of a taxi. "I suppose I do need to speak to him."

"I'll be praying for you," Caleb said.

Arthur looked up and flashed her a smile. There was a time when that smile had made her feel happy and safe, but now it meant nothing. *He* meant nothing. She thought of the loneliness she'd felt back in Missouri. It was the desire to be loved as she saw others loved that made her give in to his persistence and court him. She hadn't accepted him for anything more than a desire to escape her loneliness. She had known better, sensed deep within that their relationship would never work—that it would never be more than a temporary arrangement—but she had buried that thought in her desperation to find love.

"I hope you will forgive me for showing up without warning," Arthur said, tipping his hat to her as he entered the warehouse. "I know Mr. Coulter wanted me to stay away, but I had to see you."

"I suppose it was inevitable." Kenzie pointed past him. "If you'll follow me, I'd prefer to sit outside." He stepped back and allowed her to pass. "It's a nice day, so the fresh air will do us both good."

"But this is such a run-down, commercial area. Why don't you let me get the taxi back, and we can take a drive?"

She turned when she reached the farthest outdoor table. "Because I don't wish to take a drive with you, Arthur."

He frowned. "That doesn't bode well for me."

She sighed and took a seat on the bench. She motioned to the opposite side of the table. "Please sit."

He did and took off his hat. "I have so much I need to say."

"Arthur, please don't speak of love to me. I'm not the same girl you knew back in Missouri."

"But I have to tell you how I feel. I have to convince you that I did nothing wrong."

She almost smiled at his pleading tone. As usual, he was far more worried about his own feelings and clearing his name than about concerning himself with her. He'd always been this way, but Kenzie had overlooked it, thinking it merely the way of men. She'd been confident that in his own way, he truly did think about her needs. But of course, he hadn't.

Her silence was all the encouragement he needed. "Kenzie, we were wronged, and if you refuse me now, then my father wins. He's the one who sought to keep us apart. He doesn't realize how much I truly love you. He thought that because I had a reputation for visiting my affections on many young ladies prior to meeting you, that I was no more committed to our love than I was my previous affairs. He was wrong, and once we are married, I will be able to prove it to him."

"And that's important to you?"

His brow furrowed. "Of course it's important. He needs to realize that we belong together. It doesn't matter that you have no money. It doesn't matter that your family isn't on the social register. Nothing matters but the fact that I love you."

"Not even my feelings?"

Arthur shook his head. "I know your feelings. You love me. You may feel confused by Dr. Fisher, but that's only because you thought I had betrayed you. You sought solace with him, but it was all based on a lie."

"I was worried that might be the case at one time," Kenzie admitted, "but not now. I don't feel the same for you that I feel for him."

"But if you would just come away from here with me, I know I could convince you that you still love me. No one writes the kind of letter you did, filled with emotion and passion, without feeling something."

"I do feel something." She got up from the table. "I feel regret. Regret that I allowed my loneliness and desperation to overrule my common sense. When you first came to me and asked to court me, I told you no. I knew then that our relationship was a lost cause. I could never fit into your world. I can't play those games—pretend I'm something I'm not. I tried, and for a time I convinced myself that I could manage it, but now I see how mistaken I was. I'm sorry, Arthur. I can't marry you."

"But why, Kenzie? Why?"

"Because I have feelings for someone else."

"Dr. Fisher?" He got to his feet and reached for her. "Those feelings will pass if you just give me a chance. Think of all the fun we had together, Kenzie. I was good for you, and you enjoyed our outings and time alone. You can enjoy it again."

She backed up a step before he could take hold of her. "Go back to Missouri, Arthur. I'm confident that you will find another bride before the year is out."

"But I love *you*. I truly do. I can't go back without you by my side. We've both suffered so much, all because other people interfered in our lives. Don't let that happen now."

She felt sorry for him. She'd never seen Arthur Morgan beg. Even when she first refused his attentions, he hadn't begged her for anything. Rather, he had pursued her with relentless attention to detail. He had wooed and cajoled, but never begged.

"I'm not letting anyone interfere." She sighed. "And I certainly don't wish to cause you pain. The idea that your family could do such a heinous thing gives me a great deal of sympathy for you. We have to allow that this was neither your fault nor mine. It simply is what it is."

He moved closer. "But you pledged yourself to me. What about your word? I've always known you to be a woman of your word."

Kenzie frowned. She didn't like being reminded that she was going back on her promise to marry him—to be faithful to him forever.

"Kenzie, just give me a chance . . . just a few days to show you how much I care. Don't punish me for the mistakes of others."

Her clarity and purpose began to fade. He made a good point.

It wasn't his fault that his family had interfered. Maybe she was wrong to dismiss him without even giving him a chance. But what about Micah? Her love for him wasn't imaginary.

"Please, Kenzie. It's not fair to dismiss me without at least giving me a chance to win you back."

Her temples began to throb. Arthur had always had a way of convincing her that his way was right, but now she knew that wasn't true.

"I can't talk about this anymore, Arthur. I'm sorry that I can't do what you ask. Please excuse me."

She hurried back into the warehouse, hoping for solace. Why was it so easy for Arthur to confuse her? Everything had seemed so clear, but now it was just as murky as it had been before.

"Kenzie?" Caleb called as she hurried to her room.

She paused only a moment. "I know what you said, Caleb, but I did promise him my love, my life. How do I remain an honorable person and take that back?"

Caleb's expression was sympathetic. "How can you not? You don't love him anymore. How can you promise something that doesn't exist?"

She pressed her fingers against her head. "Never mind. I just need some time alone to think."

Victoria watched the performance from the warehouse's open window. She heard Arthur plead his case and listened as Kenzie completely disregarded his feelings. She had heard Kenzie and her friends discuss Arthur at length earlier in the day. He was rich and very handsome. She wasn't inclined to throw herself at him, but she felt certain they could help each other.

Kenzie rushed into the warehouse, spoke for a moment with Caleb, then hurried for the private quarters. Meanwhile, Caleb went to his office. With a quick glance around, Victoria could see that everyone else was occupied or absent. She smiled and made her way outside. Arthur was still standing next to the table, as if trying to figure out what to do next.

"Hello, you must be Arthur Morgan."

He turned and looked at her. Victoria was glad she'd dressed in her pink muslin with the rounded neckline. It wasn't low enough to entice, but it did show off her figure.

She sauntered closer. "I'm Victoria Whitley. You may have heard of my father, William Whitley."

He nodded. "Clark Whitley's son?"

"The same. I overheard your conversation. Not only that, but I've heard a great many other conversations, and I can't help but believe we might be useful to each other."

"In what way?" Arthur asked. His expression told her he was intrigued.

Victoria gave a seductive smile. "In the way that moneyed people are always useful to each other. The fact is, I need help getting my inheritance. My father and grandmother both died in the earthquake and now, unfortunately, my cousin Judith holds the purse strings. And you . . . well, you need help convincing Miss Gifford that she belongs with you."

"And how do you propose to do that?"

She shrugged. "I'm not without my charms."

He looked her over from head to toe and smiled. "I can see that."

"I believe we should form an alliance."

He nodded. "Perhaps you're right, Miss Whitley."

CHAPTER 14

Patrick will return every night, and we'll be over to see to things during the day," Caleb told Mrs. Andrews.

Micah stood nearby, listening to his friend give last-minute instructions to the few remaining residents at the warehouse. He had come to help move Caleb and the others back into Caleb's house, hoping he'd have the chance to speak to Kenzie about her desire to become a nurse. And if the opportunity arose to give her another kiss and remind her of what she felt for him, so much the better.

"If you have any problems at all, just send word, and I'll come right away," Caleb finished.

Mrs. Andrews chuckled. "Son, I've been taking care of myself since my husband passed on ten years ago. I'll be just fine. We'll be fine. Mr. Murdock is a good man, and my Mr. Lake will be around."

Caleb smiled. "Of course, but with the army pulling out by the end of June, I fear that the city's more unsavory types might grow bolder."

Mrs. Andrews patted his hand. "You just stop your fretting.

We're in God's hands. If nothing else, the earthquake and fires proved that to me."

He sighed. "I agree. We are in God's hands, and I won't accomplish a single thing by worrying." He turned to Micah. "Have we loaded the last of the things we're taking to the house?"

"Yes. There wasn't much left, since you took over some of the items yesterday."

"Then I suppose we should be on our way. I know the girls will want to put everything in order before nightfall."

They made their way outside, and Caleb climbed up into the wagon. Micah jumped aboard as well and took a seat beside him.

"What are your plans for this place and the future?" Micah asked.

Caleb snapped the lines. "I was just speaking to your father about it last Sunday. We both still agree that it'll make a good refuge for people who need a helping hand. Your father thinks that we should return to our original plan for it to house only women and children, however. It's difficult to provide adequate privacy for both men and women, and we want everything to be above reproach. Judith wants to add on private quarters and live there ourselves. She's amazing, the way she cares for people. God truly sent me a gem."

"I agree and feel the same where Kenzie is concerned."

"I'm praying that situation gets resolved soon. Morgan's arrival has really taken a toll on Kenzie's peace of mind."

Micah shrugged. "Better now than later. If there truly was a conspiracy to keep Morgan and Kenzie apart, then I want the details sorted out. I know she doesn't love him. She loves me."

Caleb seemed to consider this a moment, and in his silence, Micah continued. "I've got a thought to add regarding the warehouse. I'd like to offer my assistance."

Caleb glanced over at him. "In what way?"

"I'd like to be a daily presence for you at the warehouse as a doctor. I can set aside part of the warehouse for patients—an examination office, even a small area for the sick. I could receive patients there as well as take care of any residents who are sick. We could make it a hospital for the poor."

"I think that's a marvelous idea. I would happily pay you to manage the facilities as well."

Micah grinned. "And I would let you, since many of the patients I treat can't pay."

Caleb nodded. "I could provide some of the equipment and supplies you'd need as well. Judith would probably want to help. She's been after me to find ways to use her inheritance to help the people of San Francisco."

"Well, you just said she wants to have private quarters in which to live on site. Perhaps we might buy the property next door as your sister once suggested and build on." Micah grinned. "A little hospital and quarters for my family. But we can discuss that at a later date."

"Have you talked to Kenzie since Arthur came to speak to her today?"

Micah frowned. "I was livid when I heard he was here. He definitely knows how to make her feel guilty. I want to punch him in his smug face. Honestly, he makes me forget my Christian charity and Hippocratic oath."

Caleb chuckled. "I completely understand. When I spoke with Morgan, I got the sense he was hiding something. There's something that just doesn't figure where he's concerned, and I intend to find out what it is."

"I agree, but what do you have in mind?"

"I'm going to Kansas City. His family is established there. Kenzie's father and mother live close by in a smaller town. I intend to seek out information."

"About what?"

"About whatever I can learn regarding Morgan. I just can't see a man like him being fooled by his family. He's a willful person—used to getting his own way. I felt the entire time I was speaking with him at the hotel that he was giving a performance, but for what purpose, I'm not entirely certain."

"I feel the same way, but I figured it was just because I'm in love with Kenzie." Micah felt his anger grow. "He's done nothing but act out of selfishness, including coming here."

"That's just what troubles me. Why is he really here? Why is he so determined to marry Kenzie? And not just marry her, but marry her immediately before he even heads back to Kansas City."

"What motive could he have but to impose his will? Kenzie isn't wealthy. It's not like he'll gain a huge dowry or family connection."

"Yet there's something there," Caleb said, looking at Micah. "And that's why I must go see Kenzie's father, as well as learn what I can about Morgan's family and what happened last year to make them put an end to the wedding."

"When will you go?"

"I'm not sure. I need to see what's happening with the committee to oust Ruef and talk to Camri and Judith about our living accommodations. With Victoria as an addition in our house, it gives me new issues and problems to deal with. I need to make sure everything else is in order before I leave San Francisco. I'll be gone at least ten days, maybe longer."

"Well, I'll certainly do whatever I can to help. You know that."

Caleb nodded. "Thank you. I appreciate being able to count on you and Patrick. Who knows what our ladies might get up to."

Micah laughed. "That's for sure."

That evening, after everything was set to rights and Judith had made them a delicious dinner, Kenzie sat with the others in the front room while Caleb played the piano and Judith sat on the bench beside him. Camri and Patrick held hands and talked at a small table in one corner of the room, while Micah took his place beside Kenzie on the sofa. Thankfully, Victoria had retired to Camri's old room. She claimed she was feeling overly sad about her family, but Kenzie didn't believe her, nor did she think the others believed it.

"What do you think about Caleb going to Missouri to meet with your father?" Micah asked as Caleb and Judith broke into song.

Kenzie smiled at the way they seemed always to have such fun together. "I hope I'm that happy one day."

"If I have anything to say about it, you will be."

She looked at him, and her smile waned. She was still so frustrated by Arthur's reappearance. She didn't want Micah to be hurt in any of this. "To answer your question, I'm glad Caleb is going. He feels certain there is more to Arthur's arrival than meets the eye."

"I'm convinced there is too. Not that I wouldn't cross the entire world to find you if you'd gotten away from me." He gave her a wink.

Kenzie's heart skipped a beat. "Micah, I don't . . . I . . ." She couldn't figure out what to say.

His expression sobered. "Will you speak honestly with me?"

"Haven't I always?"

He gave a slow nod. "Yes, you've been brutally honest, and I trust you will be now. It's important that you are, because what I have to say will greatly affect our future."

She tensed. Was he going to propose again? She lowered her gaze and waited for him to continue. She knew she loved him, but her confusion and guilt over Arthur made it impossible to accept Micah's offer of marriage. She had to sort through those matters first, and Micah would just need to understand that.

Micah took a breath. "I want the truth. Do you still love Arthur?"

Her head snapped up. "What?"

His expression left no doubt that what he was about to say was difficult. "I want to know if you still love Arthur. If you love him, truly love him, then I don't want to cause you more pain and difficulty. I've thought about this a great deal. I don't want to lose you, Kenzie, but if you love him and you're convinced that he'll make you happy, then I'll walk away."

She couldn't hide her surprise. "Just like that?"

"I want you to be happy." He gave a heavy sigh. "I talk about not letting you go and how deeply I love you, but love doesn't demand its own way. If the only way for you to be truly happy is to be with Arthur, then I will have to trust that the Lord has someone else for me. Your happiness matters more to me than anything."

If she hadn't already realized her love for him, Micah's words would have convinced her. That he was willing to put her feelings first touched her deeply.

"No one has ever offered me such a selfless act of love," she admitted.

"No one has ever loved you as I do," he promised. "It wouldn't be easy for me to step aside, but if you tell me that you truly love him, that you want him for your husband, I will."

He looked so miserable that Kenzie couldn't keep him guessing. "I don't . . . I don't think I love him." She frowned. "Caleb spoke about true love bearing and enduring all things. If that's the basis of real love, then I can't say that I ever experienced that for Arthur. Still, with all the lies and deception his family used to separate us, I feel guilty for willingly complying and giving up so easily. I never bothered to seek him out or try to understand what had happened. I simply ran away."

"You were hurt. It's not unusual for a wounded person to want to get away from the cause of their misery."

Judith and Caleb were laughing about something, and for a moment, Kenzie focused on their joy. She loved being part of this family. She didn't regret leaving Missouri, although she did miss her mother. But when she considered everything that had happened over the last year, Missouri no longer felt like home.

"I have one more question," Micah said, pulling her thoughts back to him.

"All right." She could see he was serious. "I'll try to give you an honest answer."

"Do you love me . . . even a little?"

She swallowed hard, but the lump that formed in her throat refused to move. Could she say what needed to be said without causing him even more frustration?

"Kenzie?"

"I do," she barely whispered, "but just as I'm confused about all that transpired with Arthur, I don't want to make another mistake with you."

"What are you saying? How could loving me be a mistake?"

"It feels like my entire life this last year has been based on lies. What if my feelings for you are as well? You pursued me when I was most vulnerable. I was heartbroken—devastated by the loss of my dream of true love. You came along and insisted I let you in my life. As I got used to you and came to accept that you were a good man—that your feelings were genuine—I began to allow myself to have feelings for you."

"Although you fought it all the way," he teased.

"But what if those feelings are nothing more than emotions built on the ruins of my love for Arthur?"

"What if they are? You make them sound less valid because they came forth from the ashes. Will the city being built now have less relevance or validity just because the new is being built on the ashes of the old?"

He always had a way to explain away her concerns. "I just don't want to make another mistake." She met his gaze. "I want this to be real."

"It is real, Kenzie. Arthur is the past. Don't let him ruin what we can have together. We've always been honest with each other—sometimes painfully so. I love you, and you know that you love me. You told me so just a few minutes ago, and you cannot take it back now." He grinned.

"I don't want to. I just want to be certain it will last."

He put his arm around her shoulders and pulled her close. Kenzie let her head rest on his shoulder. She was surprised at how right it felt. She tried to remember ever feeling like this with Arthur, but in that moment, she couldn't even call him to mind. Micah's presence was too overpowering—too wonderful. She sighed.

"See," he whispered against her ear, "this is exactly where you belong."

When Victoria was certain that the others had retired to bed, she pulled on her robe and made her way downstairs. She was thankful that Camri had agreed to share a room with Judith so that Victoria could have a room to herself. It would afford her the opportunity to scout out the house without the others questioning what she was doing.

The house was dark. The electricity hadn't yet been restored, but Victoria knew where she could get what she needed. She'd made a close inventory earlier in the evening of anything she thought might prove useful. There were a few pieces of bric-a-brac she might be able to sell, and the silver candlesticks in the dining room should fetch a good sum. If she could just get enough money together, she could buy a train ticket to New York. She had friends there, and surely they would see that she gained both her inheritance and her freedom.

She felt her way along the hall and into the dining room, where she knew she'd find candles and matches. She quickly lit a small candle and glanced around the room. It was a fairly large dining room. Not anything like her Grandmother's, but it was better than she'd anticipated.

Back in the hall, Victoria headed toward the back of the house.

"Who's there?" Caleb called out.

She startled and froze in place, then drew a deep breath. "It's Victoria."

A door opened to her right, and the warm glow of lamplight illuminated Caleb Coulter. He smiled. "Is something wrong?"

She tried to figure out how to best play this hand. "I was . . . well, I couldn't sleep."

"Why don't you come in, and we can talk? I can tell you about God. You said you'd like to know more."

A sermon was the last thing she wanted to hear, but Victoria knew she would do well to play this game. "Yes, of course. I'd like that."

As she followed him into the room, she undid the sash of her robe. Her nightgown and robe were hardly appropriate attire, and should someone else see her like this, they might question what was going on between her and Caleb. She smiled and fervently hoped someone might happen upon them.

"Sit here by the fire so you won't get cold. I'll fetch you a blanket as well." Caleb crossed the room to a wooden trunk and pulled out a small quilt. "This should do the trick."

Victoria took a chair. "I'm not cold." She smiled up at him as he put the blanket across her lap. "But thank you."

Caleb picked up his Bible from the desk and joined her at the fire. "Have you had any religious training?"

She shrugged. "We attended church with some regularity. I have to admit, however, that it was all beyond me. The minister talked of one thing and another, and it always seemed so confusing. I was never able to figure out what it was all about, and no one in my family seemed even remotely interested in explaining it to me."

"Pity. But we'll rectify that as best we can. Do you know who Jesus is?"

"Of course. They call him the Son of God. He was born in a manger, and that's why we celebrate Christmas."

"Do you understand the concept of sin?"

She shrugged. "I suppose I do as well as the next person. Sin is . . . well, evil. I suppose to a religious person it would be doing anything but sitting and praying and reading your Bible."

Caleb chuckled. "Not exactly. Christians can do a great many things besides praying and reading and still avoid sin. You see, God created man in a perfect state. He made Adam and Eve as the first man and woman and placed them in a beautiful garden. Life was perfect and all was well. But then things changed."

"Oh yes. I recall hearing about Eve eating an apple that God had forbidden." Victoria tried her best to appear interested. "The serpent told her to eat it, right?"

"Yes. The serpent, or Satan, convinced her that she hadn't heard God correctly—that it wouldn't really be wrong. Satan is still doing that to each of us. He whispers in our ear that it isn't really wrong to lie or cheat. That it's not really a sin if we forsake God. His entire purpose is to separate us from God. That's what sin does. It separates us from God."

"So is there a list of rules we can follow? Something that tells us what is a sin and what isn't?" She shifted in her chair, letting her robe open even more. "I know there are those ten commandments. Is that what I have to follow?"

Caleb smiled and opened his Bible. "Once, when Jesus was

speaking to a group of people—most of whom were quite knowledgeable about the commandments God had given—one of them asked which commandment was most important."

"What did Jesus say?" She leaned forward, hoping she looked enticing.

"Let me read his answer to you." Caleb flipped several pages. "'Thou shalt love the Lord thy God with all thy heart, and with all thy soul, and with all thy mind. This is the first and great commandment. And the second is like unto it, thou shalt love thy neighbor as thyself.'"

She shook her head and laughed without meaning to.

Caleb looked at her with a raised brow. "What's funny?"

"I couldn't do that. I could maybe love God, but my neighbors were boring, insipid people who always complained about one thing or another." She frowned. "Although I suppose now that their house has burned down, I don't know who my neighbors are. But I certainly cannot love them as I love myself."

"Your neighbors are everyone around you. God wants you to show love to everyone, Victoria. Not because they're rich or poor, beautiful or plain. If you love others, then you won't be inclined to act against them in sin. You won't want to lie to them or steal from them. This is why Jesus spoke the way He did. When you love God, you will do whatever you can to please Him, which means avoiding acts of selfishness or self-centered desires."

She vaguely recalled hearing all of this before, but since it wasn't something she could ever imagine doing or even wanting to do, Victoria had disregarded it. However, this was important to Caleb, and if she was going to win his trust, she would have to pretend.

She put on a look of sorrow. "I could never be that good."

"No one could, Victoria. That's why God sent His Son, Jesus."

Caleb seemed to be waiting for her to say something. "I don't understand."

He nodded. "He knew we needed someone who could account for the sins of the world—our sins. We could never be good enough or offer enough sacrifices and prayers to be forgiven all our sins, so our heavenly Father sent His only Son, Jesus, to be the sacrifice for us all. We can never be perfect, but we should strive to live our lives to please God. Having Jesus helps us to do that."

"That was very nice of God to do that," she finally replied.

"It was amazingly nice—it was a sacrifice of love. We can't hope to have eternal life unless we accept Jesus as our Savior and allow Him authority over our lives."

"I see." Victoria looked into the fire, wondering how much longer he would drone on about God.

"Victoria, remember how I told you that I found peace in God's love? I can't imagine how you must feel without having Him to turn to. You see, I was raised by parents who believe God's Word and helped me find Him at a very young age. I've always known Him, it seems."

She could hear by the tone of his voice that this was very special to him. She nodded. "You were very fortunate. My parents were never with me very much. I had a nanny to raise me and see that I did what was proper. I don't think she knew much about God."

"I'm sorry to hear that. You lost your mother when you were very young, didn't you?"

Victoria steeled her heart. "Yes. It was the hardest thing I ever dealt with."

"I can't even imagine. Your pain must have been great. I'm sure it's still painful to recall."

Victoria started to deny it but reminded herself that having Caleb's sympathy would be to her advantage. Then another thought came to mind.

"It is. When Mother died, I sought comfort where I could. I had a friend whose mother was very understanding. She invited me over to their house often and she showed me all the love that I was missing. Grandmother, you see, was far too worried about Cora. Our family never recovered from Judith being taken, and that remained our grandmother's concern, even after I lost my mother. My friend and her mother were all that got me through my grief. That's why I long to go to them now. I know they would offer me great comfort in my time of loss."

"I didn't know that," Caleb replied. He looked at her for a moment. "Do you believe they would take you in?"

She felt her heart beat a little faster. "I do. They now live in New York City, and I know they would have me. They've told me as much on many occasions." It wasn't a complete lie. She did have friends there, and with the right things said, she was certain they'd allow her to come stay for a time.

Caleb nodded. "Then perhaps we should consider it. Why don't you write down their name and address? I'll make some inquiries."

"You would do that for me? What if Judith doesn't approve?"

He smiled. "Judith wants you to be happy, Victoria. Despite whatever else you believe about her."

Victoria rose and stood in front of him. "I don't know what to believe about Judith, but I think you truly care about me. I shall try to put my trust in you."

"Better you should put it in God, Victoria."

He rose, and Victoria pretended to stumble. She swayed to the right as if she might fall. Caleb easily caught her, and Victoria grabbed on to his shirt.

"I'm so sorry. I didn't mean to be so clumsy."

"No harm done." He released her, but she continued to hold on to him.

"Thank you, Caleb. You are wonderful. I can see why Judith loves you." She stretched up on tiptoe and kissed his cheek before he could protest. "I think I could love you as well."

CHAPTER 15

The next morning at breakfast, Caleb was caught up in his newspaper while Kenzie listened to Camri and Judith talk about their renewed wedding plans. Micah had once suggested Kenzie consider making the affair a triple wedding, but so far she hadn't allowed herself even a sliver of a dream in that regard.

"I know it may sound silly," Judith said, helping herself to a plate of biscuits, "but I'm content for our wedding to be very simple. After all we've been through this last year, having a big event with all sorts of frippery and finery isn't important."

"I agree," Camri said, nodding. "It's amazing how the earthquake and fire changed my perspective. When I see people digging in the ruins of their former lives—finding so little to rebuild on—it just doesn't seem right to spend a fortune on a wedding."

Victoria came into the dining room. She was dressed in a powder blue gown much nicer than the occasion called for. Kenzie could see she had attempted to dress up her hair. Without someone to do it up for her, however, all she had managed was weaving a ribbon through her blond locks and tying it in the back.

"Good morning, Victoria." Judith gave her a smile. "I was beginning to think I'd have to come wake you again."

Victoria suppressed a yawn and took a seat opposite Caleb. "I apologize, cousin. I'm afraid I was up rather late." She smiled at Caleb. "I want to thank you for our time alone last night, Caleb. You certainly made me feel better."

Judith wasn't able to hide her surprise. Neither was Camri. Kenzie knew by the look in Victoria's eyes that she enjoyed their shock.

"I very much enjoyed the fire and the quilt you insisted I have. It was much warmer than my nightgown."

Caleb raised a brow and looked at Judith. "Victoria found me in my office quite late last night. She told me she wanted to know more about God. I thought perhaps if you ladies were going to start again on your Bible study, you might include her."

Kenzie saw a mix of emotions cross Victoria's face before she looked away. It was clear she wasn't interested in a Bible study.

"I think that would be very nice," Kenzie said, reaching for her tea. "What is it that the Bible says about training up a child when they're young? Victoria could benefit greatly from such study."

"I agree," Camri said, nodding as she closed ranks around Judith. "It's important for the older women to teach the younger. We'll have to figure out a good time. Today won't work, however. Patrick is coming for me soon. We're going to take advantage of our Saturday and spend the entire day together. Caleb, you and Judith should join us. We can take the ferry to Oakland and get away from all the destruction and noise. I think we need to refresh ourselves in order to have strength to move ahead."

"I think you should do exactly that," Kenzie declared. "I'm going with Cousin George and Mrs. Andrews. They intend to be married today by Judge Winters."

"What?" Camri cried. "Why didn't they tell us? We might have planned a celebration!"

Kenzie laughed. "Because we might have planned a celebration. They just wanted a very quiet arrangement. Otherwise I should be here the entire day."

"We can hardly leave Victoria behind," Judith said, still appearing confused by what her cousin had said earlier.

"Oh, she can come with me to see Cousin George married, and then we'll return to the house. You all go and enjoy yourselves," Kenzie insisted. She looked at Victoria, who was watching her with a look of displeasure.

"I don't know," Caleb said. "There's a lot of work I should be doing."

"It'll keep, brother dear." A knock sounded on the front door, and Camri jumped to her feet. "That will be Patrick."

After breakfast, the plans were finalized, and the foursome took off for their day of fun. Victoria moped around the house as if she'd been asked to attend her own funeral. Kenzie thought about confronting her regarding her performance at breakfast but thought better of it. It might be wise to let Victoria think she had the upper hand.

"Do I really have to go to your cousin's wedding?" Victoria asked as Kenzie came downstairs with her hat and gloves.

"What else would you do?" Kenzie paused in the hall to put on her hat. She could see Victoria's scowling face in the mirror.

"Stay here." Victoria crossed her arms, and Kenzie turned to face her. "In fact," the girl continued, "that's exactly what I intend to do. You can hardly force me to go." She marched into the front room and plopped down in one of the stuffed chairs.

Kenzie wasn't sure what to do. If she didn't get a move on, she would be late, and that in turn would delay the wedding. She looked at Victoria and shook her head. "Have it your way. I hardly care one whit what you do, but if anything is amiss when I return, you can be certain Caleb and Judith will hear about your behavior."

Victoria looked at her as if she'd lost her mind. "I'm not causing any trouble at all. I just don't feel like attending a wedding. I just lost my family. Have you no mercy? No compassion?"

Kenzie pulled on her gloves. "Just make sure you give me no reason to tell them."

She left the house and was only a few steps down the street when she heard Micah call her name. She turned to find him driving up behind her.

She smiled. "I see you got your automobile back."

He stopped and leaned across the seat to open the passenger door. "Let me drive you."

"You don't even know where I'm going."

"I do too. You're going to your cousin's wedding."

Kenzie moved to the car and looked at Micah. "I said nothing about that."

"You didn't have to. I'm going as Mrs. Andrews's guest." He shrugged. "She wanted me to stand as her witness. We've been friends for a very long time."

Kenzie rolled her eyes. "Are you sure this isn't just a ploy on your behalf to get me up before a judge?"

He laughed. "The thought had crossed my mind."

Kenzie slid gracefully onto the seat. Before she could completely close the door, Micah leaned across her and did it for her. As he straightened back up, he quickly touched his lips to hers.

"I'd like to spend more time on that effort," he said in her ear, "but we'll be late."

The kiss left her unable to think or speak. She hadn't expected to even see Micah today, and yet here he was, and she couldn't deny she was pleased. His kiss, even abbreviated, sent a tingle through her like an electric current.

"Aren't you going to at least chastise me?" he asked, still not putting the car into motion.

Kenzie shook her head and met his gaze. "No. The thought never crossed my mind."

His eyes widened and his brow shot up. "Well, I'll be. The lady is finally coming around to my way of thinking." He rubbed his gloved hands together and put the car in gear. "We may have to talk to that judge after all."

Victoria peered from the front window to see which direction Kenzie had gone. She saw a car stop and recognized Dr. Fisher as the driver. Maybe Kenzie wasn't going to a wedding at all. Perhaps she was running off for a day of fun with the good doctor. Either way, with Kenzie in the company of Micah Fisher, Arthur Morgan would be very unhappy. Perhaps he'd like to know about it.

When the car moved off down the street, Victoria put her own plans into motion. She knew where she could find Arthur Morgan, and with any luck at all, she could get there and back before Kenzie returned. She was desperate for his help, and now she had some information he might like to know.

Just in case Kenzie came back early, Victoria decided she would pull one of the same tricks she had at home when she'd wanted to go out unnoticed. Hurrying upstairs, she arranged her bed in such a fashion that the pillows gave the appearance of a body beneath the covers. Next, she changed out of the gown she'd been wearing and draped it across the foot of the bed. She positioned her shoes next to the bed, then retrieved another pair from one of her many clothes trunks.

Once she'd redressed in her black mourning clothes, Victoria went downstairs to the kitchen level. Camri had mentioned an exterior door, and Victoria wanted to make certain it was unlocked. Now when she returned, she could sneak in that way, and no one would be any wiser about her absence.

She wasn't used to having to do for herself, but she could manage. Anyone who thought otherwise was a fool. She had been giving her family the slip for more years than she could remember.

Laughter bubbled up inside her at the thought of what she was about to do. She would let Arthur know that Kenzie would be home later that day—and alone. Victoria frowned. At least she hoped Kenzie would be alone. Arthur had told her it was important that he find a way to get Kenzie away from the others, and this opportunity was too good to pass up.

She made her way to Arthur's hotel wearing her mourning clothes and veil. She ignored the doorman when he asked if he might help her. Arthur had given her his room number, and while it was scandalous for her to go to a man's hotel room, she didn't have time for proprieties. If she asked the front desk clerk to have Arthur notified and brought to the lobby, it would only expose her presence at the hotel. Hopefully this way, no one would pay her any mind.

When she knocked at his room, Arthur opened the door and stared at her for a moment as if not recognizing who she was.

Victoria raised her veil and pushed past him. "Shut the door, you fool. We don't need anyone recognizing me."

He did as she commanded. "What are you doing here?"

"You told me to let you know when Kenzie was alone. She'll be alone this afternoon. At least, I believe she will be. The others have gone to Oakland for the day, and Kenzie just left to attend her cousin's wedding. I have to be quick about this, and you must pay for a taxi for me to return."

He smiled. "You have definitely captured my attention."

She crossed her arms. "I thought we agreed to be useful to one another."

"Of course. I'll do as you say. So Kenzie will be at the house alone?"

"I'll be there, but I'll conveniently disappear and leave you two alone. I honestly don't know why you want her. She's dull as dishwater and has a voice like a harpy."

He laughed and casually took a seat. "Kenzie is my business. What I want to know is what you expect me to do for you."

Victoria cocked her head. She crossed to where he sat and took the chair opposite him. "I need help to get my inheritance. I want you to find me someone—a lawyer or a judge or someone with power who can be bought. You'll have to front the money, but I assure you that once I have mine, you'll be paid back."

"Perhaps you should give me the details of why you can't access your funds without legal aid."

"My cousin Judith has the advantage of age. I'm only nineteen, and therefore they're holding my money in trust until I reach my majority. However, I think with the right incentive, we should be able to convince a judge to let me have my money and freedom. A great many young women set out on their own prior to reaching the age of twenty-one. Given my circumstances—my family having been killed and Judith being a stranger—I can't help but believe some sort of arrangement could be made. For the right price, of course."

Arthur's expression turned wolfish. "I'd arrange for you myself if I didn't have Kenzie to contend with. You're exactly the kind of young woman I enjoy spending time with. Perhaps I could set you up somewhere in Kansas City."

Victoria smiled in her most seductive manner. "We shall see. First things first. You, for whatever reason, need to get Kenzie to marry you, and I need my funds released from the care of my cousin. Can you find me a lawyer?"

"Of course. My family has any number of connections here in San Francisco, but as I recall, one man in particular seems able to accomplish almost anything. I'll get in touch with him immediately."

Victoria got to her feet. "Thank you. What's his name?"

"Ruef. Abraham Ruef."

"So, did that give you any thoughts as to saying yes to my proposal?" Micah asked as he drove Kenzie home from the small ceremony.

"I'm still surprised at the quickness of Cousin George marrying Mrs. Andrews. I never thought him the marrying type. He's been single all these years."

"When a man has had enough loneliness and solitude, he can't marry fast enough."

She looked at him. "Is that why you want to get married?"

Micah turned a corner and barely missed a stack of debris. Some of the streets were still barely passable, so he kept his eyes on the road ahead. "I think you know me better than that."

"Cousin George is such a strange man anyway," Kenzie continued. "He's spent so many years caught up in his belief that someone is out to do him in. He was always certain that someone was trying to ruin his chocolate business, and now he's working for the very man he called the enemy."

"Sometimes enemies can become quite chummy." He touched her cheek and smiled when she didn't jump back as she used to.

"We've never been enemies, Micah," she countered.

He nodded. "True. Perhaps *adversaries* would be a better term. Like in a game of chess. We both had our pieces and our moves, and the challenge was to see if we could endure to the end."

"I thought the challenge of chess was to put the king in checkmate."

"Well, you did that the very first time I met you." He glanced over long enough to see her blush. "Why don't you tell me something about your childhood? Share a memory."

Kenzie said nothing, and Micah worried he'd offended her. He looked over again to find her deep in thought.

"Tell me why they named you Kenzie."

She shook her head. "I've always hated my name. Who in their right mind names a little girl after a commanding officer in the army? My father wanted a son, and when I was born, he was very disappointed, but my mother, hoping to assuage his wounded spirit, suggested he give me the name he would have given a son. She knew it was important to him. So they named me Merton Kenzie after the man my father so admired—who saved Father's life at Gettysburg. But it didn't help. He still regretted me. I tried hard to win him over, but I wasn't a boy."

Micah heard the sadness in her voice. "I, for one, am very glad you aren't a boy." She looked at him, and their eyes met for a moment. He could see that the memory troubled her greatly. "I'm sure you were a beautiful little girl."

"I was as I am now. Red-haired and freckled. I take after my mother's grandfather. No one else has this curse, as my father calls it."

"I love your red hair. Your freckles too. I intend to count each and every one of them, in fact." He grinned. "After we're married, of course."

"You, Dr. Fisher, are quite out of line. I shall think twice before agreeing to ride with you again."

He laughed heartily, pulled up to the curb in front of Caleb's house, and turned off the motor. "Did your father ever get his boy?"

"Yes and no. When I was five, my brother James was stillborn. It was my father's greatest sorrow. My mother had had several miscarriages prior to that, and afterward there were no more children. I grew up an only child, and my father did his best to tolerate me."

"I'm so sorry. You deserved much better."

She shrugged. "I know he loved me in his own way. Especially once I grew old enough to be useful. He worked for his uncle, running a mercantile, and he put me to work there doing any number of things. Still, I always knew I wasn't truly what he wanted. When Arthur stood me up on our wedding day, I figured I wasn't what he wanted either."

"You're definitely what I want." Micah took hold of her chin and turned her to face him. "Kenzie, you are everything I ever dreamed of when I thought of a wife. You're all I'll ever want."

She searched his face as if trying to ascertain the truth of his words. He wished she could see into his heart and know exactly how much he loved her.

"Please, Kenzie, say you'll marry me."

"I . . . I . . ."

He thought for a moment she would agree, but then just as quickly, she opened the door and got out of the car. "I have to go."

He watched her race up the steps to Caleb's house and wondered if he shouldn't chase after her. To what purpose though? He could hardly force her to agree.

Micah heaved a sigh. Somehow he had to prove to her that his love was real—that he wouldn't be one more disappointed man in her life.

CHAPTER 16

Kenzie could hardly still her trembling after leaving Micah. She entered the house and closed the door with a sigh. She leaned back against the cool wood and wondered when she'd ever feel free to give Micah the answer he longed for.

"Kenzie."

She jumped at the sound of Arthur whispering her name. He stood in the archway of the front sitting room just a few feet away, watching her.

"What in the world are you doing here?" she demanded.

"I had to see you. The young lady staying with you let me in. She said I could wait for you to return. I see you were with that doctor again."

"'Again'? Are you spying on me and keeping a record?" Anger gave her strength. She straightened and pulled off her gloves. "Arthur, you have no business being here."

"Of course I do. You're my business, and at the moment, the only one I can focus on. I think about you every moment of the day."

He gave her his lopsided boyish smile. How she used to love

it. He seemed like such a sweet innocent boy when he smiled like that. Kenzie put her gloves aside and removed a long pin from her hat.

"It isn't appropriate for you to be here, Arthur. You need to go." She contemplated the hat pin in her hand before stepping back and opening the door.

"It isn't fair that you give that doctor a chance to woo you, but you won't even speak to me." Arthur moved closer, and Kenzie tightened her grip on the hat pin. "He doesn't know you like I do. He can't possibly care for you as I can."

"I'm not going to discuss Dr. Fisher with you."

"I can give you anything you want," Arthur said, standing within inches of her. "I'll build you a new mansion. I'll give you furs and jewels. I'll set you up with your own bank account and fill it with more money than you could ever spend."

"Those things would mean nothing without love."

"But we'll have love too." He reached out to touch her, but she held up the pin. He stepped back. "I know you love me."

"Arthur, what has become apparent to me is that I do not love you. I don't think I ever did—not the way I should have."

"How can you possibly say that? I remember our time together. I remember our talks. You seemed to like my kisses well enough." Again he grinned.

She remembered those times too. They now paled when she thought of how Micah made her feel. "Maybe growing closer to God has helped me better understand what love really is . . . and what it's not."

"If religion is important to you, it'll be important to me too," he said, his voice desperate. "I'll build you your own church—a grand cathedral. It'll be the most beautiful in the world, I promise. I'll accompany you there every Sunday. Just say you'll marry me."

Kenzie thought of Satan tempting Jesus with the world, if

only He'd fall down and worship Satan. "No. I will not marry you, Arthur. Now please, just go."

His expression grew sad, but there was something else in his eyes. Anger. She'd seen that anger many times when he'd dealt with issues that didn't go his way.

"Kenzie, just—"

"Good-bye, Arthur." She turned and walked away. When she reached the stairs, she called over her shoulder, "Make sure you close the door behind you."

Victoria knew the minute everyone returned to the house from their day of fun, due to the laughter. Kenzie soon joined them, and Victoria heard her telling them how Victoria had refused to go with her to the wedding and then allowed Arthur into the house. No doubt Kenzie would encourage them to lock her up somewhere or get her a nanny who would see that she did no further harm.

It made Victoria angrier than she could say that they held the power to command her. She had thought she'd be rid of them all by now. Hopefully with Arthur Morgan's help, it would happen, but it didn't hurt to try to hurry things along. If she could set them all against each other instead of against her, then maybe she could win her freedom. Better still, if she could convince her poor little cousin that Caleb was losing his interest in her and preferred Victoria, then Judith would be desperate to let Victoria leave.

Victoria frowned. "Of course, she could send me away somewhere awful." There were plenty of schools where people sent their adult children to be rid of them. Finishing schools, like the one in Switzerland where Grandmother had sent her because she knew it would keep Victoria under tight control until her wedding to that fat toad Piedmont Rosedale.

Uncertain of what kind of reception she might get, Victoria stayed in her room, contemplating her situation, until Kenzie came to tell her supper was ready.

Victoria lifted her chin. "I thought maybe you'd have them banish me to my room for allowing your Mr. Morgan to wait for you."

Kenzie looked at her blankly. "If your conscience is bothering you, perhaps you should stay here."

"Oh, bother!" Victoria pushed Kenzie aside. "I'll never understand you—or them."

Victoria made her way down to the dining room and found the others already seated. Caleb and Patrick stood when she and Kenzie came into the room, and Caleb pulled out her chair while Patrick helped Kenzie.

"I hope you had a pleasant day," Caleb said.

Victoria nodded. "It was nice to have some time to myself without having to worry about pleasing others."

She sat and noticed the strange array of food on the table. There was a large sliced ham and several loaves of various breads. Along with this were a dozen or so pastries and fresh fruit.

"What kind of supper is this?"

"We thought we'd keep it simple," Camri declared. "It's sort of an indoor picnic."

"I forgot the mustard," Judith said, getting to her feet. "I'll be right back."

Camri began pouring lemonade into Patrick's glass. "I wish we had ice, but I'm sure it will be just as delicious without it."

Patrick took the full glass and handed Camri Kenzie's glass. Judith returned with a pot of mustard, then took her seat. Once Camri finished seeing that everyone had lemonade, Caleb suggested they pray.

Victoria bowed her head slightly but refused to close her

eyes. She watched the others, trying to figure out each person's weakness. Camri was an intellectual who thought everyone needed education. Her weakness was clearly her feelings for Patrick. Patrick was Irish, so his weakness was probably liquor, although Victoria had never seen him drink. How strange that an educated woman would lower herself to marry an Irishman. Victoria remembered a dalliance she'd had with an Irish stable boy and smiled. Maybe she could understand Camri's interest after all.

"Amen," Caleb declared, and the others murmured the word in unison.

"Before we begin to eat," Caleb said, turning to Victoria, "I need to say something. Kenzie tells me that you allowed Arthur Morgan into the house while we were gone. I don't want that to happen again. He's not welcome here."

Victoria frowned. "I'm sorry. I didn't realize. I didn't even know who he was. He said he was a good friend of Kenzie's, and I thought you'd want me to extend charity." She lowered her gaze and drew her hand to her right eye as if to blot a tear. "I apologize."

"I'm sure you meant no harm, but now you know. It's not wise for any young woman at home alone to allow a stranger entrance," Camri said, slathering mustard on a slice of bread. "Kenzie shouldn't have left you alone."

"I didn't have much choice," Kenzie muttered.

Victoria wanted to counter with something snide or hurtful, but that wouldn't gain her much. She nodded and looked around the table. "I'm sorry about that too. I was cross with Kenzie. She didn't want to leave me here, but I was rather childish. I'm trying to change my behavior though. Caleb, the things you told me about God really made me think about how I'm living my life. I want to do better. I am trying."

Caleb gave her a smile, but the others looked surprised. "That's all any of us can do. Now, let's enjoy our meal and forget about Morgan and all that."

A sense of satisfaction coursed through Victoria. These people weren't anything like her family. She had accomplished what she wanted with her family through pouting and demands, but Caleb and his friends were cut from a different cloth. This obsession they had with pleasing God seemed to be the perfect venue for Victoria to exploit. Especially with Caleb. His weakness was God, and of course Judith. And likewise, Caleb was Judith's weakness. That just left Kenzie and Dr. Fisher. The conflict with Arthur Morgan was no doubt Kenzie's Achilles' heel.

Later that evening, when the other women began to discuss wedding gowns and receptions, Victoria made her way to Caleb's study, where he and Patrick were playing a game of chess. Victoria knew they wouldn't want her there, but she felt it important to keep at Caleb regarding her future.

"Please excuse the intrusion, but I wonder if you had a chance to speak to Judith about my friends in New York." She tried to make her voice as sweet and demure as possible.

Caleb looked up from the game. "No. It didn't come up in our conversation. Did you write down their name and address for me?"

Victoria shook her head. "I can give you their name. I'm not sure of the address."

"Given their social standing is equal to the Whitleys', I'm certain it will be easy enough to locate them." Caleb turned his attention back to Patrick's move. "Aha! I've got you now." He moved his bishop. "Check."

Patrick frowned and bent closer to the board. "How could I be missin' that?" He moved his queen to block the bishop.

"And now it's mate." Caleb took the queen with his rook and pushed back from the table. "I think I'll build us a fire. It's kind of chilly this evening."

"Let me," Patrick said, getting to his feet. "I'm the loser."

Caleb laughed and headed for his chair by the fire.

Victoria followed like a puppy. When he sat down, she knelt at his feet. "I hope you know how much I appreciate you. Your help means so much to me. I think you're the only one who really cares about me."

Patrick got the fire going and took the other chair, chuckling. "Victoria, ye remind me of a china teapot full of spiders."

She looked at him with a frown. "That hardly sounds very nice. Whatever do you mean?"

A smile edged Patrick's lips. "Ye're very pretty, but full of danger."

She shrugged. "A little danger now and then is hardly a bad thing. I like adventure in my life."

"Adventure has its advantages," Caleb agreed. "But in moderation."

Victoria got to her feet and looked down at him. "I've never met anyone quite like the two of you."

She heard someone in the hall. "Caleb?" Judith called.

Victoria used the opportunity to her advantage. She whirled on her heel and fell into Caleb's lap. "Oh my. I'm so sorry." She put her arm around his neck. "I shouldn't startle so easily."

Judith came into the room and gaped at Victoria on Caleb's lap.

Victoria gave her a smug smile. "I'll just be going," she said, getting up. "Thank you for . . . a wonderful evening."

She strolled past Judith, keeping her smile fixed. She could see the doubt and worry in Judith's expression. Satisfaction gave Victoria the edge. She had planted seeds of discord . . . something she was an expert at growing.

"I hope I didn't . . . ah . . ." Judith looked out the door after Victoria.

Patrick got to his feet and shook his head. "This is a matter for the two of ye. I'll be goin' now. I need to get back to the warehouse and make sure everyone's tucked in for the night."

Caleb chuckled. "Give 'em all hot milk and cookies while you're at it."

"Oh, for sure now, I will." Patrick headed for the door. "Judith, I'll be prayin' for ye."

"Thank you." Her gaze followed him until he'd passed from the room.

Caleb watched her for a moment. "Come here, Judith."

She looked hesitant, but he motioned her to join him. He could see the doubt in her eyes. Victoria had made her question the situation, and he intended to set her straight.

"I didn't mean to disturb you, Caleb," she said, coming to stand beside him.

Without giving her a chance to protest, Caleb pulled her onto his lap and smiled at her stunned expression. "Don't give it a second thought." He kissed her hand. "And don't give your cousin's antics a second thought either."

She blushed. "I know she hates me."

"And she'll do whatever she can to come between us. Don't let her. I know full well what Victoria's doing and why. She's even using my desire to share God with her. She wants to convince you that she has somehow wormed her way into my heart, or at very least my interest. However, it isn't true, nor could it ever be. I am completely devoted to you, and no other woman will ever have my heart." He gently stroked her cheek and felt her fears slip away. "I do believe that the sooner we figure out what to do with her, the better off we'll all be."

"What do you suggest?" Judith put her arm around his neck and toyed with the hair just above his collar.

"I can't suggest much of anything with you here like this. I think it would probably be prudent for us to say good night and start again fresh in the morning." He stood, lifting her in his arms as he did. Judith's expression was surprised, which only made him laugh. "You're as light as a feather." He kissed her gently on the lips, then put her down.

She smiled and turned crimson all at the same time.

"Your innocence and sweetness is such a blessing to me," Caleb said, shaking his head. "Victoria is lucky to have you as her guardian. Another woman in your position might not be so forgiving."

"Another woman would have just sent her back to Switzerland."

He kissed her forehead. "Perhaps you will do just that. Now go. I need to check on some papers, and tomorrow is church."

"Thank you, Caleb."

He shook his head. "For what?"

"For being you. For caring about us all, but especially for your patience with me. I can't lie and say I don't feel out of place at times. Everyone here has had such a different life from mine. But you always make me feel as if I belong."

"That's because you do, Judith. You belong here with me."

CHAPTER 17

After a subdued Fourth of July, Caleb boarded a train to Kansas City. Kenzie was grateful for his help, and yet she was concerned that with him gone, Arthur might get it in his head to impose himself at the house. Without a man in residence, they would be more vulnerable. After all, Caleb would be gone for at least ten days, possibly two weeks or more.

"Why is Caleb going to Kansas City?" Victoria demanded.

Camri looked up from the ledger she'd been going over. "He has business. Why is it of any concern to you?"

"He's supposed to be helping me locate my friends."

"I'm sure he's doing that too." Kenzie looked up from the quilt square she'd been stitching. "He probably hasn't discussed it with you so that you wouldn't get your hopes up."

"Or because he didn't feel a nineteen-year-old girl needs to stick her nose in his business," Camri replied matter-of-factly. "By the way, Victoria, how much education have you had?"

The girl rolled her eyes with an exaggerated sigh. "Don't start your crusades with me. I have no interest nor need for education. I have money, and money trumps schooling."

Camri stared at her. "You really believe that, don't you? You think so long as you have a fortune, you can sit and simper and pout, and everything will just drop into your lap."

"Well, it has so far. If I could just get my inheritance released, you would see for yourself how quickly things would go my way."

Kenzie shook her head. "Don't waste your time, Camri. She'll find out soon enough that just as she uses people, people will be only too happy to use her."

"Benjamin Franklin said, 'Experience keeps a dear school, but fools will learn in no other.'"

"I don't care what your friends say," Victoria countered. "I know quite enough to take care of myself, and you can tell Mr. Franklin I said so."

Camri and Kenzie exchanged a glance. Victoria had just proven Camri's point. Kenzie turned her attention back to her stitching.

A knock sounded at the door, and Victoria turned as if to answer it, but Judith came down the stairs. "I'll see who that is," she called as she passed the sitting room.

Kenzie prayed it wasn't Arthur. The last thing she wanted was to throw him out again. Within a moment, Judith appeared with a large bouquet of flowers.

"Oh, how beautiful," Victoria said, coming to see them better. "Are they for me?"

Judith shook her head. "No, they're for Kenzie, from Arthur Morgan. I tried to refuse them, but the deliveryman said Mr. Morgan told him that he was to leave them on the doorstep if we wouldn't take them."

"Very well." Kenzie got up and put her sewing in the basket beside her chair. "Give them to me. I'll put them in the trash."

"No!" Victoria wrenched the flowers out of Judith's hands. "You all are too cruel. That poor man has given you his heart, and you do nothing but crush his spirit with your snobbery. I'll take the flowers to my room."

Kenzie watched her disappear up the stairs and looked at Judith. "I think you should just let her have her inheritance and send her on her way. She's going to be nothing but trouble to all of us."

"I know, but Caleb said we were responsible for her. She's just a spoiled child, and I'm the only family she has left."

"I believe she'd happily rectify that if given a chance," Camri countered. "I agree with Kenzie. Maybe you should discuss the matter with Judge Winters. There's bound to be something you can do now that you're her guardian. Caleb has a good heart and more confidence than I do that Victoria can change. I'd hate to see her hurt him."

Judith nodded. "So would I."

Another knock at the front door caught everyone's attention. "I hope it isn't more flowers," Kenzie said, moving to answer it.

She opened the door to find Mrs. Fisher, Micah's mother, along with several other ladies from the church. "Good afternoon, ladies. Won't you come in?" Kenzie stepped back and admitted the women. There were five in total, and all seemed to be speaking at once.

"Please forgive our unannounced arrival," Mrs. Fisher said, giving Kenzie a gentle pat on the arm.

Camri and Judith appeared in the sitting room doorway. "Mrs. Fisher," Camri said, then nodded to the others. "Ladies. To what do we owe this pleasure?"

"We were working on some of the donations for the shelter and had an idea about hosting a party at the church to encourage the community to help. Even though our community is currently burdened with the recovery from the earthquake and fires, we heard that the relief camps will soon be discontinued. I don't know if those are just rumors or true, but it got us thinking."

Camri nodded. "Well, the army has pulled out. It surely won't be long before they demand their tents and other supplies back. Why don't we arrange ourselves around the dining table?"

"I'll gather some refreshments," Judith said smiling. "Kenzie, would you help me?"

Kenzie dutifully followed Judith into the kitchen, wondering at the strange pounding of her heart. She'd spoken to Mrs. Fisher on many occasions, but this was the first time since she had nearly accepted Micah's proposal after Cousin George's wedding. Would Mrs. Fisher someday be her mother-in-law?

Then she remembered the flowers Victoria had taken to her room, and her heart sank. Until she'd resolved this situation with Arthur, she wouldn't be able to give Micah the answer they both desired.

Victoria had come to the top of the stairs and watched silently as the women chattered on and on and finally adjourned to the dining room. With all of them busy at whatever it was that had so captivated their attention, she would be able to slip out of the house. If they found out later that she was gone, she'd deal with the consequences then.

She waited nearly ten minutes, just to make sure they were fully ensconced in their discussion, before tiptoeing down the stairs. She paused at the front door, waiting to see if anyone would hear the floor creak and come to investigate. When no one did, Victoria eased the door open and stepped outside.

The skies looked like rain, but she couldn't let that stop her now. She needed to see Arthur Morgan and learn if he'd arranged for his lawyer friend to help her. She had the feeling that Caleb's trip to Kansas City was probably to arrange to put her in some dreadful finishing school, and if so, she desperately needed to have her options lined up.

She hurried down the street and made her way to Arthur's hotel. The lobby was surprisingly deserted, and the clerk eyed her immediately upon her entrance. She had no choice but to speak to him.

"May I help you?" he asked in a curt tone that suggested he didn't approve of her being there.

Victoria turned on the charm. "Oh, I do hope so. My brother Arthur Morgan is staying here, and Mama sent me to speak to him. Could you have him come downstairs to see me?"

The clerk smiled. "Of course." He checked the boxes of keys. "It appears he's here. I'll send a boy to bring him down. Why don't you have a seat over there?"

Victoria looked at the plush sofa and chairs in the corner of the lobby. "Thank you. You are ever so helpful."

She took her seat, hoping Arthur would be quick about it. The last thing she wanted was to have to deal with her three jailers when she returned to the house.

Within a matter of minutes, Arthur made his way down the stairs. He went to the front desk, and the clerk pointed him to Victoria even before she could call out his name.

"I didn't expect to have my *sister* come to see me," he said, joining her.

Victoria jumped up and hugged him. "Oh, brother dear, I'm so glad you were here." She noticed the clerk smiling their way. "I need to know what you've found out for me." Her voice was barely a whisper.

Arthur nodded and waited until she'd positioned herself again on the sofa before he took the chair to her right. "You're taking a big risk coming here."

"It can't be helped. I must get away from those people. They have no intention of giving me my freedom, and I abhor them."

"Well, then you'll be happy to know that Abraham Ruef is checking into what can be done."

He smiled, revealing perfect white teeth. Victoria thought him very handsome. He wouldn't be a horrible choice for a husband, and he had spoken of establishing her in Kansas City. That reminded her of Caleb's trip.

"He can't be quick enough. Mr. Coulter has gone to Kansas City and—"

Arthur frowned. "Kansas City? Why?"

She shrugged. "I think they're trying to arrange a place to put me. They were all very hush-hush about it."

His expression turned into a scowl. "No doubt he's up to no good. I'm afraid, however, it has more to do with me than you. It would seem we're both running out of time. When did he leave?"

"Yesterday. But why would his trip have anything to do with you?"

"Because that's where I live, you ninny." His tone was impatient. "I should have known something like this might happen."

"Well, he'll be gone for ten days—possibly longer," she said, trying to ease his concern. "I still think it's got more to do with me than you. They've been impossible to live with, and every time I do the slightest thing wrong, they threaten me." It was a lie, of course, but she figured it might bring his attention back to her. "In fact, Judith slapped me the other night and told me she was going to put me away so that she could have all my money."

"Yes, well, power does corrupt," Arthur murmured. "I wonder, do you know where the good doctor lives?"

She raised her brows, hoping to look surprised. "Oh . . . oh, I do. He was at the house just before Caleb left. In fact, he's been at the house quite a bit."

"No doubt," Arthur growled. "Just tell me where I can reach him."

"He's at the warehouse where we first met. Apparently he's

going to open a hospital there or something. I don't know the details, but he's definitely living there. I heard him discussing it and how he and that Irishman would take care of everything while Caleb was away."

"Good. Then I shall have to pay him a visit."

"But what about me?" She hadn't meant to speak with such a whine, but she was sick and tired of everyone thinking more about their own problems than hers.

"I'll get word to you when Ruef is ready to meet with you." He got to his feet. "Right now, I have other things to handle." He took her arm and pulled her to her feet.

Victoria noticed the clerk watching them and smiled. "Thank you. I'll tell Mother that you'll be in touch."

He frowned down at her, then seemed to understand. He bent and kissed her cheek. "Run along, now. Do you have fare for the ride home?" Victoria shook her head, and Arthur immediately turned to the clerk. "My sister needs a cab."

The clerk signaled the doorman, and Arthur walked Victoria outside, where the doorman had already hailed her ride. Arthur handed the driver money and gave him the address, then helped Victoria up into the carriage. "Good-bye, sister."

Victoria gave him a wave. "Good-bye, brother."

She sat back in the carriage and smiled, filled with elation. Mr. Ruef was already at work on her situation. She could imagine the looks on everyone's faces when she told them that she was rid of them.

"Oh, what a happy day that will be."

Micah hadn't expected to receive an invitation from Arthur Morgan, much less to have it delivered at the warehouse.

"It would seem I've been summoned," he told Patrick. "Arthur Morgan has asked me to come to his hotel. Perhaps he intends to challenge me to a duel." Micah couldn't help but smile. "See for yourself."

Patrick looked at the invitation. "For sure that would be his kind of game. Are ye going to go?"

"I suppose I will. I was going to go to Caleb's house with you, but maybe I'll go speak my piece with Mr. Morgan and then come over. It'll depend on how long of a chat we need to have."

Patrick laughed. "I'm thinkin' my evening will be much more pleasurable than yers."

Micah figured as much too, but there was no denying he was curious as to what Arthur wanted.

The hotel seemed quite the gathering place that evening. Men and women dressed in their finery appeared to be trying to move on with their lives and forget that just beyond the doors, the city was still in disarray.

Micah stopped at the front desk. "I'm Dr. Fisher. I'm supposed to meet Arthur Morgan. Can you tell me his room number?"

"Of course, Dr. Fisher. Mr. Morgan said to send you up straightaway." He gave Micah directions and sent him upstairs.

When Micah reached the room, he wondered for a moment if it had been a mistake to come. The last thing he wanted was to get in a fist fight with Morgan. Perhaps he should suggest they go downstairs. There was a dining area off the lobby.

The door opened, and Arthur Morgan nodded at him. "Thank you for coming. I wasn't sure you would be willing."

"I must say it was a surprise."

"I've arranged a supper for us here. Won't you come in?"

"I didn't come for supper."

Morgan paused and gave a slight shrug. "It's of no concern to me, but I thought perhaps you'd enjoy it." He continued toward the table. "The normal fare in San Francisco hasn't been very appealing, according to what I've heard. You'll find that I have only the very best."

Micah followed him into the large suite, wondering at Morgan's game. He acted congenial enough, but Micah wasn't about to let down his guard. Not while he was in Morgan's hotel room—alone.

"The food arrived only a moment before you did, so it should still be hot." Morgan moved to his place at the table and motioned Micah to do the same. Morgan lifted the silver domes off each plate to reveal a thick steak, creamed peas with tiny pearl onions, and fried potatoes. In the middle of the table were rolls and butter. Micah couldn't remember the last time he'd had butter or anything quite this grand.

Micah took a seat and had to admit the aroma of the steak on his plate was mouth-watering. Morgan offered no prayer or even comment, but simply dug into the meal with great gusto. Micah prayed silently and picked up his fork and knife. What harm could come from enjoying a steak?

The filet was tender and cut so easily that Micah almost didn't need the knife. The piece melted in his mouth, and the flavor left him with a smile.

"I pay extra to have food brought in daily. I had the most marvelous rack of lamb last evening," Arthur said, smiling.

Micah decided to enjoy a few more mouthfuls before pressing Morgan for the reason he'd invited him here. No sense in letting a perfectly good meal go uneaten.

A man appeared moments later to pour additional wine into Morgan's goblet. He glanced at Micah's untouched glass, then left as quickly as he'd come.

"You don't drink?"

"No. Alcohol has never been to my liking, and besides, I never know when I'll be called to help a patient."

"I see. That must put a damper on parties."

Micah shook his head. "I don't attend many of those. As a doctor, I'm often busy with patients or exhausted from my day of work."

"I can imagine. It must be quite difficult right now. I heard that many of the hospitals were destroyed."

"They were, but we're getting by. Good men managed to put ideas into action, and we've arranged new hospitals. Things aren't quite back to normal, nor will they be for a while, but we've overcome the worst of it. In fact, I'm setting up a small hospital for the poor at Mr. Coulter's warehouse where you first saw Kenzie."

"New hospitals. That must take a great deal of money."

"Yes. No doubt. New equipment must be purchased, and some of it is quite specialized." Micah wiped his mouth on a fine linen napkin and placed it on the table. "But you didn't ask me here to talk about hospitals. What is it you want from me, Mr. Morgan?"

Morgan nodded. "I think you know. I want to marry Kenzie, and you are a complication."

Micah leaned back in his chair and crossed his arms. "I might say the same of you, but I don't think you are much of a complication. Kenzie doesn't love you. She loves me."

Morgan frowned. "I . . . well . . ." A forlorn expression came over his face. "You don't understand. Kenzie was my whole world. I stood against my friends and family to have her in my life."

"And they connived so that your wedding was called off and Kenzie's spirit crushed. I don't think much of friends and family who would do that. I think even less of a man who would allow it to happen and do nothing to change the outcome."

"I was a fool. It never occurred to me that I couldn't trust them. They're my family." Morgan took a long drink from his wine goblet. He held the glass and swirled the contents for a moment. "I would do anything to get her back."

"I don't intend to let her go, if that's why you've asked me here tonight."

"What if I made it worth your while?"

Micah's eyes narrowed. "I'm not for sale."

"Even if I were to build you your own hospital, complete with every possible piece of modern equipment? I could arrange for it to be named after you. I could speak with my father's cousin, J. P. Morgan. With his help, we could make it the grandest hospital west of the Mississippi. If you truly care about treating the sick and injured, how could you refuse such an opportunity?"

Micah could hardly believe what Morgan was suggesting. "Let me understand you. If I give up Kenzie, you'll give me a hospital?"

Morgan seemed to think Micah was actually considering the bribe. "Yes! You can see for yourself the opportunity. Imagine how much it would mean to the community. You would have the ability to help thousands, and it wouldn't cost you a dime."

"It would cost me much more than a dime—it would cost me a lifetime of happiness. I love Kenzie and intend to marry her." Micah got up from the table. "There is nothing you could offer me that would make me walk away from her as you did."

"But I never meant to." Arthur Morgan hung his head. "I know you don't care, but she's the only woman I've ever really loved. The only one I will ever love."

Micah felt sorry for him. He appeared to be genuinely bereft. "I'm sorry you feel that way."

"At least you aren't without compassion," Morgan said, looking up. He gave a long breathy sigh. "I suppose there is nothing left for me to do but go home."

"That would be best," Micah agreed. He certainly wasn't going to suggest otherwise. "If you'll excuse me now, I should be going. Thank you for the meal. It was delicious."

Morgan looked at him with the same lost expression. He nodded but said nothing, and Micah took that as his cue to leave.

He made his way down the grand staircase, wondering if it

would really be that simple. Would Morgan finally admit defeat and go back to Kansas City?

"Dr. Fisher!" the clerk called to Micah just as he reached the front doors. Micah looked up and saw the clerk making his way across the lobby to him. "Dr. Fisher!"

"What is it?"

"A young woman was just here. She was looking for a doctor and thought perhaps we had one staying here. She said her mother is very ill. The situation is desperate."

Micah looked around the lobby. "Where is she?"

"She just left, but she gave me the address." He handed Micah a piece of paper. "It's just down the street two blocks, then turn right. I'm sure if you hurry, you can catch up to her."

Micah nodded. "I'll see what I can do."

He raced from the hotel, glancing around to see if the young woman was still in sight. The darkness made it difficult. A few of the gaslights had been restored, but not all of the streets had them.

He picked up his pace and headed toward the address, though he wasn't sure he could even help. He'd left his bag at the warehouse, certain he wouldn't need it, so he would be limited on what he had available.

The next street was his destination. He didn't know the exact location of the patient, but figured as quickly as he'd followed, he might find the young woman just now reaching her door. He strained to see in the dark and finally spied a female figure.

"Miss! I'm a doctor!" he called.

She turned, but Micah didn't know anything else. A heavy blow to the back of his head made him sway, and then blackness engulfed his vision and he fell to the ground.

CHAPTER 18

"Yes, sir," a suit-clad man told Caleb, "Mr. Morgan plans great things. He's arranged to buy up most of the area near the river in a little town about ten miles from here. Folks thought he was crazy, but recently plans were announced to incorporate that area into the city limits. Morgan is always one step ahead of everybody else. He's going to have the largest locomotive shops west of the Mississippi. Not only to repair them, but build them." The man shook his head. "He'll make a fortune to add to the one he already has."

Having connected through friends, Caleb found the private investigator, John, to be a wealth of information. He reached into his wallet and pulled out several bills. "And you say he's been having trouble with one individual?"

"Yes. Joseph Gifford owns about eighty acres of prime real estate and won't sell. Morgan considered just rearranging his plans and going around the old man's property. He had people out there surveying the entire lay of the land, but it proved impossible to change his location without it costing twice as much. Gifford has remained a hold out, and it would seem no matter what Morgan offers him, he refuses to sell to him." The investigator took Caleb's money. "However, I've heard tell it won't be a problem much longer."

Caleb cocked his head. "Why's that?"

John stuffed the bills in his pocket. "I'm not entirely sure. I just know from what's being whispered about that Morgan believes he's found a solution."

"I see."

And he did. Caleb believed Kenzie was at the center of that solution. If Morgan got his son married to Gifford's daughter, no doubt he believed there would be a compromise. And if not willingly, then by making Kenzie miserable and forcing Gifford's hand.

"And what of his personal life?" Caleb asked. "Is Morgan stable? Does he manage his family well?"

"From what I've seen, he rules them pretty much with an iron fist. They do his bidding or suffer the consequences. He has several children, some married, some not. All his boys are in the family business and answer to the old man."

"Do you know anything about their business dealings?"

John shrugged. "A Morgan is a Morgan. They go after what they want and usually have little trouble getting it. They're related to J. P. Morgan, you know, second cousins or something along those lines, and when they can't get matters done on their own, they aren't shy about seeking his help. I figure that's how they plan to have this matter with Gifford taken care of."

Caleb hadn't known about the connection with J. P. Morgan, probably the most powerful man in the United States. During the depression of the 1890s, he'd single-handedly saved the U.S. government from complete financial failure by putting up his own money. He had his hands in everything lucrative—steel, railroads, shipping, and anything else that tickled his fancy. If he truly were related to the Kansas City Morgans, they shouldn't have any trouble at all in accomplishing what they wanted.

"Let me know if you get any more information that you think I should know," Caleb said. "I believe I'll ride over to see where Mr. Morgan wants to set up his shops."

The investigator nodded. "I'll keep on it."

"Thanks, John. Oh, and I appreciate the loan of your horse."

"You'll be glad for him instead of my car. The roads are laid out well enough, but not always maintained, especially once you leave the city."

Caleb bid John farewell, then mounted the black gelding. It had been a while since he'd been on horseback. He nudged the animal into a trot and headed out to find Kenzie's folks.

Kansas City was hilly and packed with people. Everyone seemed to be anxious to be somewhere, and most appeared to be late. A few people were rude and intolerant of those around them, as was true of most large cities, but most were congenial. Unlike San Francisco, there was no ocean or even large open bay. The muddy Missouri River flowed along the northern edge of the city, offering river travel to the mighty Mississippi. The geographic position of Kansas City made it a nearly perfect center mark for the entire nation, and every major railroad had connections to the town. If Morgan could control even a part of that, he would not only make a fortune, he would control a vital part of the country's transportation. It gave a clear motive to Morgan doing whatever he needed to do in order to get what he wanted.

John's directions out of the city were easy to follow. The farms and pasturelands picked up almost immediately where the city's buildings left off. Occasionally, rocky ravines and thickly forested areas offered contrast, but this was still agricultural land. Acres and acres of wheat and corn made a patchwork of the landscape, and from time to time there were open meadows with herds of horses or cattle feasting upon thick green vegetation. It was pretty country, but hot and humid, and Caleb found himself longing for a bath.

He felt fairly confident of what he'd hear about Joseph Gifford. Given what John had relayed, it seemed Morgan had given up conventional means of getting the property and now approved of the marriage of his son to Kenzie. If Morgan had truly interfered in his son's life and Arthur knew nothing of his role, then Kenzie's letter had no doubt awakened her former fiancé to what had happened. Arthur had probably confronted his father, and Morgan, being in a bind with Gifford, had used it as a means to get what he wanted. Maybe sacrificing the family's social status by allowing his son to marry beneath him was worth it in lieu of getting the Gifford land.

After an hour's ride, Caleb reached the tiny town where all the trouble was centered. It was quaint, typical of the Midwest, showing both a mixture of agricultural as well as river interests. There was a town square with a bandstand, and all around this were a variety of businesses. The library where Kenzie had worked was at one end of the square beside the post office. Gifford Emporium was across the square from that, nearer the river port and small train depot. There were a variety of other buildings—general stores, a bank, a barber's shop, and a butcher. Caleb counted at least three churches, several cafés, and a book and toy store. Not far from the depot was a grain elevator and what looked like a hardware store. Houses were arranged beyond the city square in beautiful tree-lined neighborhoods. All in all, it was a charming place.

He spied a man wearing a star-shaped badge on his suit coat and stopped to inquire. Tipping his hat, Caleb asked, "I wonder if you could direct me to the Gifford residence."

"Joseph Gifford?" the man asked. "I'm the law here. May I ask your business?"

Caleb smiled. "Of course. I'm a good friend of his daughter's. I promised her I'd look him up when I came to town. Actually, he's expecting me. The name is Caleb Coulter." He leaned down from the horse and extended his hand.

The thick-waisted lawman shook his hand. "Always glad to meet a friend of the Giffords." He smiled and pointed. "You see the Emporium at the end of the street? Just turn there and head two blocks down. You'll see a large two-story white house trimmed out in green. Has a white picket fence that runs the length of the front yard."

"Thanks. Nice town, by the way."

"It is, although I don't know how long it'll stay that way. Kansas City plans to expand its territory. We're soon to become a part of their fair city. Big men with big money want to change our way of life."

"I can well imagine. Still, I suppose it could be good for you in that there will be plenty of jobs and new people wanting to come to the area."

"There's plenty of folks here already. If I wanted to live in a big city, I'd have settled in Kansas City to begin with. I prefer my small town. Less trouble and crime. Kansas City always has one problem or another. Big bunch of hoodlums in and out of there all the time, and the Pendergasts make sure things always break their way."

Caleb had heard of the Pendergast family. They reminded him of Ruef and his style of politics. "Seems every big city has their power-hungry folks." He tipped his hat. "I'm obliged for the help."

The lawman tipped his hat in return, and Caleb urged his horse in the direction of the Emporium and down the street. It didn't take long to find his way to the Gifford place. He tied the horse off at the fence, then made his way through the gate and up the porch steps to the front door. The windows of the house were open, as was the inside door. Caleb could see through the screen door that two people sat in the front room. The man was already getting to his feet before Caleb could knock.

The man bore the same blue eyes as Kenzie. "Can I help you?"

"I'm Caleb Coulter. I wired you that I'd be coming."

Mr. Gifford smiled. "Kenzie's friend. Welcome." He opened the screen door. "We're pleased to meet you." He turned toward the front room. "Mother, it's Kenzie's friend Mr. Coulter."

"Please call me Caleb. I'd like to be your friend as well."

"I could use a friend. Times have been a little difficult around here." The old man led Caleb into the front room, where an older woman sat in a rocker, knitting.

She smiled up at him. "We're so glad to have you." She paused her needles for a moment and looked at Mr. Gifford. "Call Etta in here. She should meet Mr. Coulter as well."

Mr. Gifford nodded and headed back the way they'd come.

Mrs. Gifford smiled at Caleb. "My brother's child came to live with us last year. She's been mighty good to have around in Kenzie's absence."

"I can well imagine that Kenzie's absence has been hard to fill. She's a remarkable woman, your daughter."

Mrs. Gifford gave a sad sort of nod. "I wish her father might have seen her value sooner. I'm afraid he never knew just how special she was until she left us."

"Sometimes that's the way of it." Caleb heard the old man returning. "But it's never too late to appreciate someone."

Mr. Gifford reappeared with a mousy, bespectacled woman in tow. Her face was slightly bowed, but she raised her eyes to glance over her gold-rimmed glasses.

"Mr. Coulter, this is Cousin Etta. She cooks and cleans for us. Reads to us too."

Caleb nodded. "It's nice to meet you. I'm a good friend of Kenzie's."

Etta seemed too timid to speak, but she gave a slight nod of her head before doing an about-face to leave the room.

"Etta's fixing supper. I hope you like fried chicken," Mrs. Gifford said.

She looked up to see his reaction, and Caleb beamed at her. "I do. In fact, I'd go so far as to say that I love it."

Kenzie helped Judith put supper on the table. The poor girl was a nervous wreck with Caleb gone and Victoria tormenting her.

"This stew looks delicious," Kenzie said as she placed a big platter of biscuits beside the pot.

"I hope it is. I can't remember if I salted it. You might want to taste it."

"We can salt it when it's in our bowls. Why don't you let Camri know the table is set, and I'll go fetch her highness?"

Judith giggled and relaxed a bit. "I appreciate that, Kenzie. You've been so good, helping me deal with her."

Kenzie shook her head. "It's not right for her to treat you as she does. She ought to be grateful, given the situation."

"Well, thanks just the same." Judith had started for the stairs when a loud knock sounded at the front door. "I'll get it," she said.

"I've got it," Camri announced, coming from the front room.

Kenzie left them to figure it out and made her way upstairs. She knocked on Victoria's door. "Supper is ready."

Victoria opened the door. "What are we having this time?"

"Stew and biscuits." Kenzie looked past her at the messy room. "You really should learn to pick up after yourself."

"Sensible people would have a staff to do those things," Victoria countered.

"Well, until you find some, you'd better see to it yourself."

Kenzie made her way back downstairs, spying Patrick, Camri, and Judith talking in hushed tones at the entryway. They all looked up in unison with the same worried expression on their faces.

"What's wrong?" Kenzie didn't need to be told it involved Micah. He hadn't been around in days, and she'd felt uncomfortable ever since Patrick had mentioned him going to see Arthur.

Camri answered. "Micah hasn't been back to the warehouse since the night he went to the Arthur's hotel."

Kenzie bit her lower lip and forced all sorts of unpleasant thoughts from her mind. "He's probably just been too busy." She walked down the last few steps.

"I was thinkin' much the same," Patrick said, "but then one of his doctor friends showed up at the warehouse this morning. He said Micah hasn't been to work—not since that day."

"Patrick also spoke with Pastor Fisher," Camri added. "They haven't seen Micah either."

Kenzie nodded. The truth was too obvious. "Arthur's done something with him."

"With who?" Victoria asked, coming down the stairs. She looked at each person's face, then settled on Kenzie.

"It's none of your concern." Kenzie turned back to her friends. "Do you know anything else, Patrick?"

"No, I'm sorry to be sayin' I don't. I wasn't even worried about him—knowin' how he can be with his work and all."

"Micah wouldn't let people worry about him if he had the ability to do otherwise." Kenzie went to the door. "I'm going to see Arthur and find out what he's done."

Patrick reached out and stopped her. "You can't be goin' to the hotel alone, especially if that man has done somethin' to Micah."

Camri took hold of Kenzie's arm as well. "He's right. If

Micah's disappearance is Arthur's doing, then he's already done whatever it is he's done. If you show up without protection, he might very well hurt you."

"Then what do you propose I do?" Kenzie looked from Camri to Patrick.

"Let's sit down and discuss it sensibly and come up with a plan," Camri suggested. "Maybe you could send Arthur a message to come here. At least that way you'd have all of us nearby, and we could help you in case something went wrong."

What Camri said made sense, but Kenzie wasn't feeling sensible. Especially when Micah might be in trouble.

"You people are all fools," Victoria declared, bringing everyone's attention to her. "Isn't it possible that Dr. Fisher has simply tired of you? Honestly, Kenzie, it isn't that difficult to believe he might have found someone else to be interested in, especially given that you hardly seemed inclined to give him the time of day."

"That isn't true," Judith said, positioning herself directly in front of Victoria. "You can say and do what you like where I'm concerned, but you have no right to hurt my friend. Now, go into supper or back to your room, but you aren't part of this conversation."

Kenzie had never seen Judith take such a stand. It was impressive, and even Victoria seemed to realize she'd gone too far. Without another word, she made her way into the dining room.

Judith turned back to face the others. "I'm sorry for what she said. You know it's her goal to make us all miserable. I'll go keep her company while you decide what to do about Micah."

Victoria had seen the anger in Judith's eyes and knew it was no time to make a scene. She needed to bide her time just a little longer, until she could meet with Abraham Ruef. If she caused too much trouble, they might find a way to keep her from ever having that meeting.

She sat down at the table and took a biscuit from the plate. Without worrying about the others, she began to nibble on it. It was light and fluffy. Actually, it was delicious, but she wasn't about to admit as much. Judith had made them, and Victoria wasn't going to praise her for anything.

"How can you be so cold and indifferent to the pain you cause others?" Judith asked in a hushed voice. "I have never met anyone with less compassion than you."

Victoria stopped eating and shook her head. "I wasn't trying to be hurtful, simply truthful. You all presume that because Dr. Fisher isn't around, begging crumbs from Kenzie Gifford, that something bad has happened to him. I merely suggested that it's possible he got tired of waiting for her to make up her mind."

Judith sat down across from her. "But your intent is to cause pain and problems. It's one thing for you to hate me. I completely understand, and were I not a Christian woman, I might return the favor. As it is, I can honestly say there is nothing about you that I like. You are mean-spirited, vindictive, and hateful. However, given your upbringing and the people who were responsible, I have to pity you."

"Don't." Victoria hated the very idea of Judith pitying her. She could deal with hate and anger, but not pity. No one pitied Victoria Whitley. "I don't want your pity. I don't want anything from you, except my money and freedom."

"Believe me," Judith said with a sigh, "I want that too. I want to give you both and send you as far away from me as possible. And just speaking honestly about that makes me sad. We might have been friends—true family. We might have shared laughter and stories—daily events and memories. We might have offered each other comfort in our times of loss." Judith shook her head in disappointment. "But instead you treat me worse than you would one of your servants. Frankly, I'd rather be completely without family than try to nurture something with you."

Victoria kept her expression blank, but Judith's words stung. "Then we're in agreement on something."

"Well, you need to be in agreement with something else." Judith pointed a finger at Victoria. "You will leave my friends alone, or I will do whatever it takes to see you put where you cannot hurt them. It's already been recommended that I send you back to that finishing school in Switzerland, and I just may agree to that."

Victoria felt a momentary twinge of panic. She wouldn't show fear, no matter what. She was better than Judith and more capable. She wasn't going to be cast aside.

"You have all the power right now, Judith, but just keep in mind that I'm not without my ways." Victoria smiled. "If you aren't careful, you might even find yourself without a fiancé, and wouldn't that be sad?"

Judith laughed, which wasn't at all the reaction Victoria had hoped for.

The others came into the room, still discussing Micah and what was to be done. Shaking her head, Judith continued to smile. The others ignored Victoria but looked to Judith.

"What's so funny?" Camri asked.

Victoria wondered how Judith would respond. She didn't have to wait long.

"Victoria is threatening to take Caleb away from me."

Victoria raised her chin and met Camri's gaze. To her utter frustration, Camri's lips raised at the corners. Not only that, but Patrick and Kenzie were smiling too.

Camri shook her head. "My brother has no interest in selfish little girls, Victoria. However, he is a great advocate of education, as I am. I believe the time has come for you to advance your learning. I think tomorrow we should arrange for you to return to the finishing school."

"I think so as well," Kenzie concurred.

Victoria couldn't control her rage. "You can't do that! I won't go. I'm not going to be forced back there, no matter what you say. I have friends in this town who will keep you from it. You'll see. You'll all be sorry that you ever took a stand against me."

She dashed from the room and up the stairs to the protection of her bedroom. It wasn't much in the way of safety, but Victoria locked the door behind her and leaned back against it. She wanted to scream and cry all at the same time. Why couldn't they just leave her alone?

Pushing away from the door, she began to pace amidst the mess of gowns and shoes, stockings and hats on the floor and strewn over the furniture. She looked at her half-emptied trunks. First things first. She would put her things in order. That way she could be ready to leave at a moment's notice. She could never hoist the trunks downstairs on her own, but if all else failed, she would stuff what she could in her small traveling case and send for the rest later.

Of course, they might not allow her to have her things. She frowned and considered that for a moment. Her wardrobe was expensive and fashionable, even if Grandmother had chosen rather modest designs. Victoria didn't want to lose any of it.

"I must be calm," she told herself. There was no sense in worrying about something that hadn't happened yet.

She picked up a large green hat and placed it in an empty hat box. She'd never had to look after herself, and it stirred her anger to have to do so now. Nevertheless, she bent and picked up a pair of gloves. They weren't mates, so she placed them at the foot of her unmade bed and looked around the room. She spied one of the matching pieces and retrieved it. She continued searching until she found the other, and as she worked, she formed a plan.

By one means or another, she would get word to Arthur Morgan and explain the urgency of her situation. She would offer him whatever he desired, so long as he came and took her from this place.

CHAPTER 19

Micah wasn't entirely sure how long he'd been a prisoner in the small, bare-walled room. There wasn't a single window, nor a clock. His watch and wallet had been taken from him, along with his clothes. When he'd first come to after being hit on the head, Micah found he'd been dressed in canvas pants and a broadcloth shirt, the typical garb of local sailors, and manacled at the ankle. There was hardly even enough chain to walk. Probably to ensure he did nothing to try to escape.

The worst of it was the darkness. It was like being entombed. He sat alone in the dark, hour after hour, wondering when someone might come. It gave him a great deal of time to pray, which at the moment was all that was keeping him from complete despair.

The only way he could gauge time, the only reprieve from the darkness, was the daily visit from his jailers. There were two men, one large and barrel-chested, the other short and wiry. One held a gun on him while the other brought him a tray of food. They hung a lantern on the outside doorknob in order to give them enough light by which to work.

While Micah ate or pocketed the food on the tray, the same man who brought the tray took his waste bucket and empty water pitcher away. Both men would leave him in the damp darkness with his food and reappear later with the empty bucket and refilled pitcher. They'd leave those and take the tray away, and Micah wouldn't see them again for what he deemed to be a full day.

If he used their visits to calculate, then he'd been a prisoner for five days. From the stubble of growth on his face, that seemed about right.

At the sound of a key in the door, Micah straightened where he was sitting on the side of the bed. The door opened with a groan, and the two men appeared. Light filled the room, causing Micah to blink several times as he adjusted to it.

"Well, it looks like you survived another night," the man with the tray of food said. He plopped the tray down at the foot of the bed. "Hopefully you won't be with us much longer."

"Why is that?" Micah asked. "Are you going to move me to a hotel?"

The large man with the gun chuckled. "Yeah, that's right. Gonna put you up at the finest hotel at the bottom of the bay."

Micah shrugged. "It's got to be better than this place."

"I wouldn't be talkin' so ungrateful-like if I were you. If we weren't bein' paid to bring you food, you'd be mighty hungry."

"Speaking of being paid, how about I pay you to let me go?" Micah looked at the big man at the door while his partner retrieved the waste bucket and water pitcher, both of which sat on the floor—one at the end of the bed, the other at the head.

"We're being paid well enough," the man replied. "I don't have any interest in renegotiatin'."

"Well, what if I can top the amount?"

The man laughed. "Ain't likely. Now, you behave yourself, and we'll be back shortly."

The duo exited the room and relocked the door. Darkness settled over Micah like a thick fog. He had already looked over the contents of the tray. It never changed all that much. A small loaf of bread, a couple of boiled eggs, and a piece of fruit. Once they'd brought cheese instead of eggs. The fruit varied or was absent altogether. Today they'd brought a rather sorry-looking orange.

"Well, beggars can't be choosers." He felt his way around the tray. He put the orange and one of the boiled eggs under his pillow for later. Next, he tore the loaf of bread in two and began to eat half while saving the other.

He'd managed to finish off the bread and second egg by the time his jailers returned. This time the smaller man held the gun while the big man came in with the bucket and pitcher. He dropped the bucket on the floor at the foot of the bed, then handed Micah the water.

Micah's eyes adjusted faster this time. "I don't suppose I could have a bath and a razor? Maybe a good bar of soap? A lamp of my own and a book?"

The big man looked at Micah and rolled his eyes. He didn't even bother to reply. At the door, he motioned for his partner to move out of the way, then handed him the lantern and pulled the door closed. The sound of the key in the lock sent a wave of melancholy through Micah. Another twenty-four hours before he'd see light again.

He had no idea where he was or where the men went after seeing him. He figured he was in a cellar or basement somewhere. Occasionally he heard muffled noises, and the few times he had, Micah had called out, but no one ever seemed to hear him.

Every day after the men left, Micah worked on two projects. One was to free himself from at least one of the shackles, and the other was to try to open the door. He'd tried ramming the door with his body, but it was sturdy and he only wound up with a sore shoulder. He'd felt around the room, trying to find something that would make a decent tool with which he could pull loose the hinges, but there was nothing. The room had been depleted of anything save the bed, bucket, and pitcher.

The bed was little more than ropes and frame with a thin mattress and pillow. There was a moth-eaten blanket that did little to stave off the damp cold at night, but at least it was something. The waste bucket was wooden with a rope for its handle, and the pitcher was glass. The bigger of the two men had already told Micah that if he broke the pitcher, he'd have no more water, and given that broken glass would do little to aid his escape attempts, Micah wasn't about to risk his water supply. The fiends hadn't even left him the comfort of his shoes.

For a time after the men had gone, Micah sat in the dark and thought about Kenzie and his parents. He knew they'd be worried. They'd know by now that he was missing. The hospital would surely have gotten in touch with his father to find out why he hadn't reported for work. He hated to think of his mother sobbing at the fear that he might be hurt or dead.

He knew without a doubt that his situation was Arthur Morgan's fault. There had never been a sick woman. Morgan must have made arrangements with the clerk to tell him about the medical emergency. There was no other explanation. Morgan had known Micah would never agree to walk away from Kenzie—not even for a hospital of his own.

Frustration and anger were quickly giving way to discouragement, and Micah knew he couldn't let that happen. He had to figure out some way to escape. It wouldn't be easy to attack the duo, especially with chains around his ankles and no weapon. But he needed some sort of plan. He eased back on the bed, careful of the leftover food.

"Lord, You've been my mainstay all these years. I need help now like I've never needed it before."

Kenzie looked over the short note Arthur had sent only hours earlier. He said he had something imperative to tell her related to Dr. Fisher. She had considered discussing it with the others, but given everyone was setting off to tend to their own business, Kenzie said nothing. Instead, once they were gone, she hailed a boy on the street to run a message to Arthur at his hotel. A quick glance at the clock on the mantel told her that Arthur should be arriving at any time.

She didn't like the idea of entertaining him without someone nearby to remind him of the proprieties, but given all of San Francisco was still in some degree of chaos, it didn't seem quite so important. Besides, she could always imply that the others were upstairs or down in the kitchen. If Arthur thought that someone else was in residence, then he would surely abide by the rules of proper society. At least she hoped he would.

She knew it wasn't wise to be alone with him, but if he had the answer to Micah's disappearance, then she had to at least try to get it. If he tried anything untoward, Caleb still kept his revolver close at hand, and she knew where to find it.

The knocker sounded, making her jump. Even knowing Arthur would be arriving hadn't kept her from being nervous about the meeting.

She opened the door to find her former fiancé on the porch, hat in hand. He gave her his charming smile. "Kenzie, my love. I'm so glad you agreed to see me."

She fixed him with a look of annoyance. "I didn't have much of a choice. You said you had something to tell me about Dr. Fisher."

Arthur frowned. "I was hoping you'd want to see me."

"Come in." Kenzie left him at the door and moved into the front sitting room. Her mind raced with thoughts of how to keep the upper hand. She took Caleb's chair by the fire and sat before Arthur could try to coerce her into joining him on the sofa.

Arthur stared at her from the doorway. "You are beautiful, you know. I've always loved you in green."

Kenzie made a mental note never to wear the color again. "Say what you've come to say. Where is Micah? Is he all right? Have you hurt him?" She knew Arthur to be capable of stalling for time, but she wasn't going to tolerate it. "I want answers now."

"Very well, you shall have them. Although I had hoped to ease your pain at hearing them."

She leaned back in her chair, hoping to look completely unconcerned. "You let me worry about my pain. Where is Micah?"

"I'm afraid he won't be coming back. You see . . ." Arthur pulled a ladderback chair to within inches of Kenzie. "I made him a deal."

"What kind of deal?" She didn't believe a word he said, but she was determined to hear him out.

Arthur sat before continuing. "I told Micah that I'd never stopped loving you and that I knew you loved me as well, but the pain of thinking I'd betrayed you made you afraid of that love and of me."

"I'm not afraid of you, Arthur." She could hardly bear to sit next to him and his condescending smile. If it weren't for the fact that he was the only one who could give her answers about Micah, she would never have let him in the house.

"I'm glad to hear that. I told him we were meant for each other and that I felt confident that if he would step out of the picture, you would no longer be confused about your feelings for me."

"Arthur, I haven't been confused about my feelings for you in a long while. Now tell me where Micah is." Her patience was quickly coming to an end.

He held out his hands, palms up. "I'm afraid I can't do that. You see, I don't know. I asked him to go away, and he did." He let his hands rest on his lap and shrugged.

"Just like that?" She raised a brow in disbelief. "Do you really think me such a simpleton as to believe that?"

"Well, there was a bit more to the situation." He smiled and shrugged. "I know you might think it underhanded." He paused as if waiting for her to assure him otherwise. When Kenzie said nothing, he continued. "You see, I offered to build him a hospital. His very own—named after him. It would be the best that money could buy, with every piece of equipment possible. You know Dr. Fisher's devotion to healing."

Kenzie frowned. "I do." She fixed her gaze on the hearth. Micah loved medicine more than life itself.

"Well, when I told him I would do this for him—free and clear—if he would just walk away—give you up—I suppose it was more than he could resist." Arthur had the audacity to grin. "Everyone has their price."

For a split second, Kenzie thought it might be true. But somewhere deep inside, she could hear Micah's hopeful voice. *"I love you, and you know that you love me."* It cleared away all doubt.

"And . . . Micah agreed to have you build him a hospital?" Kenzie questioned, stalling for time. It dawned on her that she might get more answers if she pretended she believed him. She sighed and let her shoulders slump. "I suppose you're right and a hospital was his price. I'm sure it would have been almost impossible to resist such an offer. Micah is completely devoted to medicine."

Arthur nodded, doing his best to look penitent. "I know you must think it terribly unfair of me, but I had to do whatever I could. I love you and can't live without you. I knew his love for you wasn't as strong as mine. I knew that if I offered the proper enticement, he would give you up and prove me right." He leaned closer. "I did this for your own good. I knew his love wasn't true—not like my own. If a man can be bought off, he can't be truly in love."

"No, I don't suppose so." Kenzie shook her head. "Still, I never expected you to take such a devious turn."

"But, my dear, it wasn't devious. It was done out of sheer desperation and the love I hold for you. You must see now how ardently I adore you. I want you to be my wife. Please, Kenzie, say you will."

"I don't know." She touched her hand to her forehead. "I need time to think. This is all so shocking, and I have a terrible headache. I must go lie down." She got to her feet, and Arthur did likewise.

He pulled her into his arms before Kenzie could say or do anything. "Kenzie, I love you. Search your heart—you know it's true. Remember all of our good times—the hope we had for the future. We belong together. I know you love me."

She remembered a time when someone had gotten sick at the library while Arthur was there to see her. He hadn't been able to stomach the scene. She put her hand to her mouth and closed her eyes. "I think I'm going to be ill. The shock—you understand."

He abruptly let her go, as she'd hoped. "Yes, of course." He quickly stepped away and pulled a handkerchief from his pocket, holding it to his mouth. "Rest and then come to me or send word. We can leave as early as tonight."

She opened her eyes. "If you don't mind . . . show yourself out. I wouldn't want you to see me . . . sick."

He moved in a hurry toward the hall. "I'm sorry to have distressed you. Please feel better and send word when you've, ah, recovered."

Kenzie nodded, but held her pose until she heard the front door open and shut. She went to the window and saw Arthur all but running down the front steps. She knew he had Micah under his power. No doubt that meant Micah was imprisoned somewhere. But where?

"Oh, Micah, I'm so sorry to have put your life in danger." She turned from the window and shook her head. "But I promise I will find you. I will make this right."

CHAPTER 20

Hiram Morgan intends to own most everything you see," Joseph Gifford told Caleb as they walked around town.

Caleb studied the small community. "Did he explain his plan to the townspeople when he arrived?"

"Not at first. When he showed up, asking to speak to the mayor and city council, he only talked like he wanted a small section of land along the river. Eventually, that small section expanded to taking over everything."

"And how did the people react?"

Joseph Gifford shrugged. "Most of them didn't care, as long as there was plenty of money being offered. Some were more concerned about continuing to make a living. Morgan made promises, however. He told them they'd keep their jobs."

"Then he means to keep the businesses running?"

"After a fashion. He only wants certain businesses and plans to bring in others. He promised folks that if their current jobs became obsolete, he'd put them to work elsewhere."

"And you are the only holdup in him moving ahead?" Caleb asked.

The older man nodded. “He thinks it’s purely vindictive.” He grinned and scratched his chin. “I confess there’s a healthy portion of that spirit in me, but it’s not the only reason. My family has lived here since the territory was open to settling. My uncles and father inherited all the land the town is situated on, and then some, when my grandfather died in ’70. Over the years, they’ve sold off pieces. They encouraged the growth of the town—it was always at the heart of what they hoped for.”

“How long has Hiram Morgan planned to uproot everything?”

“Nearly two years. He and his son Arthur—the one who wronged Kenzie—showed up here one winter to discuss their desires. We had a big town meeting, and Morgan told the people what he wanted and why. There were those like me who were opposed, but in the end, he offered so much money, they couldn’t refuse. What Morgan didn’t realize was that a good number of properties that my uncle sold include the proviso that first right of purchase comes back to our family. I took advantage of that right and bought up two of the businesses and a half-dozen houses. I also bought back the Emporium I’d sold to one of my cousins. When Morgan learned what I’d done, he was livid.”

“I knew you owned the house and possibly the Emporium, but had no idea about the other locations.” Caleb frowned. “I’m sure that must be quite a thorn in Morgan’s side.”

Joseph smirked. “I’m sure it is, and he’ll probably move ahead with legal proceedings to force me to sell. I’ve heard him making noise about it.”

“I hardly see how he can force you to sell. At least not legally. How did Arthur figure in?”

Joseph glanced at Caleb. “If you want my honest opinion, I think Hiram saw the potential to have Arthur woo my daughter. I think he figured that if those two got married, I’d feel obliged to give in.”

It was easy to see that a man with Morgan's reputation wouldn't think twice about using whatever means he had at hand. "But if that were the case, why did Arthur change his mind? Or as he told Kenzie—why would his father dupe him into believing she canceled the wedding?"

They came to a bench near the bandstand, and Joseph motioned to it. "If you don't mind, I could use a rest."

"Of course." Caleb waited until the older man had taken a seat before joining him on the bench.

"Morgan made it known that he disapproved of them marrying," Joseph said. "Whether that was just part of the act, I couldn't say. Marrying Kenzie might have all been Arthur's idea. I have no way of knowing. But about a month before the wedding, Morgan got the notion he would build farther to the east. Everything looked like it would go that way. Folks who'd already sold feared he'd want to back out of their contracts, but he said no, he would honor them. He came across all gracious and generous. He told me that he wanted our families to be at peace for the sake of Arthur and Kenzie."

"And he was sincere?" Caleb found it hard to believe.

Joseph laughed. "I never trusted anything that came out of that man's mouth. A week later, Morgan was breaking ground to the east, and new rail lines were being surveyed into the area. Then, the day of the wedding, Kenzie got a letter from Arthur, telling her the wedding was off and, well, you pretty much know the rest."

"Arthur swears he came to you, begging to see Kenzie."

The older man shook his head. "Nothing came except for that letter. Kenzie was heartbroken. A lot later, months afterward, Arthur did come to the house. He apologized for having left Kenzie at the altar and said the circumstances had been beyond his control, and he wanted to speak with her to explain. I told him she wasn't there, and I wouldn't tell him where she'd gone. He went away, and I never heard from him again."

"So what happened to bring Hiram Morgan back to wanting your land?"

"I can't say for certain. I've heard gossip that the lay of the land wasn't suited to his needs—that the ground wasn't good and fixing it would triple the cost. Who can say? With Hiram Morgan, it could just be that he doesn't like that I have the upper hand. Could be he stands to make a bigger profit now with the city wanting to incorporate this area. All I know is his lawyer showed up here last March and offered five times as much money for my land as it's worth. When I told him no, he told me that I'd be sorry—that they'd find a way to best me. That's the last I heard from any of them."

"Arthur told Kenzie that everything that happened was his father's fault—that he's never stopped loving her."

"Hogwash." Joseph got to his feet. "That boy never loved anybody but himself. I'm guessing his pa sent him to win Kenzie back so that he can get to me."

"It would answer why Arthur insists she marry him before returning to Kansas City."

Joseph's expression remained stoic, but there was fear in his eyes. "You've got to keep her from doing that. He can't be trusted. I'd be willing to bet everything I own that it's all a ruse. He'll marry Kenzie and then threaten to make her miserable unless I give in. You can't let him marry her. I haven't always done right by that girl, but I wouldn't be able to bear seeing her hurt again."

Caleb chuckled. "I don't think that's a problem. You see, there's someone else who wants to marry Kenzie. My best friend, Dr. Micah Fisher, has fallen hard for your daughter."

"And he's a good man?"

"He is. He's a good, God-fearing man, and he loves Kenzie.

I've no doubt of his sincerity. He's worked hard to get Kenzie to notice him." Caleb grinned. "She hasn't made it easy."

"I don't imagine so." Joseph smiled. "Do you think she'll give him a chance?"

"I believe she already cares for him a great deal. I think she's just been afraid to trust another man after Arthur. Then Arthur showed up, telling her that it was all a lie—that he still loves her and never intended to end their relationship. It's got her pretty shaken up, but she's got a good head on her shoulders. I think in time, it'll all come around right."

"I was always disappointed that she wasn't a boy," Joseph admitted. "I'm sorry to say she knew about that disappointment too. She did whatever she could to try to please me, to win my approval. I wish I'd made it easier on her. She's a good daughter. She's always done right by us, and it grieves me to think that my attitude might have caused her to seek solace with the likes of Arthur Morgan."

"We all make mistakes. Maybe one day you can tell her that you're sorry and ask her forgiveness. I'm sure it would go a long way to healing that wound."

Joseph rubbed his chin and nodded. "No doubt you're right."

Victoria couldn't believe her good fortune. The day before, she'd received a letter from Arthur telling her he'd arranged an appointment for her with Abraham Ruef. He would send a carriage for her, and it would be up to her to figure out how to get away.

She had worried about that very thing, especially after Camri Coulter demanded to know who the letter was from. Victoria had lied and told them it was from her former fiancé, who'd gotten in touch with Mr. Bridgestone and learned where she was.

"You surely don't want to see him again," Judith commented

as Victoria prepared to leave. "I don't know that I should let you go by yourself. If Kenzie hadn't left this note saying she needed to speak to Camri and me as soon as she got back, I'd go with you."

"I'll be perfectly fine." Victoria had quickly landed on the perfect excuse for going to see Piedmont Rosedale. "I must return his ring and some of the other jewelry he gave me. He's sending a carriage. I won't be unescorted. Not only that, but he lives with his two maiden sisters, and they will be there as well," she added, though anyone who was anyone knew Rosedale had no sisters.

Fortunately, her cousin was a nobody.

Judith frowned. "I didn't see his sisters when we were there. Of course, it is a very big house." She wrung her hands. "I do wish the others were here to consult. Why didn't you tell me about this yesterday?"

Victoria wasn't about to admit that she hadn't mentioned it because she knew this would be the kind of argument she'd face. "I'm sure I'll be back within the hour, and I'll be supervised at all times."

Judith finally raised her hands in defeat. "Just get back as soon as possible. I don't want it said that I kept you a prisoner in this house, but neither do I want to be accused of not looking after your welfare."

Victoria smiled as the clock in the hall chimed three. "I'm sure no one would accuse you of doing anything improper." She walked to the front door and opened it. The carriage was just coming to a stop at the curb. "Good day, Judith *dear*." Her voice dripped sarcasm.

The short ride didn't culminate at Arthur's hotel as she'd thought it might, but rather at an office building only a few blocks away. The driver helped her down from the carriage, and Victoria was relieved to see Arthur waiting for her at the lobby door.

"I wasn't sure if you'd manage your escape," he said with a grin and a tip of his hat.

"Judith was bothersome, wanting to know all the details, but I gave her a satisfactory story, and that was that. It really isn't all that hard to handle her. She's not very bright."

"But she is quite lovely to look at," Arthur said with a smile.

"Do you think her prettier than me?" Victoria watched for his reaction.

Arthur looked shocked. "Hardly. She could never hold a candle to your beauty."

Victoria returned his smile. "I knew you were a man of sophisticated taste."

They stepped into the building, and Arthur pointed the way. "Mr. Ruef is meeting you in the office of a friend. I told him discretion was important."

She clutched his arm and simpered. "You are truly amazing. I'm ever so grateful for your help in this matter. I have to admit I find you quite captivating."

Arthur's voice grew husky. "I was thinking much the same about you."

They entered the office, where a stern-faced matron in a rather manly brown tweed suit looked up from her typewriter and ordered them to sit. She then got up from her desk and exited the room through the door behind her desk. When she returned, she left the way open.

"He will see you now." She reclaimed her seat and immediately went back to work as if they didn't even exist.

Victoria allowed Arthur to lead the way. He walked in and greeted the stranger with an extended hand and a broad smile. "Mr. Ruef. My father speaks so highly of you."

"I don't suppose he accompanied you to San Francisco?" Ruef asked.

"No, sorry, but circumstances beyond his control kept him

too busy to leave Kansas City. However, I believe you'll enjoy the company I've brought you. Miss Victoria Whitley, this is Abraham Ruef."

Victoria considered the older man. He had a thick head of dark hair combed straight back and an equally thick mustache. He stared at her with an intensity that would have intimidated a weaker woman, but Victoria wasn't at all concerned.

"Mr. Ruef, thank you for agreeing to see me."

"Miss Whitley. I knew your family. A fine family indeed."

She touched her gloved hand to her throat and sighed in the way she'd learned delicate women could use to gain great attention. "I'm so relieved. Does that mean you'll help me?"

He smiled. "It has been my life's work to help those who are being put upon by others." He motioned for them to sit. "I've already reviewed your situation and believe it will be expensive but not impossible to rectify."

Victoria sat and smoothed out her skirt. "I don't care at this point what it costs. I simply want my inheritance and my freedom."

Ruef gave her a broad smile, but his gaze remained cold and calculating. "Then I am certain we can do business. I've already gone through the details of your situation. The fact that your father and brother are deceased, as well as your grandmother, clearly cuts the ties where your family is concerned. This Judith Whitley has no proof of being your cousin and, although I'm far too busy to see to it, should you desire to pursue action to reclaim the entirety of your family's fortune, you might fare well. It will probably take a great deal of time, perhaps years, but we could try."

As tempting as that sounded, Victoria knew there were too many people who would come to Judith's aid to declare her a Whitley. She was an identical image of her twin sister, and those who'd known the family realized exactly who Judith was.

Besides, wouldn't it be better to just take what she could get now and then maybe try to get the rest at a later date?

"I'd prefer just to get my share for the time being. I want to be rid of this town and my cousin as soon as possible." Victoria smiled. "Is it something I might consider later?"

"Of course." Ruef leaned back in his leather chair. "In the meantime, I can have this matter wrapped up before the end of the week."

"The end of the week? Then I'll have my money and freedom to do as I wish?" Victoria could scarcely believe she'd heard right.

"Absolutely. I have a judge who's a good friend. He'll see the matter pushed through. Of course, there is an expense to expedite this matter. It will require a considerable fee."

"I don't care," Victoria said, shaking her head. "I'll pay you as soon as I have my inheritance."

Ruef nodded and pushed a detailed invoice toward her. "I'll need you to sign this."

Victoria scanned the itemized list of expenses. She forced herself to remain expressionless as she looked at the total, which amounted to fifty thousand dollars. She had no idea how much her inheritance was, but she had a feeling Ruef did and had charged accordingly. She glanced at Arthur Morgan, and when he smiled and nodded, she signed the paper.

"In just a few days, you shall be a free woman, Miss Whitley," Ruef said.

"Thank you, Mr. Ruef." She got to her feet. A huge burden and obstacle had been taken from her. "I look forward to hearing from you once matters are settled."

He considered her for a moment, then nodded. "Yes. I'll be in touch very soon."

"I'll be ready." She looked at Arthur. "Thank you for assisting me with this matter."

They exited the office together and made their way outside. Already Victoria was making plans.

"I wonder if you would do me another favor?" she asked Arthur.

"And what would that be?"

"When we hear from Ruef, arrange a room for me at your hotel for that evening. After we see Ruef, I don't intend to return to Mr. Coulter's house. I'll send for my things when I send Judith proof of my freedom."

Arthur frowned. "But I need you there to be my eyes and ears. At least until Kenzie agrees to marry me."

"I can tell you that the entire house is in a tizzy since Micah disappeared. I know you told Kenzie you offered him a hospital and he agreed to go away, but somehow I doubt that's the truth. Dr. Fisher isn't the kind to just walk away."

"No, indeed he wasn't."

"Wasn't? Does that mean Dr. Fisher is no longer alive?" She watched him carefully. She was picking up on his idiosyncrasies. He had a way of darting his gaze left and right when he lied and a slight tic in his right cheek when he was angry.

This time he only smiled. "It means that he will soon no longer be a problem."

She shrugged as he hailed a cab. "Well, I hope you can find a way to wrap things up by Friday. I have no desire to remain in that house one second longer than I have to." He helped her into the carriage, and she sat back on the leather upholstery and smiled. "I presume you'll send a cab for me once our meeting is settled."

Arthur handed the driver money for the ride. "You can rest assured. Haven't I seen to everything so far?"

She nodded. "Yes, but I have yet to see your itemized list for repayment."

He smirked. "Oh, but you will. I have a very specific repayment plan in mind."

Victoria laughed as the driver put the team in motion. Arthur Morgan might think he was going to take advantage of her, but he wouldn't. She'd had other men try to compromise her, and they hadn't won. Arthur Morgan wasn't going to win either.

CHAPTER 21

The clock had chimed four by the time Kenzie was finally able to sit down with Camri and Judith. She'd been formulating a plan in her head since talking with Arthur. She knew Micah was in danger, and it was up to her to see him rescued. After all, she was the reason he was in trouble.

"You invited Arthur here?" Camri shook her head.

"I'm convinced he's done something with Micah. He must have him locked up somewhere." Kenzie tried not to let her thoughts go to anything worse than imprisonment. "You know Micah too well to believe he'd leave of his own volition. He wouldn't hurt his mother and father this way."

"He wouldn't leave you for ten hospitals," Judith replied.

"I agree," Camri said. "Micah isn't that kind of man."

"No, he's not." Kenzie smiled. "I knew Arthur was lying when he said it." She sobered. "I don't know if he's hurt Micah, but I have to find out. I've come up with an idea."

Judith leaned forward. "How can we help?"

A knock interrupted them before Kenzie could reply. The trio exchanged a look of concern.

"You don't suppose Arthur has returned?" Camri asked, getting to her feet.

"I hope not." Kenzie stood too.

Camri left them for a moment and then returned alone. "It's a telegram." She held it out so they could see the envelope. "It's from Caleb."

Relief washed over Kenzie. "I'm glad." She sat back down while Camri read the message aloud.

"'Morgan is lying. Catching train. Do nothing until my return. Caleb.'" She glanced up. "Well, that suggests he's found out something."

"I've no doubt Arthur is up to no good." Kenzie shook her head. "When he was here earlier, it was as if scales had fallen from my eyes. I don't know what I saw in him before. I think his declarations of love have always been a lie. I wish I had realized that when I first met him. I'm such a fool."

"There's nothing to be gained by that kind of thinking," Judith declared. "We must look to the future."

Camri lowered the telegram. "She's right. Micah may be in a dire situation."

"I'm certain he is. Arthur wouldn't have come to me so confidently if Micah weren't under his control. That's why I'm going to move ahead with my plan. I'm going to see Arthur at his hotel."

"But Caleb said not to do anything until he returns," Judith protested. Kenzie got to her feet again, and Judith jumped up as well. She put her hand on Kenzie's arm. "He wouldn't want you to get hurt."

"I know, but I don't want Micah to get hurt, and that's more important."

"But how can going to speak with Arthur again help you?" Camri asked. "It's not like he'll confess that he has Micah."

"No, but that's where my plan comes into play." Kenzie met

Camri's concerned expression and then Judith's. "I will agree to marry him."

"What? No, Kenzie, you can't do that. You love Micah." Judith's eyes filled with tears.

"I'm not really going to marry him," Kenzie said, giving Judith's hand a squeeze, "but I'll make him believe it. However, I'm also going to make it a requirement that I get to see Micah one last time so I can tell him to his face how awful I think he is for taking Arthur up on his offer."

Both women looked at her as if she'd lost her mind.

Kenzie drew a deep breath. "Look, I know Arthur. He won't produce Micah for me unless it suits his purpose to do so. Arthur will be thrilled to have me reject Micah in his presence. It will feed his sense of accomplishment. I'll convince Arthur that I want to make Micah regret his choices and that without that satisfaction, I won't marry him."

Camri still looked skeptical. "Do you think he'll agree?"

Kenzie nodded. "I know he will. Arthur loves to see his enemy laid low. This will be the icing on the cake for him, so to speak. Once I see that Micah is safe, then I can turn the tables on Arthur. We can probably have him arrested for whatever he's done to Micah, but we'll need Micah's testimony to prove that."

"You can't go alone," Judith said. "There's nothing to stop that man from . . . well, he might try to force you to his room."

"We'll go with you," Camri said, surprising Kenzie. "If we're with you, he won't do anything untoward." She glanced at the clock on the mantel. "Patrick mustn't know. He wouldn't understand. Thankfully, he won't be home until after six. If we hurry, we can get to the hotel and back before then."

"I don't know if it's wise for you to go." Kenzie considered for a moment. "Arthur might feel like we're ganging up on him."

"Not at all," Judith interjected. "It wouldn't be appropriate for you to be at the hotel by yourself. We'll sit apart from you, but we'll be your chaperones."

Kenzie nodded. "But what about Victoria?"

"At this point, I don't care," Judith replied. "She ventured out on her own earlier, so perhaps she'll be content to remain here. Especially if we tell her we'll be back soon."

Camri nodded. "I agree. We'll tell her that we're just going down the street to see someone and we'll be right back. I'll take money for a cab to bring us home, and we can walk at a fast clip to get to the hotel. We won't be gone long at all, and she won't have time to cause too much trouble." Camri headed for the stairs. "I'll go get my purse."

And with that, the matter was settled. Judith followed Camri upstairs to explain the situation to Victoria, and then both women joined Kenzie at the door. They took up their hats and gloves and made their way outside.

At the hotel, the clerk seemed more than a little surprised to have three women asking for Arthur Morgan. He grinned as if they'd just suggested he escort them to Arthur's room. "I'm sure you realize, ladies, that it's hardly appropriate—"

"We're not here to entertain him in his room," Kenzie interrupted. "Send him a message to meet me in the lobby. He will be quite angry if you fail to do so, I assure you."

"Never seen a man have so many women come to visit him at a hotel," the clerk said, shaking his head. "Even his sister was here."

Kenzie couldn't imagine that Arthur's sister had come to San Francisco. She had been expecting a baby in January and surely wouldn't travel with one so young. But Kenzie said nothing to challenge the clerk. She fixed him with a scowl. "I don't care who else has come to see him. Get upstairs and give him my message. Tell him Miss Gifford awaits his company in the lobby, but will only wait three minutes."

The clerk considered this for only a moment, then nodded. He called to a bellboy and whispered something in his ear. The boy scurried up the main staircase without a word.

"There you are, ladies. Now, if you don't mind, I've other things to tend to." He smiled again at Kenzie. "I must say that red hair of yours does your temperament justice."

Kenzie rolled her eyes and turned to survey the lobby. "Over there," she said, motioning Camri and Judith to a quiet corner of the room. "You two can sit there, while Arthur and I sit in the little alcove."

They quickly took their places before someone else managed to claim the seats for themselves. The lobby was bustling, but given the hotel had a restaurant and ballroom, it wasn't surprising to find the place filling up with evening visitors.

Arthur appeared in less than two minutes. He was breathless and still buttoning up his coat, but he looked delighted. Kenzie had known that if he were in the hotel, he wouldn't pass up an opportunity to see her.

"I knew you would come to me." The look on his face was elated. He figured he'd won, and his smug greeting irritated Kenzie.

He tried to take hold of her, but Kenzie waved him off. "Please sit. We wouldn't want to cause a scene." She waited for him to pull up a chair.

"I'm so happy you've come," He perched on the edge of his seat. "I hope you've come to give me the answer I long to hear."

"I'm here to discuss it, yes."

"What's to discuss? I will take you from here right now. We'll go be married. I have all the proper papers."

She held up a gloved hand. "No. First things first. I won't do anything until I have a chance to speak to Micah."

"But why, my dear?" He leaned forward and reached for her hand. "He's no longer important to us."

Kenzie allowed him to take her hand, but she could see from the look on Camri's face that she was just as unhappy about it as Kenzie was.

"Perhaps he's not important, but what I want to say to him is. I never settled matters with you, Arthur. You and I parted without any explanation or farewells between us. It nearly killed me. I suffered terribly this last year."

"I know, but I've already explained that it wasn't my desire to hurt you. It wasn't my fault."

"No. Of course it wasn't. But if I had sought you out and spoken my heart on the matter, we would never have been parted. Isn't that true?"

"And if you speak your mind to Dr. Fisher, you think you'll change his mind?"

Kenzie drew from her limited skills to appear completely shocked. "Of course not! Why would I want that man to change his mind? He threw me over for a hospital, of all things. Another woman would have been bad enough—but a building?" She was pleased by how indignant she sounded.

Arthur relaxed and chuckled. "So you wish to reprimand the greedy doctor. How perfect." He paused, and his demeanor changed. "Still, I don't, ah, know that I can reach him. He did promise me that he wouldn't see you."

"Oh, Arthur, I've never known any challenge to be too great for you. Goodness, but you even convinced me to come here." She smiled and patted his hand when she really wanted to slap his face. "I've no doubt you'll be able to find him. I want to tell him exactly what I think of him. After that, we can be married."

She fully meant that she and Micah could marry, but she let Arthur presume what he would.

"Wonderful. My darling, you won't regret it. You can even ask your friends to bear witness to our marriage." He glanced over at Camri and Judith and gave a nod.

Kenzie started to get to her feet, and Arthur jumped up to assist her. "I'll get word to you first thing in the morning," he promised. "Oh, my darling, you've no idea how happy you've made me."

She looked up, forcing herself not to cringe at his arrogant expression. "Thank you, Arthur. It has made me quite happy, as well. This shall be very satisfying."

He lifted her hand to his lips. "The satisfaction shall be all mine."

Camri was still laughing as they entered Caleb's house. "You really should perform on the stage, Kenzie. I never knew what a great actress you could be."

"I wanted to slap him," Judith added. "He just puts me out of sorts."

"Well, that'd be two of us feelin' that way," Patrick said, coming from the dining room. "Where in the world have the three of ye been? Victoria had no idea where ye'd gone."

"We are grown women, fully capable of going out without you needing to raise an alarm," Camri said, stretching up on tiptoe to kiss his cheek. "There's absolutely no reason for you to fret."

She stepped back, and Patrick eyed them all with great suspicion. "Right. So who was it ye wanted to slap, Judith?"

All eyes went to Judith, who immediately paled. "I . . . well . . ."

Patrick sighed and pointed to the front room. "Why don't the three of ye sit down and tell me what ye've gotten yerselves into?"

The girls hesitated only a moment before parading into the front room to sit side by side on the sofa. Patrick towered over them for a moment, then finally took a seat in Caleb's chair.

"Now—who's gonna be tellin' me about this?"

"It's my fault," Kenzie piped up. "I don't want you to blame Camri or Judith. They went with me because they were worried about my safety."

"Well, that makes me feel so much better." Patrick glared at his wife-to-be. "I thought ye had more sense than to put yerselves in danger."

"It was important that we do this." Camri softened her voice. "I'm sorry you were worried."

"I'll get back to ye later," he said, shaking his head.

"Micah's in danger," Kenzie continued before anything else could be said. "Arthur has him but won't tell me where. I went to see Arthur at his hotel. In the lobby," she added quickly. "Camri and Judith went with me in case he tried to do anything untoward."

Patrick nodded. "Tell me the rest."

"Caleb sent a telegram telling us that Arthur was up to no good," Camri offered. "He came here earlier, telling Kenzie that Micah had agreed to give her up and never see her again in exchange for a hospital that Arthur would build him. You know Micah has been missing and that he'd never worry his parents like that."

"And he would never take a hospital if it meant giving up Kenzie," Judith added.

"Indeed, he would not." Patrick let out a long sigh. "So what did ye do?"

"I told him that I would marry him, but not until after I saw Micah and let him know exactly what I thought of him. Arthur is a prideful and vindictive man. I appealed to his sense of revenge. This way, Arthur will have to produce Micah from wherever he's holding him."

"So ye're certain he's holdin' Micah against his will."

"Of course he is," Camri interjected. "You know as well as I do that wild horses couldn't keep him from Kenzie."

"But to tell the man ye'd marry him." Patrick shook his head. "I don't mind sayin' that's not so wise."

Kenzie leaned forward. "Patrick, will you help me?"

His brows knit together as he frowned. "How would I be doin' that?"

"I'm not sure. Arthur said he'd arrange a meeting tomorrow. I don't want to go alone. If he has taken Micah, as I believe he has, then he no doubt had help. He'll probably have someone there to make certain Micah can't get away or cause Arthur harm. If you could follow us to wherever Arthur takes me to meet Micah, then maybe you could help me set him free."

Patrick rubbed his chin. "For sure, I know that if I don't, ye'll be findin' a way to do it behind me back."

"We should also involve the police," Camri declared. "Or at least get some men to come with us. There's power in numbers."

"Aye. That's true enough." Patrick's expression was one of deep contemplation.

"Then you'll help me?" Kenzie didn't hide the hopefulness in her tone.

Patrick's blue eyes narrowed. "But what if I lose ye on the way to wherever Arthur is takin' ye? Ye'll be plopped into a hornet's nest, and there'll be no one to help ye."

"That's why we should all go," Camri said. "We'll rent a horse for you, then Judith and I will take Caleb's car." She smiled as if it were the perfect solution.

"Ye don't know how to drive. Besides, there's no need for the two of ye to go."

"Of course there is," Camri said, looking to Judith for help.

Judith nodded and parroted her friend. "Of course there is."

Patrick shook his head. "No need that a reasonable man could be thinkin' up."

Camri lifted her chin in defiance. "Either we figure out a plan together, or Judith and I will figure one out separately.

You know we're capable of it. And for your information, Mr. Murdock, I know very well how to drive."

He looked at each of the women and sighed as he cast his gaze heavenward. "God help us."

Kenzie smiled. "I'm already assured of His assistance, but what of yours?"

Patrick shrugged. "What choice would I be havin'?"

CHAPTER 22

The door to Micah's cell opened, flooding the room with light. He couldn't be sure, but it didn't seem like the regular twenty-four hours had passed since he'd last seen his jailers.

Micah scooted to the edge of the bed and touched his bare feet to the cold, damp floor. "Well, I must say this is a surprise." He tried his best to sound nonchalant. "If I had known I'd have company this early, I would have straightened up."

"We're taking you for a little ride," the big man said, moving toward Micah. He yanked him to his feet.

"And where would we be going on this fine day?" Micah squinted, still trying to get his eyes to adjust to the light.

"The boss wants to see you."

"Arthur Morgan?"

The man grinned. "Come along like a good fella. Don't be causing me any trouble. I'd hate to have to mar that handsome face."

Micah wasn't sure what to make of the situation but knew if he was to have any chance of escape, he needed to be free of this room.

He walked with exaggerated slowness, hoping it would draw attention to his shackles. He stumbled a couple of times for effect. Finally, the larger of his jailers stopped him.

"I'm going to take these off, but if you try anything, it'll be the last thing you do."

Micah gave him a look of surprise. "What would Mr. Morgan say if you killed me?"

The man smiled. "He plans to pay me to do exactly that. Leastwise, that's my understanding. If it happens sooner rather than later, well, that's just the way it goes."

"So Arthur Morgan *is* the one I have to thank for these long days of rest."

"Shut up and keep moving," the man growled and gave Micah a hard push.

They climbed one set of rickety steps and then another. At the top of the second one, Micah could see they were in some sort of warehouse. It was filled with crates of every size, but otherwise the place was deserted.

He figured Morgan would step out of the shadows at any moment, but he didn't. They passed through the warehouse to the doors and then out to a small wagon.

"Climb up there. You'll sit between us."

"There isn't room," Micah said, looking at the big man as if he were crazy.

"He's right," the smaller man said with a shrug. "I'll get in back and keep my gun on him. He won't jump over the side without a bullet following him."

Micah took his seat but did his best to look for a chance to escape. He wasn't going back into that cell, nor was he going to sit idly by and let these two kill him.

His heart raced as he considered his odds. He wasn't in the best of shape after several days of little food and no exercise. He would have to find a place where he could not only jump from the wagon, but do so in such a way that he had immediate coverage to protect him from the gun. He also needed to pick a place that wouldn't risk the lives of anyone else.

"Where are we going?" he asked.

"It's not important. Just keep quiet and don't do anything that will get you or someone else killed," the big man replied, nodding toward the street market just ahead.

From that point on, Micah kept his thoughts and questions to himself. He figured by the growth of beard on his face and the number of times the twosome had brought him food that he had been captive for at least ten days. By now his family would be frantic, and his friends would know something was wrong. He was counting on that and hoping that the police were looking for him. Still, the two men who guarded him would most likely do as they threatened, and innocent people might be harmed if Micah made the wrong move. He had to wait for just the right opportunity.

When they made their way out of the burned-out section of the city and into one of the remaining middle-class neighborhoods, Micah straightened a bit in the seat. His movement caused the man behind him to press the revolver into the space between his shoulder blades.

"Don't be moving around," the man warned.

It wasn't long before they pulled up to the back of a large three-story house. The white clapboard was trimmed with black shutters. The big man at his side all but dragged Micah from the seat and held him fast as they made their way to the back door. Once inside, the man shoved Micah forward until they were standing in the middle of the kitchen.

At the opposite side of the room stood Arthur Morgan.

"I see you've survived," the blond man said with a smug look. "Despite your meager accommodations."

"Yes, well, I hadn't planned to accommodate you with

anything but a grave. However, it seems my hesitation has paid off."

Micah tried to assess his surroundings without appearing to do so. He shrugged and leaned back against a wooden table. "So why am I here now?"

"You're going to clean up and dress properly, and in one hour you are going to meet with Kenzie for the final time. You see, she has agreed to marry me. We will be wed at exactly ten thirty this morning."

Micah frowned. "Why would she ever agree to marry you?"

"I like to think it's because she loves me, and in your absence, she was able to realize that. Of course, I helped her along by explaining that I had bought you off with a hospital."

"I see. And she was gullible enough to believe you?"

Morgan crossed his arms and gave a casual shrug. "She's always been gullible. She believed I was in love with her a year ago—that I'm still madly in love with her now."

"But you weren't and you still aren't. So why are you determined to marry her?"

"If you must know, she serves a purpose in a bigger scheme. I'm bringing her here to tell you good-bye and to give you a piece of her mind. She's very put out with you." He laughed. "As she well should be."

"I'll tell her it's all lies."

Morgan's eyes narrowed. "You will—if you want her to remain safe and unharmed—convince her that you no longer love her. You will tell her that the hospital I offered to build you was too big of a prize to let go. You'll wish her well and tell her you knew we were always meant to be together. You will convince her that nothing is amiss and that this is what you want—no matter what she says to you. Do you understand?"

"I'm beginning to." Micah knew Kenzie would never believe him—he wasn't a good actor.

"Good. Please understand that I will make her miserable if you do anything to interfere with my plan. I'll start by having you killed in front of her." Morgan smiled, and his nostrils flared. "Although as angry as she is at you, she very well might enjoy that." He looked at Micah's guards. "But enough of this tea talk. Boys, take him upstairs and see that he's properly groomed. Shave him yourself, lest he get his hands on the razor and make a fool of himself. I'll be back in twenty minutes, so waste no time. Have him positioned exactly as we discussed. That way you'll have no trouble keeping your guns trained on him."

It was nearly a half hour later when Micah sat dressed and ready to receive Kenzie. He wore an expensive black wool suit with a vest of green striped silk. It wouldn't have been his choice, but Morgan had guessed his size adequately, and the suit fit him well. He'd been instructed to take a seat near the fireplace and to look relaxed—disinterested.

Micah knew it would be impossible. How could he look disinterested when Kenzie's life was on the line? He eased back in the chair and undid the buttons on his suit coat. Next he crossed his legs and waited. He knew his guards were hidden close by. They had strict instructions to shoot him if he did anything wrong.

He laced his fingers and prayed. There had to be a way to save Kenzie and himself. There had to be a way for them to escape Morgan. He glanced around the room. Four windows. Two . . . no, three different exits.

The front door opened. A shadow fell across the polished floor, and then Arthur Morgan swept into the room with Kenzie on his arm. She was dressed beautifully in a short-jacketed walking suit of navy plaid. A large straw hat trimmed in navy and green graced her auburn hair.

They locked gazes. Micah could see the pain in her expression and wanted nothing more than to wipe away the doubt and hurt Arthur had put in her mind. Could she really believe the worst of him?

"It took some doing to convince Dr. Fisher to meet with us," Morgan began, "but when it comes to pleasing you, there isn't much I wouldn't do."

Kenzie turned to look at him, and her expression changed completely. "Thank you so much. You're a dear." She patted his arm, then stepped away from his side and returned her gaze to Micah. With a haughty tilt of her chin, she narrowed her eyes. "While you, on the other hand, have been nothing but a source of irritation to me."

Micah forced back the words he wanted to say. He looked at his fingernails instead. "Life isn't always what we wish it would be." He glanced at Morgan and shrugged.

Kenzie stepped toward him, then stopped. She pointed a gloved finger at him. "You have wounded me deeply. You left me heartbroken and abandoned. When I think of all the flowery words you spoke—the promises you made—it's enough to sicken me."

Micah swallowed hard. Could she really believe him capable of giving her up for a bribe?

"Arthur told me how easily your love can be bought and sold. You should be ashamed, Micah Fisher. What a fool I was to believe anything you ever said to me. You never cared one whit about me, did you?" He opened his mouth, and she held out her hand. "No, don't speak. I don't want to hear your excuses or words of apology."

Micah didn't know what to do. He could tell her what had truly happened, but he'd probably be shot, and she might be hurt as well. He didn't trust Morgan not to punish her just to further hurt him. As if seeing Kenzie on Morgan's arm wasn't bad enough.

"I always knew you were a doctor for the money and prestige," she continued. "When I think of how you badgered your patients for pay before you'd even look their way—well, it's shocking to say the least, and I should have known you could be easily bought."

Micah bit his tongue lest he laugh out loud, and all his doubts slipped away. Kenzie was playing a game with him, but even more so with Morgan. Micah wasn't sure what she was doing, but he didn't intend to ruin her excellent performance. She was quite good at playing the part of the woman scorned.

"I can't bear to think about how I let you wear me down with your false love." She put her hands over her heart. "It's a wonder Arthur would even want me back, given my undeniable ridiculousness where you were concerned. And to think I would have married you had Arthur not helped me see your flaws."

Micah smiled. "Oh, my dear Kenzie. You know very well what's most important to me in life. How could I possibly have passed up the opportunity to have a hospital built—a hospital named after me?" He glanced heavenward. "The Fisher Hospital. Just think of all the sick who will find refuge there. Surely you can't fault me when you consider all that I might accomplish."

Kenzie frowned. "I'm so glad I did not yield my heart to your pretense of passion. When I think of how you might have ruined me for Arthur . . . well, I can't speak of it."

Morgan snorted a laugh.

Kenzie put the back of her hand to the corner of her eye. "I'm quite beyond words."

The clock struck ten, and Kenzie shook her head and turned back to Morgan, who was grinning from ear to ear.

"I'm so glad you allowed me this moment, Arthur. I will always remember what you did—the sacrifice you made to see me returned to you. When I think of how your family might have kept us apart—how you were willing to defy them—it truly touches me."

Morgan chuckled. "I'm just glad I'm not on the receiving end of your temper. Dr. Fisher may have his hospital, but he also has your disdain, and I wouldn't be in his shoes for all the world." He extended a hand. "But now we must be on our way. We're to be married in half an hour."

Micah wasn't sure how Kenzie intended the situation to play out, but he couldn't stand by and let Morgan take her away. He jumped to his feet.

"Wait!"

Kenzie turned, and Arthur immediately stepped to her side. He put his arm possessively around her shoulder. "Surely you wouldn't want to delay our nuptials, Dr. Fisher." Morgan's voice was tight with an unspoken threat.

"Everything he told you is a lie," Micah said.

Kenzie smiled while Arthur scowled. To Micah's surprise, Kenzie turned her face upward. Arthur couldn't help but meet her gaze.

Kenzie's smile faded. "I know."

CHAPTER 23

Victoria answered the door to find a smartly dressed chauffeur. "Yes?"

The man gave a slight bow. "I've come with a message for Miss Victoria Whitley."

She nodded. "I am she." Victoria glanced back over her shoulder, then relaxed. Thank goodness Judith and her friends were gone.

The chauffeur handed her a piece of paper. The note was from Abraham Ruef. Victoria unfolded the paper and read.

Everything has been arranged. Come with my driver to the office, and you will be a free woman this day.

Victoria smiled. "Wait here. I'll get my hat and gloves."

The driver nodded, and Victoria shot up the stairs in a very unladylike fashion. Freedom! She was soon to be free of Judith and all these horrible people. She was so glad she'd sorted and packed her things back into their trunks. Kenzie thought Victoria had simply taken her advice and picked up after herself. She'd even commended Victoria for her hard work. It had taken all of Victoria's constraint not to blurt out the real reason she'd tidied the place. Wouldn't they all be surprised when they learned the truth?

She looked in the mirror. Her hair was a mess. Oh, to have someone to style it again. She took the time to pin up several errant strands of hair, then glanced over her dress. A lady's maid, that was what she needed more than anything else. How marvelous it would be to have a competent lady's maid again. She would have to locate one, but that shouldn't be too difficult. She could call on some of the family's old friends—if she could find them. The earthquake and fire really had reordered her once perfect world.

There was so much to tend to. Perhaps it would all have to wait until she could get out of this wretched city, but soon no one would be bossing Victoria Whitley around. A giggle escaped her.

"Oh, but this is glorious!" She pulled on her gloves and clapped her hands.

She looked at her various trunks. Should she ask the driver to take them down? No, they would keep, and then she'd have the satisfaction of watching Judith's stunned expression as she moved out of the house.

Victoria pinned her hat in place and then picked up her small purse. She had no idea if Ruef would actually furnish her money today or just papers to take to the bank. Grandmother seldom handled actual cash. She usually just signed for things or told people to submit a bill.

Victoria frowned. She knew so very little. It was hard to admit she was ill-prepared to face her future. Her brother Bill had once told her she would be better off if she studied the way their grandmother managed the estate and their servants rather than fighting the old woman. Victoria had thought it a waste of her time, however. She had always known she would marry and her husband would attend to such things. Now, at nineteen, she was about to embark on a life of her own, free from the oppressive restrictions of her grandmother and father. The very idea thrilled and terrified her to the core of her being.

"I can't rely on anyone else," she told herself. She drew in a deep breath. "I will be my own mistress." She squared her shoulders. "No one will ever again order me about."

She gave a curt nod, then made her way downstairs. The driver stood waiting at the door, just as she'd left him.

"Let us be on our way. I wouldn't want to keep Mr. Ruef waiting."

Kenzie felt Arthur tense beside her. He shook his head and looked down at her in confusion. "Kenzie, I think you're mistaken. He's the one who's lying."

"No, Arthur. You are the liar, and I want nothing to do with you. I have no idea what you and your father are up to, but it won't involve me."

"You don't know what you're saying. You've listened to your friends and their lies. I'm the right man for you, Kenzie."

"Hardly," Micah said, moving toward them. "You've kept me prisoner for nearly two weeks, as best I can tell. You've lied to the woman I intend to marry and made plans to kill me." He looked at Kenzie, and she warmed under his scrutiny.

Morgan scowled at Micah. "You'll pay for this with your life." He let loose a stream of curses, then called again for his men. "Ramus! Bardsley!" He looked at the opening behind Micah's chair. No one appeared. He called out again. "Ramus! Bardsley! Get in here and do your job!"

Kenzie reached into her pocket, causing Arthur to lose his grip on her shoulder. "Goodness, Arthur, who in the world are you yelling for?"

Instead of Arthur's henchmen, Patrick, Camri, and Judith appeared in the archway that led into another room. "I'm afraid," Patrick began, "that yer boys are a bit tied up at the moment."

Arthur stared at them for a moment and then bared his teeth. Shaking with rage, he produced a small derringer and waved it. "Get back! I have a gun."

Kenzie cleared her throat and smiled. "What a coincidence, Arthur. So do I." Her hand closed around the butt of the pistol in her pocket as she shoved it against Arthur's rib cage. "And just so you know, mine is bigger and will cut you in half."

He paled and lowered the derringer. "So this was all a ruse?"

Patrick quickly stepped up and disarmed Arthur.

"I don't understand." Arthur looked at her, shaking his head. "You really don't love me?"

"No. I thought I did once, but it was never real. Just as your love for me was never real."

Despite Patrick holding fast to his arm, Arthur turned to Kenzie. "I only did what I had to. You don't understand." He sounded desperate. "It's not too late. Perhaps we don't love each other, but marrying me will be to your benefit. I can give you anything you want—believe me."

Kenzie shook her head. "That's the whole point, Arthur. I don't believe you. I don't know why it is so imperative to you that we marry, but it isn't going to happen. I'm glad you stood me up at the altar. For all the humiliation and shame, I faced—for all the pain and sadness I endured—I'm glad things worked out the way they did. Otherwise I might never have known what real love was all about."

There was a commotion at the front door. Furious pounding seemed to rattle the entire house. Judith hurried away. "I'll get it." When she returned, there were six uniformed policemen behind her. The police had already been apprised as to what was going on, and with very little ado, they took Arthur Morgan into custody and escorted him from the house.

Kenzie didn't care what else happened. Micah was safe, and that was all that mattered. She looked him over from top to bottom to assure herself that he wasn't hurt.

Micah ignored the others and swung Kenzie into his arms. Unashamed, he kissed her. Kenzie held tightly to him, thanking God that he was alive and hers.

"I was so worried about you," he whispered between kisses.

She pulled back. "Me? I was perfectly safe, but you . . . where have you been?"

"I don't know. I was locked in a room without windows, but none of that is important now. I'm just so glad he didn't hurt you. So glad you believed in me enough to know I'd never willingly leave you."

She smiled. "When Arthur told me you jumped at the chance to have a hospital named after you, I knew he was lying."

"But how could you be sure?" he asked, smiling.

"Just as you once suggested, my heart told me. Or perhaps I should say God made it clear to my heart."

He pulled her close again, then jumped back. She frowned, but when he reached down to remove the revolver from her hands, she had to smile.

"Sorry."

"You've been known to react rather recklessly."

"Oh, is that so?" She cocked her head. "And why would you say that?"

Patrick didn't give him a chance to answer. "For sure it might be because of the gun in yer hand, lass. I thought we agreed ye wouldn't be bringin' it."

"Well, you should be glad I did. I knew Arthur wouldn't risk being unarmed." Kenzie looked at Patrick, who stood watching the scene play out, and then realized Judith and Camri were watching as well. She shrugged. "Sometimes drastic situations call for drastic measures."

"And this was definitely one of those." Camri stepped forward to hug Micah. "We're all so relieved to find you unharmed."

Judith nodded. "Caleb sent a telegram to tell us that Arthur Morgan was lying."

"He also made it clear that they were to do nothing until his return, but ye can see for yerself how well they heeded that," Patrick added. "And with Caleb's own gun."

"Just have a look at the gun if you're really all that bothered," Kenzie said. "It isn't even loaded."

"What good is an unloaded gun?" Patrick questioned. "Faith, woman. What if Morgan had pressed ye to shoot?"

Kenzie's confidence faded. "I guess I don't know the answer to that."

Micah shook his head. "I don't suppose any of us will ever know the answer to that." He looked at the other women. "I wish you hadn't put yourselves in harm's way, any of you. But I'm very grateful for the rescue."

"You would have done it for any one of us," Camri countered. "So stop fretting about it." She looked around. "What is this place? Who owns it?"

Micah shrugged. "I have no idea. Arthur mentioned it being on loan to him for a few hours, but nothing else. He probably arranged it through a friend of the family or his other connections." He pulled on the striped vest he wore. "He furnished this as well."

"It doesn't suit you," Kenzie said, shaking her head.

He laughed. "I didn't think so either." He looked at Patrick. "So what happens now?"

Patrick shrugged. "Morgan and his men are in custody. I'm sure ye'll be havin' some legal statement to make."

"Yes, in fact, we need to be on our way. Judge Winters has all the information we could provide him prior to this encounter, but he told me he'd need to get a statement from you before formal charges can be made against Arthur Morgan," Camri announced.

Patrick offered Camri his arm and headed for the door with Judith following. "I wish I could have Victoria dealt with as neatly," Judith said. "I'm so weary of her battles."

"Who knows," Camri called out over her shoulder, "Caleb may return with a solution for that as well."

For a moment, Micah and Kenzie just stood, gazing into each other's eyes. Kenzie could see the love in his expression. "I'm sorry," she whispered.

"Sorry?"

"Sorry it took so long to believe in you—in us."

He touched her cheek. "It doesn't matter. The past no longer concerns us. We're together now, and if I have anything to say about it, we'll soon be man and wife. If you'll just say yes."

"Do you suppose I would go to all this trouble if I didn't intend to marry you?" Kenzie smiled and planted a quick kiss on his cheek. "Now, come along, Dr. Fisher. We have a triple wedding to plan."

Victoria listened as the judge, a staid and homely man in his sixties, explained the details of her liberty. He droned on and on, and she had no idea what he was really saying, but she figured she could get Arthur to explain it once he bothered to arrive. Where in the world was he, anyway? Thankfully, Abraham Ruef sat with her, or she might have despaired of ever understanding.

Finally, the old man closed the file he'd been reading from and looked at Ruef. "That should see the matter through to conclusion. I trust you have everything else in order for this young woman?"

"Yes," Ruef said, getting to his feet. "Thank you, Your Honor."

He pulled out an envelope and placed it on the desk. "I'm sure you'll find this to be satisfactory."

Ruef then turned to Victoria. "Come along. I'll explain in a way that you'll understand while we make our way to lunch. I'm famished and presume you are as well."

Victoria had no desire to eat with Abraham Ruef, but she felt she owed him at least that much. She allowed him to escort her back to the privacy of his car and began to assault him with questions as soon as she'd settled in.

"So am I now finally able to draw on my inheritance? Will I have money in order to purchase train tickets and arrange for a hotel?"

"Yes. It's all yours. The matter has been completely taken care of. Your cousin has no more say over anything you do. The money is already sitting in your personal account at the bank, and you can draw from it any time you like. In fact—" he reached into his coat and produced another envelope—"I have some ready cash here for your immediate use. I know you mentioned wanting to leave the city. I can help you with those arrangements as well. Generally speaking, genteel women do not carry money on their persons. It's too much of a temptation for ruffians to take advantage of them. You could, however, have a trusted servant carry it for you. Once you establish your household, you'll no doubt have a driver, and he could manage it."

"Thank you." She took the envelope and looked inside. There was a great deal of money, and she smiled, feeling suddenly empowered. "I'll hire a driver when I settle in New York City. Right now, I want to have my things moved from the Coulter house to the hotel where Arthur Morgan is staying. He promised he would have a room put on hold for me there. Then I'll need a lady's maid. Perhaps you could advise on how I could go about that? Afterward, I will make my plans."

"You remember there is still the little matter of settling our account for services rendered. I have papers at my office. I also have your new bank book. You can write me out a draft for the money you owe."

"Yes, of course. We can go there directly and forget about lunch, in fact. I'm sure you're quite busy."

He smiled and patted her hand. "I would never deny a beautiful young woman the enjoyment of a meal. Especially one at the Cliff House. Besides, there are several investment ideas I think we should discuss. You wouldn't want that newfound fortune to simply dwindle away for lack of proper care. I think I can take that modest fortune and help you turn it into more wealth than you'll ever know what to do with. You might want to stick around San Francisco. We might be in pieces at the moment, but the potential to make a great deal of money is quite high. I promise you, we could triple what you currently have by making just a few prudent choices."

She shrugged and eased back against the leather seat. "I suppose it couldn't hurt to hear what you have to say."

It seemed the right thing to do for now. She didn't like the idea of being manipulated, but she was quickly learning that sometimes it was best to appear cooperative. She could always make her desires known when the situation was a little more stable. Besides, he might very well be able to do what he promised. Then again, after taking nearly twenty percent of her inheritance, Ruef might have bought her freedom, but she had no desire to join him on his other schemes.

"Will Mr. Morgan be joining us?" she asked.

Ruef shook his head. "I have no idea where he is. Last I heard, he was to be married this morning."

Victoria frowned. "To Miss Gifford?"

"I suppose so, if that's the young woman he came to town to find." Ruef smoothed his mustache. "He seemed dedicated to no other purpose."

Victoria considered the passing scenery as she thought about Arthur Morgan and his determination to marry Kenzie. She'd have known if a wedding were in the works. None of the women at the house seemed to have that in mind. There was still talk about the trio sharing their nuptials in one large, hideous arrangement, but Arthur Morgan's name was certainly no part of it.

She shrugged. Arthur's situation with Kenzie wasn't her problem. He, like Ruef, had served his purpose, and she couldn't care less if she ever saw him again.

CHAPTER 24

That afternoon, after Micah had seen his parents and changed into clothes of his own choosing, he escorted Kenzie to the Solid Rock warehouse. He wanted to tell her about his desire to add a hospital to the warehouse to serve displaced women and children.

Mrs. Andrews, now Mrs. Lake, met them at the door of the warehouse. She was harried as usual, but happy to see them. "You both look quite jolly. I do hope that means you've come to your senses, dearie, and decided to marry this young man."

Kenzie looked at Micah and nodded. "I have. He's finally worn me down."

The older woman had no idea what they'd just gone through, and Micah saw no reason to enlighten her. He wanted nothing more than to put it all behind them and plan for the future.

"She finally came to her senses, Mrs. Lake. And I don't mind saying I'm exhausted from all the effort. I'm going to see that she makes it up to me."

Mrs. Lake laughed.

"How are you and Cousin George enjoying your new house?" Kenzie asked.

The older woman smiled. "He's concerned about the chimney. He's not entirely convinced it remained undamaged from the earthquake. I told him I'd have it checked a second time, but you know how he can be."

Kenzie nodded. "Indeed. Well, if anyone can settle his nerves, it's you. I've never seen him so happy."

"He's happy with his work as much as with me. He seems to enjoy not having all that responsibility. Now he can just sit around dreaming up ideas and mess up my kitchen. If you'll excuse me, I need to get back to work. However, Mr. Murdock left you a ledger to write your ideas in, Dr. Fisher. It's just over there on the table by the kitchen. He said to sketch out what you had in mind." She pulled a pencil from her pocket and handed it to him. "I found this for you in case you didn't have one of your own."

"Thank you, Mrs. Lake."

Kenzie looked at him oddly. "What's this all about?"

Micah led her to the table where the ledger waited. "Have a seat. I want to talk to you about some ideas I've had."

She looked skeptical but nevertheless did as he asked. Micah sat beside her and opened the sketchbook. "I spoke to Caleb about a possibility and want to talk to you about it as well. After all, since we're to marry, you have a say in the matter."

Her brow raised. "What matter?"

"Living here."

Her eyes widened in surprise. "Here? At Solid Rock?"

"Yes." He kept his expression serious. "You see, I'd like to expand the operation to include a hospital. I did a lot of thinking while enjoying Mr. Morgan's hospitality. A hospital focused on helping the poor—regardless of their ability to pay—is much needed. Not only that, but it ties in nicely with what Caleb and Camri hope to accomplish here. Caleb told me that he finally feels clear on God's direction for him. He wants to make this entire area a haven for those in need."

"I see."

He couldn't tell from her short statement whether she approved or not. "I'd like very much for you to be my nurse and help with the patients."

"Show me what you have in mind?"

He smiled. "Just like that? No argument?"

She crossed her arms. "I don't always argue with you."

"You used to."

A thin smile touched her lips, and she batted her eyes in a coquettish manner. "All right. Would you *like* me to argue with you?"

He laughed. "Not really. I suppose I'd do better to just explain my ideas, eh?"

"Indeed."

Micah sketched out the dimensions of the present warehouse and then added on an entire wing. "I thought we could build our own quarters on the backside, overlooking the water. Caleb has an idea for buying up all the land around us. He's working on it now. He wants to create a park, as well as a small house for himself and Judith. He wants to make a place of rest and tranquility that will minister to the hearts and souls of the poor women and children who come here for help. My father even plans to hold services here—after his regular services at the church, of course. Oh, and Camri wants a little school, as well."

"What a surprise." Kenzie laughed, shaking her head. "She would put us all in school desks if she had her way."

"Patrick said she wants to start a free school for adults who had to quit at a young age. I think it's a very good idea, myself."

Kenzie nodded. "As do I. Don't tell Camri, but I happen to agree with her defense of education."

"And what do you think of my idea for a hospital?"

She looked at the rough sketch he'd made. "How big would you want it to be?"

"I'd like there to be room for fifty beds in four different wards."

"Fifty? That big?"

Micah nodded. "Caleb said we might as well think big and do it right the first time. Besides, there's so much need. You have no idea what I see in my job, even before the earthquake. Many people don't even attempt to get treatment because they don't have the money to pay for doctors and medicine."

Kenzie considered this for a moment. "I think it sounds very wise to make it large."

"Judith wants to use her money to benefit the needy, so we have the perfect opportunity to do this in grand style. It would be a charity hospital. We would solicit funds from the wealthy and the government to help pay for things. We won't get rich doing this, but I never figured to have a grand fortune."

She smiled in such a loving way that Micah knew her heart was in agreement with his own. "If I wanted money, I could have married Arthur."

"I would never have let that happen," he said matter-of-factly. Micah looked down at the drawing, making it clear such thoughts weren't even up for discussion. "I want a ward for men, one for women, and another for children. And the fourth will be for critical care and surgery. Over here we'll have a small laboratory. Depending on the equipment we can purchase, we might very well be able to do almost everything the larger hospitals can do, but on a limited scale."

Kenzie looked up, and he could see the admiration in her eyes. "I think it's a wonderful idea. But don't you think I'll need to get some better training before I'll be of much use to you?"

"Many nurses are doctor-trained. There are a growing number of nursing schools, but regulations and training haven't yet been standardized." He grinned. "I think I can teach you everything you need to know, and if the time comes that more is required, we'll cross that bridge then. I've considered getting some additional training back east as it relates to blood typing and transfusion. We could go east while the hospital is being built, and you could take classes at the same hospital I'm studying . . . if you think me incapable."

She rolled her eyes. "You know very well what I think of your abilities. Now, is this where you would want our quarters?" She put her finger on the drawing.

"Yes. I think we could arrange a lovely apartment of rooms. We could have our own private living and dining area, although Caleb did mention that shared meals here with the others would be more cost-effective and less time-consuming."

Kenzie nodded. "But we'd have our own private bathroom?"

"Of course."

"And how many bedrooms?"

He laughed. "How many do you need?"

She shrugged. "I don't know, but it seems we should be mindful of children we might have."

His voice became soft and serious. "I am very mindful of that idea. I would love to have a large family. What about you?"

She nodded but didn't look up. "I suppose we should have at least a couple of extra bedrooms then . . . if you intend for this to be long-term."

He lifted her hand to his lips and pressed a kiss to her fingertips. "Ah, Kenzie. Where you're concerned, I want everything to be long-term. I want it to be forever."

She finally raised her eyes to his, and he'd never thought her more beautiful—flushed and bright-eyed, a look of hope in her expression. "I want that too."

"Judith, this roast is meltin' in my mouth," Patrick said, helping himself to another slice of beef.

She looked up in relief. "Thank you. I was nervous, leaving

it to cook while we were dealing with Mr. Morgan, but I honestly didn't know what else to do. It would never have cooked in time if I'd waited."

"I marvel at how tender it is," Camri agreed. "You're going to have to teach me how to cook. Otherwise my poor husband will starve."

Kenzie glanced up from her plate. "Well, now that Micah and I are making plans to live at Solid Rock, I wonder if the two of you won't do the same. Then we could just all plan our meals together."

"'Tis a possibility," Patrick agreed, ladling more potatoes onto his plate. "But with all that's happened, we've scarce had time for talkin' about it. Once Caleb is home, we'll be discussin' it for sure."

Judith looked at the clock for the tenth time and shook her head. "I don't understand Victoria being gone all this time. Where could she be?"

"My guess is that she's gone out with friends," Camri answered with a shrug. "She's made it clear she won't be kept as a prisoner."

"Yes, and I have no intention of being her keeper. I know that it's my responsibility to look after her, but she's two years from her majority. I don't think I can endure her that long." Judith put down her fork. "She's making this so hard on everyone."

"God will be providin' an answer," Patrick assured her. "We have to have faith."

The diners startled as the front door opened with a bang.

Patrick immediately got to his feet and moved toward the open hall.

Victoria appeared in the doorway, followed by two broad-shouldered men. She smiled in that self-confident way they'd all come to recognize.

"Where have you been?" Judith got to her feet. "We've been worried."

"Well, you needn't ever do so again." Victoria looked over her shoulder at the men behind her. "My trunks are upstairs. Turn left, and then the first room on the right past the bath." The men nodded and took off up the stairs.

"Wait just a minute, fellas," Patrick commanded. The men stopped. "What's this all about, Victoria?"

"Today I received my freedom from Judith. Abraham Ruef and Arthur Morgan arranged for a judge to make me free of your guardianship. My inheritance was released, and I am moving to a hotel. Arthur secured me a suite of rooms there, and I won't have to live in this abhorrent little house any longer."

Judith shook her head. "Do you have proof of this?"

"I do, but none that I feel inclined to show you. I don't owe you anything, cousin. I am a woman in my own right. I have a lawyer who will happily sue you, should you try to impose any of your restrictions on me."

"This house still belongs to Caleb Coulter," Patrick reminded her. "So before ye have yer goons traipsin' upstairs, ye'd do well to get Miss Coulter's permission, since he's absent."

"I say good riddance," Camri said, putting aside her napkin. "Let me show you the way, gentlemen." She got up and brushed past Victoria without another word.

Judith remained in place. "I'm sure you realize by now that Arthur Morgan is under arrest."

Victoria laughed. "He was detained but not arrested."

"What?" Micah jumped to his feet. "What do you mean, he wasn't arrested?"

Kenzie took hold of his arm. She felt a tremor run through her. Of course Arthur wouldn't be arrested. He was wealthy and could pay his way out of anything. Especially when a corrupt government was otherwise preoccupied with the city's resurrection.

Victoria laughed. "Honestly. Did you think you could defeat a Morgan?" She shook her head. "You have no idea what that man is capable of. The two men who held you hostage told the judge they alone were responsible. They assured the judge that Mr. Morgan was in no way their acquaintance nor their employer. They threw themselves on the mercy of the court, explaining that sheer hunger and loss drove them to their woeful deeds." She offered a smug smile before adding, "Arthur is happily dining with Abraham Ruef this evening to discuss filing charges against you all for your terrible treatment of him this morning."

"Of all the nerve!" Micah declared and looked down at Kenzie. "Are we never to be rid of this miscreant?"

Kenzie didn't want to add to Micah's discomfort, so she merely shook her head. "It's not important. We needn't let Arthur or Victoria ruin our happiness."

"What's this about ruined happiness?" Camri asked, returning to the dining room as the two men carried Victoria's trunks to the door.

"Apparently Mr. Morgan is free from responsibility in holding Micah against his will," Judith told her. "He's even considering suing us for our part in rescuing Micah and having him arrested."

Camri looked at Victoria askance. "I'm sure once Caleb returns, he'll be able to manage all of this easily. Mr. Morgan isn't the only one with friends."

"Friends can't accomplish what money can. Arthur has enough wealth to see you all ruined," Victoria reminded them.

Judith crossed the room to her cousin as the men stomped back upstairs. "You might remember that I have plenty of money now, myself. I won't let you or anyone else cause problems for this family. Now, take your things and go. I hope in time you will mature into a woman half as noble as our grandmother, but I have my doubts." She grabbed Victoria's shoulders and turned her without warning. "Leave. You may wait in the car for your things." She gave Victoria a hard push, which caused the younger woman to gasp.

"And you claim to be such a good Christian," Victoria said sarcastically as she moved toward the front door.

Judith shook her head. "No, not at all. I'm a sinner saved by grace. Nothing more. If not for the love of Jesus in my heart, I would do more than show you the door."

Victoria paused and glanced over her shoulder. Apparently Judith's look of fierce determination was her undoing, and the younger woman hurried from the house without another word.

Judith went back to the table and took a seat, while Patrick waited in the hall until the last of the trunks had been delivered from upstairs. He locked the front door and returned to the dining room just as Micah sank back into his chair beside Kenzie.

For several minutes, all they could do was look at each other in stunned silence. It was hard to look back on the day and all that had happened without feeling a sense of disappointment in the news that Arthur was free. Kenzie wanted nothing more than to see him pay for his treatment of Micah. What if he'd ordered Micah killed? How could she have ever survived that pain?

They all slowly began eating again, but there was no real enthusiasm or conversation. No doubt everyone felt the same way Kenzie did.

Lord, we need Your comfort and guidance.

Kenzie glanced at Micah and could see the tic in his cheek. He was so angry. No doubt he had thought catching Arthur in the act would assure legal justice.

Calm his spirit, Lord. Help him to see that none of this matters anymore.

After several minutes of uncomfortable silence, Judith jumped to her feet. "I nearly forgot." She rushed from the room with everyone gazing after her. When she returned, she held a pie pan aloft and smiled. "I made dessert."

This broke the tension, and one by one, they burst into laughter.

"For sure, a little sugar should put a better taste to the day," Patrick said.

Kenzie took Micah's hand and smiled as he turned to face her. "Don't give Arthur any kind of hold on our life. I won't allow him to come between us."

Micah nodded. "I had just hoped that he would pay for his wrongdoing and the way he hurt you."

She shrugged. "He is paying, whether he realizes it or not."

A look of understanding broke across Micah's face. "Indeed, he is. He doesn't have you."

Caleb returned late the following Tuesday, and after a night of rest, agreed to go with Judith to the hotel to check on Victoria. To both their regret and relief, they learned that she and Arthur Morgan had departed on Sunday. They were bound for Kansas City, the clerk explained.

"Can I help you with anything else?"

Caleb shook his head. "No, thank you." He pulled Judith's hand through the crook of his arm. "What say we go to lunch and discuss your accounts, Miss Whitley? Our business here is apparently finished."

Judith nodded. "I suppose there's no way of finding out exactly where she's gone."

"Oh, there are ways," Caleb said, leading her to his car. "The real question is whether or not we care enough to utilize them."

"I worry she might be in danger. I didn't like her very much—in truth, not at all—but I still don't wish her harm."

"Which is far from her regard for you and the others." Caleb helped her into his car. "There are always going to be cold-hearted people like Victoria. She's a victim of her calloused upbringing and the loss of her mother at such a tender age. All we can do is pray for her and hope for the best."

He got the car started and maneuvered down the street. Every day the cleanup was returning the city to better order. It would be a long time before San Francisco regained her former beauty, but the people were hardy and willing to work.

"Where are we going for our luncheon?" Judith asked as they headed north.

"Mr. and Mrs. Wong invited us to share Chinese food with them. Have you ever eaten it?"

Judith was wide-eyed at this question. "No. But I'm intrigued."

He smiled. "Good. I think it's just the diversion we need. Besides, I thought you might like to see what's happening in Chinatown. You might just be of a mind to arrange some aid for them as well as what you're doing for Solid Rock."

She seemed momentarily surprised, then gave him an assuring nod. "I would very much like to help the Wongs and their friends. They were wonderful to us when we first arrived in the city last year."

When they arrived, Mrs. Wong pushed open the tent flap and welcomed Caleb and Judith to their temporary home. She was dressed in a floor-length plum-colored skirt with a short robe-style top that crossed her body and was tied with a sash. The sleeves were long and slightly belled at the bottom. Her black hair, liberally salted with gray, was combed back and styled in a perfect bun.

"You come and sit as honored guests," Mrs. Wong told them with a wide smile and a bow. "We are very happy to share our home with you."

Caleb returned the bow. "We are honored to be invited."

"We've missed you very much," Judith added.

"Mr. Wong and Liling will be with us in a moment. You come and sit." Mrs. Wong motioned to a simple plank table set with plates and teacups.

Her husband entered from the back of the tent.

"Mr. Wong." Caleb bowed and then extended his hand. "I am glad to see you are doing so well." Their daughter, Liling, entered behind her father with a simple teapot.

"It is good to see you, Mr. Caleb," Mr. Wong said. "I hope the wild radishes are not choking out the flowers."

"I've scarcely had time to check on that, but I promise I will." Caleb smiled at Liling and gave a slight nod. She smiled and returned the bob before stepping to the opposite side of the table with the tea.

"You sit here, Mr. Caleb," Mr. Wong told them. "Miss Judith, sit here."

They took their seats, and Mr. Wong did likewise. Liling began to pour the tea as Mrs. Wong filled the table with several dishes of food.

Once everything was served and Judith was instructed on the use of chopsticks, the meal began. Mr. Wong explained all that was happening to retain their rights to Chinatown, at least all that he knew. Caleb figured he knew more than the older man, but it would have been dishonoring to suggest as much. Instead, Caleb promised any help that he could give and praised Mrs. Wong and Liling on the meal.

"We have plans to expand the warehouse grounds and put in a hospital and school for the poor," Caleb told them as the meal neared conclusion. "I will have jobs for anyone who cares to come and apply. I want to create a beautiful park area, so I will need gardeners too, and of course there will be other jobs as well."

"You will hire Chinese?" Mr. Wong asked.

Caleb smiled. "I'll hire anyone who is willing to give me an honest day's work."

The older man smiled. "I have many friends."

This brought a chuckle from Caleb. "And I will have many jobs." They all laughed at this.

"And you will all marry?" Mrs. Wong asked.

"Yes. Judith and I, Camri and Patrick, and now Dr. Fisher and Kenzie. We will have a triple wedding."

Mrs. Wong smiled and nodded. "And when you do this?"

Caleb looked at Judith and realized he had no idea. "Have we set an exact date?"

Judith shook her head. "No. But now that we've managed to put most of our troubles in order, I think we should do exactly that."

"Perhaps this evening we can rally the others and figure it out." He looked at Mrs. Wong and then at her husband and daughter. "And of course, you are all invited."

"It's a very nice house," Camri said, following Patrick from room to room. It wasn't all that big, but the craftsmanship was excellent due to Patrick's father's skills.

"It pleased my mother," Patrick admitted. "Ophelia too. They were so happy to live here." He ran his hand along the fireplace mantel, but he stared off toward the wall, not seeming to even see it. By the set of his jaw, Camri could tell he was deep in contemplation. He had grown melancholy since their arrival, and she wondered if the memories, both good and bad, were a little overwhelming.

She went to him and put her arms around him. "It feels like a very happy home."

He held her in return but said nothing for a long time. "'Twas once, but I don't know that it could be again. There are things here I'd just as soon not remember. For sure, I didn't expect to be thinkin' this way."

Camri glanced up and saw his eyes dampen with tears. "Patrick, we don't have to live here. Just because you've been given the house doesn't mean you have to keep it or live in it. You could lease it out and see how you feel about it later."

He looked down at her. "But then where would we be livin'?"

"Why, at Solid Rock. The others plan to live there. Why don't we join them? We could build a little space for ourselves, and you could headquarter your construction company out of the same location. We're already surrounded by commercial businesses and structures. Your company would fit in quite nicely."

"Ye're an odd one, Miss Coulter. Most women would be naggin' for their own cottage."

"I would think by now you'd have realized that I'm not like most women."

He nodded and pulled her close. "Aye. Ye're not at all like most. Although, I will say ye remind me a good deal of my mother. She never let me da take her for granted."

"You may always count on me, Patrick, but I would never allow you to take me for granted. Nor would I do that to you. God has given us a precious gift in each other, and I will always remember that."

He touched her cheek and smiled. "Ye're a fine lass. My sister knew ye'd be the right one for me, even when I couldn't see it for meself."

"I miss Ophelia," Camri said toward the ceiling. "I knew her such a short time, but it was enough to fill me to overflowing. I'd like to think she's able to look down from heaven and see how well things have turned out. I know she'd be pleased."

"Aye. She'd probably be a sight more pleased if we'd get on with sayin' our vows."

"Oh really?" Camri pulled back with a grin. "Now who's anxious to be settin' the date?" She attempted an Irish brogue. "And after ye kept me waitin' for so long?"

He laughed and lifted her in his arms. He whirled her in a circle, then plopped her back down. "Come along then, Miss Coulter. Let us go speak to the others and get this marriage arranged. I'm not of a mind to keep ye waitin' any longer."

CHAPTER 25

The wedding was set for Friday, the thirty-first of August. None of the couples felt it necessary to have a grand affair, considering the city was still working to overcome the devastation from the earthquake and fires. San Francisco would no doubt bear her scars for years to come, and recovery often seemed painfully slow, given the political nonsense that continued to plague them.

Kenzie questioned the sanity of planning a second wedding in twelve months. When she thought of all she'd gone through in less than a year's time, she marveled that she could even consider giving her heart to another, much less that she'd done so with great abandon. However, it was easy to see that her love for Micah was nothing like the love she'd thought she'd held for Arthur. With Arthur, there had always been the feeling that she didn't deserve him—that she was so far beneath him. Whenever she thought of their time together, the word *sacrifice* came to mind. She had always thought Arthur was sacrificing his future because of her. Now Kenzie could see that the real sacrifice would have been hers. She would have given up true love in the hope of having something remotely similar.

"I can hardly believe the wedding is just days away," Judith said. "Aren't you excited, Kenzie? You've hardly said two words this morning."

Camri and Judith were like giddy schoolgirls, sharing thoughts and ideas about the upcoming day. Since breakfast, they'd been talking nonstop about the wedding.

"I'm very excited," Kenzie assured her.

"Well, you looked rather sad for a moment," Judith noted.

"Just reflective. This last year has been quite busy for me."

Judith nodded. "It has been for all of us. When I think we haven't even known each other a full year yet, it amazes me. I've never been closer to anyone than I am you two."

"I feel the same way," Camri said. "You two have taught me so much. I'm so blessed that God saw fit to put us together." She arranged several pairs of gloves on the dining room table. "I'm also very glad we decided against having fancy wedding gowns made. If we'd done that, we'd be half mad with fittings and worries. It was hard enough just to pick a hat, and now I'm overwhelmed just trying to figure out which pair of gloves to choose."

Judith giggled. "I'm glad too, although my dress will be new. Nothing I had seemed appropriate for a wedding, and since Grandmother's dressmaker was able to get back to business so quickly, I figured it didn't hurt to order a new gown."

"I think it's a lovely dress," Kenzie offered. "With your blond hair, you always look so sweet in pale blue. Just like a porcelain doll."

"And it isn't all that fancy. I'll be able to wear it for church and other dressy occasions," Judith replied, shaking her head. "I still remember all the money Grandmother spent on that massive wardrobe for me, and now it's nothing more than ash. What a waste."

Kenzie knew there were hundreds, even thousands of similar

stories out there. Vast amounts of art had been lost, hundreds of thousands of books. Many priceless first editions had been burned. It hurt to think about the irreplaceable things, but even more painful was the growing total of deaths. Bodies were still being found on occasion, especially in the poorer neighborhoods.

"And have you settled on your gown, Kenzie?" Camri asked.

"I have." Kenzie smiled, trying not to let herself become morose. "Remember the white sprigged muslin?" Camri and Judith both nodded. "The embroidered flowers are lavender, and I made a waistband of the same color. It's quite fetching, if I do say so. I had planned to do it before the earthquake and just forgot about it. I believe it will be perfect for the wedding, and it's one of the few gowns I own that Micah has never seen."

"You'll be in lavender, Judith in blue, and I'll be in yellow. We'll be a veritable rainbow of colors." Camri chose a pair of gloves. "I think these will go well with my dress. I might even sew on a yellow bow at the wrist. What do you think?" She had chosen a pair of cream crocheted gloves.

"I think that would be lovely," Judith replied before Kenzie could comment.

Camri turned the gloves first one way and then the other. She nodded, satisfied with her choice. "You don't suppose we'll regret not having a big church wedding with all sorts of flowers and sweeping gowns, do you?"

"I think we'll be much too happily married to care, and also too busy. Micah wants to get right to work putting together his hospital for the poor." Kenzie had to admit she was equally excited. "I think it's going to be an amazing place. Not only that, but I'm looking forward to learning more about healing. I've enjoyed helping the sick."

"Micah says you're a natural at it," Judith declared.

Camri set the chosen pair of gloves to one side and stacked the others. "I think we're going to have the most amazing ministry." She glanced up. "I want to have the school up and running as soon as possible. So many women have come to me at church and told me about women they know who want to learn to read. It's so exciting."

Kenzie glanced at the pocket watch she'd taken to wearing. "It is, but we should probably gather our things and get to the millinery shop. We'll be late for our appointment if we don't leave right away."

"I'm so glad we decided to purchase special hats for our wedding. I think it's the perfect way to celebrate," Judith said as Camri gathered her gloves.

Kenzie smiled and put her watch away. "I do too. Not too much or too little. We'll all look perfect. By the way, is Caleb going to drive us to the shop?"

"No. He's not even here. He had to attend a meeting at the mayor's office," Camri replied. "I thought we might walk, and if Providence smiles upon us, we can hail a taxi."

Providence did smile, and a taxi was easily procured. Kenzie gazed out of the carriage at the progress that had been made in the city. There were still large piles of debris and empty lots where buildings had been demolished and cleared away for the new to come. But the hard work of thousands of laborers was paying off, and she'd heard it wouldn't be long until electricity and water were restored. She'd be especially glad for that.

She thought too of the progress they'd made with the hospital plans and the expansion of the warehouse. It was going to be quite the place, and already Caleb and Micah had managed to interest a group of wealthy donors in helping to fund the project. A few had even been asked to serve on the board. The project had been given approval as a priority, due to the nature of its service to the city.

There was a great deal of work ahead of them, but Kenzie

didn't mind. For the first time in her life, she had a true sense of purpose. She was going to work at her husband's side and care for the sick. The contentment the idea provoked filled her with wonder.

"Kenzie, when will your parents arrive?" Camri asked.

"They're supposed to come in tomorrow evening. Micah and I plan to go to the station after dinner. I'm so excited to see them again. I've missed my mother terribly."

"What of your father?" Judith asked, then frowned as if she realized she'd overstepped her bounds.

Kenzie smiled. "I'll be glad to see him as well. I just know that whereas my mother will be beside herself in delight at our reunion, Father will be less concerned. I'm not sure he'd even have come, had it not been at Mother's insistence."

"But why? Surely he knows you would want him to give you away," Camri replied.

Kenzie sighed. "Father wanted a son. A young man to carry on the family name and lineage. I have always been the greatest of disappointments to him, I'm afraid."

"But that doesn't mean he doesn't love you," Judith interjected.

Camri nodded. "Of course he loves her. Kenzie is easy to love."

Kenzie smiled at their fierce defense. She put up a hand to calm them. "There's no need to worry over me. I am used to my father's regrets. Besides, I've found a man who loves me for exactly who I am—flaws and all."

"Micah really is perfect for you." Camri sighed. "Just as Patrick is perfect for me and Caleb for Judith. We are blessed, and all because of what some might consider a chance encounter on a train."

"Nothing happens by chance," Judith assured them. "I'm convinced of that. I can see now that God had a plan all along."

Kenzie nodded. "I agree. It wasn't the path I would have chosen had I known all the obstacles, but the place it has taken me is exactly what I longed for."

"I think you'll be happy to know that despite the sunny disposition of thc mayor and Ruef," Judge Winters told Caleb in a whisper as they left a meeting, "the evidence against them both is sufficient enough to move ahead."

"Truly?"

The older man nodded. "I think we'll see action within the next couple of months. How's that for a wedding gift?"

"I think it's wonderful." Caleb could hardly believe the old man was right. Everything where Ruef was concerned seemed to be the same as always.

"I suppose you're pleased that the city has approved all of your plans for the changes you'll be making at the warehouse."

"I think they were afraid to do otherwise. Once the newspapers carried the story about our plans, they knew that doing anything but supporting it would have spelled disaster. People are feeling generous right now, but it's fading fast. Earthquakes and fires cause the masses to rally for a time, but they soon forget the need and start to think only of their own little part of the world."

"Well, the donations have been significant. As a member of your board, I can honestly say that I'm impressed by the generosity."

"I am too. I only hope we can make a difference. I know the city board makes noise about keeping the Barbary Coast businesses from ever coming to power again, but already there are dens of iniquity rising up all over the place."

"Vice will always be with us, son. There's no getting around that. Evil begets evil, and people will seek their entertainment in the darkest places."

"They need God's light." Caleb glanced down the street as they stepped outside into the sunlight. "We all need God's light."

"And Solid Rock is a wonderful way to reflect that light," the judge replied. "Perhaps you should even consider installing a beacon light. Imagine that."

Caleb couldn't contain a smile. "A beacon light? I like that idea very much. It will be a signal of both hope and warning."

"A very appropriate symbol."

When Caleb arrived back at the house, the chaos was more than enough to send him to his office. Before he could close the door, however, his sister appeared.

"Did things go well?"

He looked up as he removed his coat. "They did. We have the last of our permits in place and the city's full approval and cooperation."

Camri smiled. "That's wonderful news. And what of Victoria? Have you managed to get any information on her?"

"I was just coming to ask that very question," Judith said, sweeping into the room. She crossed to where Caleb stood, her eyes shining in adoration for him.

He kissed her hand before answering. "She's in New York City. Apparently family friends have taken her in. She's quite the toast of the town and has no less than twenty suitors vying for her attention."

"That sounds like Victoria." Camri rolled her eyes. "I hope some of those family friends have better sense than to let her ruin her reputation and spend all of her money. Even better if they educate her in fiduciary responsibility."

"I don't think she's quite as naïve as you might imagine," Caleb replied. "After all, she is living off the money of others. The investigator I hired said she's not drawn on her own money at all. She'll probably just wander from friend to friend until she decides to purchase a place of her own or marry. Somehow, I don't see her giving up her freedom too quickly."

Judith agreed. "She told me she was determined to do things her own way, and I have no reason to think she won't see that through. Still, it makes me sad. I have a cousin out there who wants nothing to do with me. We're the only family left to each other, but she doesn't care."

"Family has little to do with bloodlines, my dear." Caleb slipped his arm around Judith's shoulders. "We have created a strong family here with our friends. We'll soon be married and working together to benefit the city's poor, and together we will strive to grow in the Lord."

Camri offered her thoughts as well. "Before you know it, we'll have children of our own, and they in turn will grow up together. Who knows, our children might marry Kenzie and Micah's children, and then we'll be bound by blood as well as the heart."

"No matter what happens," Judith said, looking up at Caleb, "I know we will be a family, and that was the only reason I came to San Francisco in the first place. To find my family."

Kenzie watched as her mother and father stepped from the train. They looked remarkably healthy—even happy. She'd never seen her father this way. He seemed years younger. When he came to her, he put his arm around her shoulders and placed a kiss on her cheek.

"My dear, you are a sight for my old eyes. Just look at how pretty you are."

Kenzie wasn't sure how to take the compliment. She could count on one hand the number of times her father had praised her for anything, much less her appearance.

"Father, it's good to see you again." She stretched up to kiss his cheek in return, then turned to find her mother waiting to greet her. "Mother." Kenzie threw herself into the older woman's arms and felt a rush of tears. "I've missed you so." She whispered the words against her mother's ear, lest her father feel offended.

The women held fast to each other for several long moments.

"Aren't you going to introduce us?" Micah asked.

Kenzie reluctantly let go of her mother and stepped back, wiping tears from her eyes. "Mother, Father, this is Dr. Micah Fisher, soon to be your son-in-law."

Micah shook hands with her father, then kissed Kenzie's mother on the cheek. "I'm so happy to know you both. You have an amazing daughter, and I love her dearly."

"I'm glad to hear that," Kenzie's father replied. "I don't want her to settle for less." He glanced around. "What say you help me arrange for the bags?"

Micah smiled. "I'd be delighted."

The men went off to collect the luggage. Kenzie had thought she'd have so much to say to her mother, but the words seemed unimportant. "I'm so glad you could come."

Mother clasped Kenzie's hand. "Your young man is quite handsome, and it sounds as if he's very much in love."

Kenzie nodded and felt her cheeks flush. "We are. I can't imagine ever loving anyone as much as I love him. He's a good man, Mother. He cares so deeply for people, and I've learned so much at his side."

"I can see how happy you are, and that blesses me more than I can say. You were never this happy with Arthur."

"No. I don't suppose I ever was." Kenzie thought back for a moment. "I never felt I was equal to Arthur."

"You weren't. You were far superior," her mother snapped back.

Kenzie couldn't help but laugh. "I've never known you to be so opinionated."

"I wish I'd been more so when the Morgan men were up to their wily tricks. But hindsight is always so clear, is it not?"

"Yes, I suppose it is."

The men returned, laughing and talking as if they'd always known each other. Kenzie marveled at the ease with which Micah conversed with her father. She wished she might one day know that feeling.

"Are you ladies ready?" Micah asked. "I think, given you've spent the last few days traveling, it would be prudent to whisk you away to your hotel so that you might recover."

"I'm absolutely ready for a proper bed and bath," Mother said with a sigh.

Micah offered her his arm. "Then allow me to show you the way." They began to walk toward the depot's entrance. "I'm looking forward to getting to know you."

That left Kenzie with her father. She looked at him and without prompting took his arm. "I'm sorry it was such a long trip here, but I'm so glad you could both come. I wanted you to be with me on my wedding day."

"I wanted that as well. I have only one daughter, and it's important to me that I approve of her husband and see her properly wed."

"And do you?" she asked as they followed Micah and her mother.

"Do I what?"

"Approve of Micah." She glanced up to see her father's expression sober. Did he not like Micah? Was he only pretending to have enjoyed their conversation? "Father?"

He stopped her once they were inside the depot. "I have something I must say, Kenzie. Something that cannot wait, although a busy train station is hardly the venue."

Nerves raced through her stomach. "By all means, tell me."

He pulled her off to the side, out of the flow of traffic. He looked perplexed for a moment, almost confused, and then a peace seemed to settle over him.

"This past year has been difficult. No. Let me start again. I have never been an easy father for you." He released her and looked at his hands. "I know I didn't offer you the comfort and reassurance you needed after Morgan left you at the altar. I've never offered you the comfort of a father to his daughter. I have wronged you, and for that I beg your forgiveness."

Kenzie wasn't sure what to say, so she remained silent. To see her father in such a state was difficult, but at the same time, her heart yearned for any explanation and apology he might offer.

All around them, people went about their business, mindless of the importance of this moment in Kenzie's life. She had longed to hear her father speak to her about his aloof and often cold behavior toward her, his only child.

Joseph Gifford straightened and stared out across the large open room. "I set in my mind aspirations for a life that I could never make happen. I saw a future with sons and the empire we would forge. My father had sons, his father had sons, and as far back as anyone can recall, there were sons."

"But not for you. Not that lived." Kenzie's voice was barely a whisper. The old empty feeling of inadequacy began to smother her.

"No. Not for me." He was silent for a moment and then turned to face her. "And for the life of me, I could never see it for a blessing rather than a curse."

Her heart sank a little further as she forced herself to meet his gaze. "I'm sorry, Father."

He shook his head. "No. I'm the one who's sorry, Kenzie. I couldn't see how my behavior destroyed the happiness of my child. I couldn't see beyond my own plans and aspirations long enough to take note of the little girl who tried so hard to win my affection and approval. I was a blind fool. The lacking was never yours, Kenzie. It was mine."

She startled at his declaration. "Father . . . I don't . . . I . . ." She fell silent. What could she possibly say?

He patted her arm. "This apology comes too late perhaps, but I want you to know that I am ashamed of how I treated you. When I looked back over the years and realized the truth of my failings . . . it was condemning."

"I forgive you." The words were simple, but they poured out from Kenzie's heart without regret.

Their eyes met, and she saw for the first time that her father's were full of tears. "I intend to take that forgiveness like the cherished gift it is," he said in a whisper. "I will endeavor to be a better man." He pulled her close and held her tight. "You'll see, Kenzie. I'll endeavor to win you back."

She pulled away and shook her head. "You needn't do that. You never lost me. All my life I've longed for this day—just to have a chance to win your approval, your love. I've just been waiting."

He shook his head. "Then wait no longer. I love you very much, Kenzie. More than I ever even knew was possible. Seeing you endangered by the Morgans made me realize that. Knowing how easily you could have been truly damaged by them makes me all the more determined to see you safely married to a man who will love you as you deserve to be loved. I believe Dr. Fisher is that man."

She squeezed his arm and nodded. "He is that man, and I think you are going to love him as the son you always wanted. Who knows, perhaps the two of you will build your empire."

Her father's words of apology and love were still ringing in Kenzie's ears two days later when she and Micah joined her parents, along with the others, for dinner. The wedding would be held the next day, and it was a time of celebration that included Caleb and Camri's mother and father as well as Micah's.

Kenzie liked the elderly Coulter couple. They were both college-educated, socially active, and yet amazingly enough, simple Christian people. They looked down on no one, even extending great affection to Camri's Irishman.

"It seems so right to have everyone here together." Camri's enthusiasm was contagious. "I'm just so happy." She clapped her hands together twice. "What a perfect gift: all of you here under one roof."

Kenzie felt the same way. The last few days had been a mad rush to make certain preparations for the wedding come together. For all their effort to keep their nuptials simple, the plans had gotten rather out of control. The ladies who had lived at Solid Rock after the earthquake had insisted on being allowed to decorate and set up the rooms for the reception. In turn, the women of the church insisted not only on creating a cake for each bride, but also on overseeing the preparation of a large wedding brunch that would hopefully be held outdoors, since the weather had been so agreeable.

Caleb offered grace, and soon the dining room was filled with a cacophony of voices and clattering plates and silver. The girls had put their best efforts together for the gathering and done what any sensible brides would do—they'd ordered the meal brought in from a local restaurant. It had cost them plenty, but in Judith's words, "What is money for, if not spending?" They had even hired two of the staff to serve and clean up afterward. Kenzie felt more than a little decadent, but she was having the time of her life.

"We're having an architect put the finishing details on the plans for the new additions," Caleb explained to the fathers. "We'll have quite the complex of buildings and grounds once we manage to complete it."

Pastor Fisher paused with a forkful of lasagna halfway to his lips. "Many people are going to benefit from this act of love. You're going to be amazed at how God returns your giving."

Micah's mother nodded and squeezed Kenzie's hand. "Already the poor who come for aid at the church are talking about the future. They're anxious to find a way to better themselves."

"Schooling will help," Camri said, passing a plate of bread to her brother. "So many of these women could acquire better jobs with even a minimal amount of training. Kenzie and Judith helped me see that we could teach skills along with book learning. We plan to employ a very talented woman from England whom I met at a lecture some months ago. She has trained up women to work in some of the finest homes in America. I think she'll be quite an asset."

"I would imagine so," her mother agreed.

And so the conversation went until the final cups of coffee were served with thick slices of cassata cake—a sweet, cheesy confection for which the restaurant was famous. Soaked in a maraschino liqueur and filled with a sweet cream and ricotta concoction, the cake was topped with candied fruits and marzipan shapes. The delightful flavor was unlike anything Kenzie had ever eaten, but she quickly decided she would have it again—hopefully often.

"It's such a joy to see you children so perfectly matched with God-fearing mates," Mrs. Coulter said, looking around the table. "I had begun to fear I might not live to see it."

Both Mr. and Mrs. Coulter had grown gravely ill when their son had disappeared the year before. Kenzie knew it was nothing short of a miracle that both had recovered their health so completely.

"It did seem to take an inordinate amount of time," Camri's father replied.

"And we both want more grandchildren to spoil," Camri's mother added.

Kenzie could see by the surprised expression on Camri's face that she hadn't anticipated this comment. A quick glance at her own mother, however, confirmed she felt the same.

"We've longed for grandchildren." Kenzie's mother smiled and looked at her husband. "Haven't we?"

"We had to wait until our Kenzie had the right fellow," Kenzie's father offered. "And I am very thankful for the man He sent to her."

Micah smiled. "She didn't make it easy on me." He winked, causing Kenzie to flush all the more.

"That just makes the victory even sweeter," Caleb threw out, and everyone laughed.

"My only regret is that Arthur Morgan is a free man," Micah said, shaking his head. "I suppose he'll go on being a thorn in our side until he and his father get what they want."

"They already have it," Kenzie's father declared. Everyone stopped eating and looked at him. He shrugged. "I sold them every piece of land I owned."

"What?" Kenzie couldn't hide her surprise. "Why would you ever do that? Arthur couldn't really hurt us anymore—could he?"

Her father shook his head. "I didn't do it out of fear. Your mother helped me realize that my previous decisions were based on pride. I had wrapped my decision in a justification of wanting to preserve the family heritage, but it was never really about that. The past is gone. The focus of our lives should be the future. You have no desire to live in Missouri, do you?" he asked Kenzie.

She shook her head. "None."

"And it turns out that neither do we. Mother and I talked it over and realized that we want to be close to you . . . and our new son."

"So you sold your land to the Morgans?" Kenzie could hardly believe it.

"Yes. You see, that was their sole ambition. They would do whatever they had to in order to have it. I decided to work it to my advantage. I sent Hiram Morgan a letter via my lawyer. I named a price ten times what he had proposed and told him the offer was good only for twenty-four hours. The lawyer returned that afternoon with the signed documents accepting my terms and a bank draft."

"That must have set back the Morgan ledgers quite a bit," Caleb said with a grin. "That's the best place to hurt a man like Hiram Morgan."

"He'll easily make it back once the incorporation is complete and his new locomotive shops are in place. Never worry for the likes of Hiram Morgan or his sons."

"What do you plan to do, Mr. Gifford? Will you purchase a house here in San Francisco or perhaps rebuild on one of the abandoned sites?" Judith asked.

"We do plan to purchase a house here, though it might suit us better to build one or remake one that is already in existence. We shall rely on all of you to help us with that choice," Mr. Gifford said. "However, most of the money from Morgan will be given to Micah and Kenzie as a wedding gift." He looked at Kenzie's mother, who nodded. He turned back to Kenzie and Micah. "We are more than a little proud of all that you want to accomplish, and we want to be a part of that as well. I intend to invest in this charity hospital of yours."

"That's wonderful!" Micah said, shaking his head. "We have been blessed by so many, and to have your help as well . . . it makes everything complete. I hope you'll consider being on the hospital board. We'll need sound thinking men like you and my father to help guide the future."

"I'd be honored." Her father's expression made it clear that he was deeply touched.

Unable to stop smiling, Kenzie eased back in her chair. A

year ago, she had been prepared to embark on an entirely different journey—a journey that she thought would make her happy. But it would have been a life without attention to God and His direction. It would have been a marriage based on a lie—nothing more than a scheme for land and power.

How odd that out of such rejection and pain, all her dreams were coming true.

CHAPTER 26

It was a glorious summer day. The kind that closed up shops, sent everyone outdoors, and put smiles on the faces of young and old alike. It was a perfect day for a picnic in the park, a swim at the Sutro Baths . . . or a wedding.

Kenzie couldn't deny the butterflies in her stomach. She tried her best not to think of how nearly a year ago she'd been preparing for an entirely different wedding, one that had ended in pain and humiliation. She knew Micah would never do to her what Arthur had done, but she couldn't help feeling a little overwhelmed by the memories. She supposed it didn't help that she'd gotten word only yesterday that Arthur was now engaged to some East Coast socialite whose family money went all the way back to Europe. The news set her on edge, because once again Arthur Morgan was getting away with all the wrongdoing he'd orchestrated, and no doubt this new woman was being manipulated just as she had been. It wasn't right that money should allow him to do as he pleased without consequences.

She forced the thought from her mind and helped Judith readjust Camri's hat. There was no sense in fretting over what might have been, nor despising what was. God would eventually exact justice, and that was worse than anything Kenzie could dream up.

"Are you girls ready?" Mr. Coulter asked. He peered into the room where Kenzie and the others had been making their final adjustments.

"Camri's hat was a bit heavy on the side," Kenzie explained, "but we've secured it now."

He stepped into the room with Kenzie's father directly behind him. Both men were quite handsome in their black double-breasted suits.

"You're all absolutely radiant," Joseph Gifford declared. "I'm sure there have never been three more beautiful brides. And what hats!"

Kenzie laughed. Her own hat had been created from a foundation of white woven straw with a wide brim and high crown. It had been covered in feathers, lace, and silver tulle, all of which had been skillfully arranged like a masterpiece of art. Camri's millinery delight was also based on woven straw, but hers was a more natural color. The width of the brim was as wide as her shoulders and intricately piled on one side with ribbon, beading, and silk flowers. Judith's was a little simpler yet still quite stunning. The base of her hat was a rigid platform of dark blue that peaked out from pale blue tulle and lace. The hat was higher than it was wide, and beautiful ostrich feathers had been painted silver and carefully placed to draw the eye ever upward. As a final detail, small white roses had been added throughout the creation.

Mr. Coulter stepped over to his daughter and kissed her cheek. "You are stunning, my dear. I shall be honored to walk you to your groom."

Kenzie's father nodded. "As will I."

For the first time, they realized that Judith had no one to

walk with her. Kenzie saw Judith bite her lower lip and quickly lower her gaze. Kenzie knew her friend would never acknowledge her situation.

"I have a marvelous idea," Kenzie said, reaching for Judith's hand. "I will walk on my father's left, and you may walk on his right. Then Camri's father will walk on your right and Camri will be on his right. We will face the altar as we have faced life here in San Francisco: united."

"I think that's marvelous," Mr. Coulter declared. "I'm sure I have never been on the arm of three more beautiful young ladies, and I will very much enjoy playing my part."

Her own father gave her a smile and nodded. "As will I."

Judith, Camri, and Kenzie exchanged a glance and smiled. They truly had become sisters. Theirs was a bond that wouldn't easily be broken.

The walk from the warehouse to the place near the shore where the others waited wasn't long. It was strange that for all its industrialization and commercial surroundings, the warehouse grounds had the feel of an isolated park. Some of the old men who'd stayed with them had been out early that morning, arranging tables and chairs. Mrs. Lake had created an arbor of sorts using bleached white sheets, ribbon, and flowers, with the bay as a backdrop. It was here that Pastor Fisher waited with the grooms.

Kenzie saw Micah standing with Caleb and Patrick and smiled. He didn't seem the least bit nervous or concerned. Standing ramrod straight in his cutaway coat, he appeared to be doing nothing more important than waiting for a cable car, yet he'd never been more handsome. Just seeing him made her feel weak in the knees. Their eyes met, and Kenzie felt her heart skip a beat. The look in his eyes left her little doubt that he loved her—that he would always love her.

Camri felt her father's firm hold on her arm and was grateful. She'd never felt so nervous, almost to the point of being overcome. The day had been full of emotions for her, some expected and others not so much. On one hand, she felt like she was finally completing a long journey, one that had taken her a lifetime to travel. One that led to a conclusion she'd never even considered. On the other hand, Camri knew this was the beginning of an entirely new adventure.

She saw Patrick try to casually run a finger under his collar and immediately felt sorry for him. He looked so miserable in his wedding clothes. He was a man of movement and hard work. Suits and ties didn't leave him with the comfort or ability to do either one. She had told him last night how much it meant to her that he was willing to wear the wedding clothes Caleb had given him, but that she would happily marry him even if he showed up in his work attire. He had teased her by saying he just might. Now, as their eyes met, she could see that the love he held for her would have gone through far worse . . . and had.

She thought about Ophelia, Patrick's younger sister who had died last year from consumption. Ophelia had known they belonged together almost from their very first encounter. She had bequeathed Camri their family Bible, no doubt anticipating that it would remain in the family. Camri had thought her mistaken, but her doubts didn't last long. Patrick had proven to her over and over that he was not only worthy of her love, but that without it, she would never be complete. Glancing heavenward, Camri breathed a prayer.

Lord, we're going to need Your help to make this marriage work. We're both headstrong and opinionated and are far too easily given to arguing. Especially me. I know I need your guid-

ance to be a good wife, and I know Patrick will need patience to deal with me from time to time. Help us both, Lord. Help us keep our eyes on You so that when we're put out with each other, we remember who has the answers.

She looked at Patrick again and found him grinning as if he had heard her prayer aloud. She smiled. Their life together was sure to be interesting.

Judith trembled on the arms of her friends' fathers. She was grateful for their support, knowing that she might never have been able to manage even the short walk to the altar without it. Her stomach was churning furiously, but Caleb's steady, approving gaze made her keep putting one foot in front of the other. She had come a long way from that dusty, broken-down ranch in Colorado. A long way from the isolation and loneliness she had known most of her life.

I'm marrying the only man I've ever loved. The man I've loved since I first set eyes upon him.

She wondered what her mother and father might have thought of Caleb. Her birth parents had never had a chance to know her, but Judith liked to think they would have approved of Caleb. Even Grandmother had liked him, after a fashion.

Judith smiled at the memory of the feisty old woman she'd known for such a short time. Grandmother Whitley would have chosen a man of high finance and social regard for her granddaughter, but Judith had made it clear that such arrangements weren't acceptable. Grandmother Whitley had marveled at Judith's strength of will—a strength Judith hadn't even known she'd possessed. A strength that she felt had come in part from Caleb's encouragement and support—and, of course, God's help.

Issues of faith had seemed relatively unimportant when she'd been a child. Now, however, she felt that God was a very real presence in her life. Not just some faceless deity people spoke of in reverence or in cursing, but a real and active force in the world. A father and guardian who loved her more than any human father could.

The short walk to the altar ended, and before she knew it, Judith was handed off to Caleb, while Kenzie was paired with Micah, and Camri went to Patrick. Judith looked up to find Caleb's brown eyes shining with love. A delicious shiver ran down her spine as he touched the hollow of her back and turned her to face Pastor Fisher. She was getting married!

"Dearly beloved," Pastor Fisher began, "we are gathered here today to join Micah and Kenzie, Caleb and Judith, and Camrianne and Patrick in holy matrimony." He paused and chuckled. "While I presided over the marriage of my other children, I've never married three couples at once. This is truly a first for me and such a blessing. I've had the privilege of knowing all six people individually and am proud to call them friends. They have shown great love for each other, for their community, and for the Lord, and I see no reason they should not be joined together. However, if anyone else has thoughts against them, let them speak now or forever be silent on the matter."

No one breathed a word, and Pastor Fisher gave a nod. "Then let us continue."

The ceremony itself was short and simple, despite there being three couples rather than one. Each of the six people repeated their vows to their fiancé, pledging their life and love, then Pastor Fisher offered a prayer and instructed each groom to kiss his bride.

Those who had come to observe the strange little wedding cheered as if they were attending a baseball game rather than a solemn ceremony. Their response made Patrick laugh heartily, which only served to make them cheer the more.

Kenzie felt the breeze pick up and tug at her hat. She reached up to hold the brim, drawing Micah's hand along with hers. He turned to see what the problem was, then grinned.

"Shall I tie it on with some rope?" he asked.

"We may have to," she replied, doing her best to secure the hat.

"Or we could just rid ourselves of it all together," he teased.

"Not until after the photographs are taken," Camri said, coming up behind them. "And let's hurry. I fear Patrick will start shedding his clothes at any moment."

"Oh dear." Kenzie put her hand to her neck as if shocked. "The journalist for *The Call* would no doubt put that on the front page." She nodded toward the man who'd come at the insistence of the newspaper's owner after hearing about the triple wedding. "Then we'd none of us ever be invited to any important social events."

"What a pity that would be," Camri said, laughing, and hurried to catch up with her husband.

"Well, just remember, we need those socialites to help fund Solid Rock," Micah said.

Kenzie looked at him and shrugged. "God will provide, as you are always reminding me." She reached up and smoothed his collar. "Are you ready to have your photograph taken, Dr. Fisher?"

"Only if you are. Is your hat secure, Mrs. Fisher?"

She nodded. "I believe so. It feels secure." She smiled, feeling truly happy. "I feel secure."

He touched her cheek. "You'll always be so with me. I'll see to it, Kenzie. Even when we're old and gray."

"Are you two coming for the photograph?" Caleb asked, leaning toward Micah. He pulled Judith along with him. "Camri said we need to hurry. Apparently Patrick is about to pass out from wearing a suit."

Epilogue

San Francisco—Christmas, 1908

The sanctuary was packed to full capacity for the Christmas service, making it necessary for everyone to squeeze together as closely as possible. Kenzie's parents sat in the aisle next to Micah. Kenzie found herself tightly wedged between her husband and Caleb, but the joy she felt could not be dimmed by the crowded pew. She shifted the sleeping bundle in her arms and smiled at the way the baby momentarily pursed his lips. Their son was just a month old, yet already he had a strong personality that matched the red hair he'd inherited from his mother.

They'd named him for their fathers, both of whom were Joseph. Joseph Micah Fisher had already become the delight of both sides of the family.

A cry of protest from farther down the pew left little doubt that Camri and Patrick's baby girl was awake. Little Ophelia Murdock had been born only two days before Kenzie's son. Micah had delivered them both. But perhaps even more exciting was that the week before either Camri or Kenzie had given birth, Judith and Caleb had become parents to twins. A boy and a girl, whom they had named after his grandfather and her grandmother. James and Ann. Both now slept in the arms of their mother and father.

It had been a surprise to learn that all three women would have babies at the same time, and even more of a shock that Judith would give birth to twins. Micah had explained that because she herself was a twin, the odds were much greater that she would have two babies rather than one, but still it amazed them all. Judith had later laughingly said that she had to have two—one of each sex—so that they could marry little Ophelia Murdock and Joseph Fisher.

The congregation sang "O Little Town of Bethlehem," and then Pastor Fisher took to the pulpit to dismiss them. "This Christmas has come with many changes both to our city and our congregation. We have seen wrongs made right in the conviction of those responsible for taking unfair advantage of our city. We have seen rebuilding and restoration that has brought this once crippled town out of the ashes and into the grace and beauty she was once known for. There is still a great deal to do, but with God's help, we will see it through."

He paused and smiled at the row where Kenzie and the others sat. "We have been blessed as God has enlarged our congregation. Enlarged it so much, in fact, that we are raising a new church building to accommodate everyone. God has already provided the funds we will need for the new building, and our own Patrick Murdock's construction company will tend to our needs."

There were murmured *amen*s throughout the crowded sanctuary. Kenzie knew that money she and Micah had donated, as well as funds from Caleb and Patrick's families, had gone a long way toward meeting the need. However, she knew others in the congregation had given just as freely. This was a collection of people who gave without reservation. They had been deeply moved by the earthquake and fire and the need to help one another, and would no doubt go on giving in the future.

"We look to 1909 with tremendous hope in our hearts, as well as joy. The Lord has provided in great abundance—given more than we could ever ask or imagine—and so I encourage each of you to do the same. Remember those in prison. Remember those in poverty. Remember those who are lost and alone. Our Lord and Savior came that we might have life in abundance, so I encourage each of you to share that life with your fellow man. Now, please stand for the final benediction."

Upon conclusion, the sanctuary filled with music as the organist played "Joy to the World." Kenzie thought she might break into tears. Her joy was indeed great, and with the babe in her arms, Christmas held a new wonder for her.

"You look radiant, my dear," her mother said as she came to kiss Kenzie on the cheek.

"Doesn't she though?" Micah commented with a grin.

"How could I not?" Kenzie looked down at her son. "I cannot imagine being any happier."

"Well, I know I couldn't be," Caleb said, holding both babies while Judith pulled on her wool coat. "I have a beautiful wife and two incredible children. Added to that, Ruef has been sentenced to fourteen years in San Quentin, and this city will finally be free of corruption."

"Oh, I don't know that I'd be goin' that far," Patrick said as he and Camri joined them. "Corruption is bound to be with us till the good Lord returns to set things right."

"I'm sure you're right, Patrick," Caleb agreed, "but I'd like to think that, for now, we are much better off than we were."

"For sure, I believe ye on that account." Patrick smiled. "But now I'm thinkin' we've a grand feast awaitin' us at Solid Rock.

I'm not usually one for rushin' right out of church, but since a good many of these folks plan to join us there, couldn't we be savin' our visitin' till later?"

"Especially since we skipped breakfast," Camri said, jostling Ophelia in her arms. "I'm half-famished myself."

"Then let's go," Caleb said with a smile. "Let's go make merry and enjoy the bounty the Lord has provided."

They headed from the church to their waiting cars. Kenzie let Micah take the baby while she arranged herself in the automobile. She looked up with a nod when she was ready, and Micah deposited little Joseph in her arms. A blustery wind whipped up, and Kenzie quickly wrapped a wool blanket around them both.

Micah got the car started, but before he followed the others from the church, he reached into his pocket and pulled out a small jewelry box. "I wanted to give you this while we were alone. I have a feeling this will be the only time today that it might happen."

She opened the box. Inside was a beautiful heart-shaped gold locket. Mindful of the baby, she opened the locket and found a photo of Micah on one side and one of Joseph on the other. Her eyes filled with tears. "It's beautiful."

"Not half so lovely as you, but a token of my love and a reminder of what matters."

She held it close to her heart. "I used to dream of such things, and now they've come true. Thank you, Micah. Thank you for pursuing me and not giving up."

He chuckled and put the car in gear. "A wise man never gives up on love—especially when there's a feisty redhead involved."

Kenzie laughed and tucked the necklace back into the box. She slipped the gift inside her coat, then noticed that Joseph was watching her. His intense blue-eyed gaze made her smile. She touched the corner of his lip. "I suppose you'll be a persistent charmer just like your father."

"Of course he'll be a charmer," Micah declared. "I'll teach him everything I know."

Joseph's lip curled upward.

Kenzie sighed in complete joy. "Heaven help us all."

Regarding the Historical Facts

The San Francisco earthquake and subsequent fires of 1906 are believed to have ended the lives of over three thousand people. Damage to the city structures, utilities, and roads topped over $350 million and destroyed 80 percent of the city. The fires were more destructive by far and left over twenty-five thousand people homeless. San Francisco wasn't the only city damaged by the earthquake. San Jose, Salinas, and Santa Rosa, to name a few, also suffered greatly. As related in this story, insurance companies were unable to meet the demand of claims, and many insured people never recouped their losses.

Even before the fires were completely out, there was a push to rid San Francisco of its Chinese population. The desire to take over valuable downtown properties owned by the Chinese was met with approval by most, but the Chinese Americans fought back. The Empress of China voiced her disapproval of what was happening to the Chinese in San Francisco, and Washington, D.C., found it necessary to step in to stop the relocation of Chinatown. Wealthy Chinese businessman Look

Tin Eli knew that Chinatown could be a tremendous boon to the city and came up with the idea to re-create it with a strong Chinese theme that would appeal to tourists. The Chinatown of today was the result.

Through the aftershocks and cleanup, San Franciscans were resilient and determined to bring their city back to life. Millions of dollars in aid and donations poured in from around the world, and by 1915, San Francisco had not only rebuilt to its original grandeur and beauty, but went beyond that to invite the world to see what they had accomplished by hosting the Panama-Pacific International Exposition.

Many of the people mentioned in minor roles in the Golden Gate Secrets series were real. Big name businessmen like Spreckels, Stanford, Crocker, and others were the very heart and financial soul of San Francisco. Newspaper men like Fremont Older were determined to see the truth come out about the city's corrupt leaders, even though at one point he was kidnapped and threatened with murder. Then, as now, political arenas were rife with corruption, and Abraham Ruef, Mayor Eugene Schmitz, and so many others manipulated the system in whatever manner needed to accomplish what they desired. As Solomon said, "What has been will be again, what has been done will be done again; there is nothing new under the sun" (Ecclesiastes 1:9 NIV).

In October of 1906, District Attorney William Langdon asked a grand jury to bring indictments against Ruef and the other grafters. He appointed Francis J. Heney as his assistant district attorney. During this time, Mayor Schmitz went to Europe, leaving Acting Mayor James L. Gallagher to run the city in his absence. Schmitz went to Europe in an attempt to get foreign insurance companies to pay fire settlements. He was unsuccessful, and in fact many insurance companies fell into ruin in the aftermath of the San Francisco disaster. Laws were later passed to make sure insurance companies had proper collateral to back claims, but millions of dollars went unpaid to those who'd lost everything after the earthquake and fire.

Seeing their days were numbered, Acting Mayor Gallagher suspended DA Langdon, claiming "neglect of duty," and appointed Abraham Ruef as district attorney—the very man at the top of the list of grafters. The public outcry turned even more people against Ruef and the city government. However, Ruef and his cronies were unconcerned, at least for a while. Ruef quickly stepped into action to dismiss Francis J. Heney. Heney countered, saying he did not recognize Ruef as district attorney, and refused to step down. The following day, October 26, at five o'clock in the morning, Judge Seawell signed an order temporarily restraining Ruef from taking his place as district attorney, and the games continued.

Both sides argued that the other had taken bribes and manipulated the system for their own gain. Court appearances and arguments played out in the newspapers, as they are wont to do today. San Franciscans watched this battle while struggling to rebuild and recover from the devastation that had taken place only six months earlier. People were outraged that their mayor was off traipsing about Europe while so much was left undone at home.

By November, Mayor Schmitz, "Boss" Abe Ruef, and Police Chief Jeremiah Dinan were indicted by the grand jury for bribery and extortion. Abraham Ruef countered that he had never taken bribe money, but rather received "legal fees" for counsel. Mayor Schmitz returned to San Francisco from his unsuccessful European trip to find himself, along with Ruef, charged with five counts of extortion. Schmitz was also accused of using San Francisco relief funds to pay for his European holiday.

In February 1907, Abe Ruef pleaded not guilty to graft charges. The trial was set for March 5, 1907. Of course, given the circus that seemed to follow Ruef, there were complications and accusations enough to go around. Judges were accused of drunken misconduct, witnesses were concerned for their well-being as threats against their lives were delivered, and Ruef even disappeared completely for a time but was eventually found and jailed.

Finally, things started coming together. Officials admitted to taking bribes, and eventually Ruef was charged with more than sixty-five counts of graft. Ruef sent word that he "might confess if granted immunity," but the district attorney refused. Various public businessmen who had paid hefty bribes over the years for Ruef's favors were soon indicted for graft and bribing public officials. Ruef eventually pleaded guilty in return for limited immunity. Mayor Schmitz was then tried and convicted of extortion, but his conviction was overturned on a technicality. Ruef failed to abide by the terms of his plea and was found guilty. He was sentenced in December 1908 to 14 years in San Quentin State Prison.

In 1912, a judge dismissed the charges against the former Mayor Schmitz after Ruef refused to testify against him. Schmitz tried twice again to run for mayor but was soundly defeated. However, he eventually won election to the city's Board of Supervisors and served several years.

Ruef served four years and seven months of his fourteen-year prison sentence, and when he was paroled, he opened a new business as an "idea broker." But the idea failed, and when he died in 1936, Abraham Ruef was bankrupt.

Tracie Peterson is the award-winning author of over one hundred novels, both historical and contemporary. Her avid research resonates in her stories, as seen in her bestselling HEIRS OF MONTANA and ALASKAN QUEST series. Tracie and her family make their home in Montana. Visit Tracie's website at www.traciepeterson.com.

Sign Up for Tracie's Newsletter!

Keep up to date with Tracie's news on book releases and events by signing up for her email list at traciepeterson.com.

Also from Tracie Peterson

After her parents' deaths, Judith Gladstone travels to San Francisco to find her last living relative. Her unrequited love, Caleb Coulter, helps her search, and when his connections lead Judith to a wealthy, influential family, she learns shocking truths about her heritage . . . and finds herself in danger from someone who wants to keep the past hidden.

In Dreams Forgotten, Golden Gate Secrets #2

BethanyHouse

Stay up to date on your favorite books and authors with our free e-newsletters. Sign up today at bethanyhouse.com.

Find us on Facebook. facebook.com/bethanyhousepublishers

Free exclusive resources for your book group! bethanyhouse.com/anopenbook

You May Also Like . . .

In the early 1900s, Camri Coulter's search for her missing brother, Caleb, leads her deep into the political corruption of San Francisco—and into the acquaintance of Irishman Patrick Murdock, whom her brother helped clear of murder charges. As the two try to find Caleb, the stakes rise and threats loom. Will Patrick be able to protect Camri from danger?

In Places Hidden
GOLDEN GATE SECRETS #1

In search of a fresh start, three sisters head to the Oregon country, where they must adjust to life in the West. As they all discover new opportunities for their lives and find healing from their pasts, each woman will unknowingly risk her life—and her heart.

HEART OF THE FRONTIER: *Treasured Grace, Beloved Hope, Cherished Mercy*

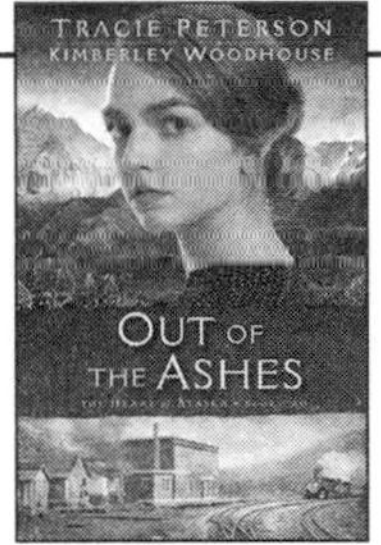

Katherine and Jean-Michel once shared a deep love that was torn apart by forces beyond their control. Reunited in the 1920s at the Curry Hotel in Alaska, have the years changed them too much to rediscover what they had? And when Jean-Michel's nightmares of war return with terrifying consequences, will faith be enough to heal what's been broken for so long?

Out of the Ashes by Tracie Peterson and Kimberley Woodhouse
THE HEART OF ALASKA #2
traciepeterson.com; kimberleywoodhouse.com

BETHANYHOUSE

More from Bethany House Publishers

In the aftermath of tragedy, Grace hopes to reclaim her nephew from the relatives who rejected her sister because of her class. Under an alias, she becomes her nephew's nanny to observe the formidable family up close. Unexpectedly, she begins to fall for the boy's guardian, who is promised to another. Can Grace protect her nephew . . . and her heart?

The Best of Intentions by Susan Anne Mason
CANADIAN CROSSINGS #1
susanannemason.com

Zanna Krykos eagerly takes on her friend's sponging business as a way to use her legal skills and avoid her family's matchmaking. But the newly arrived Greek divers, led by Nico Kalos, mistrust a female boss who knows nothing about the business. Yet they must work together to rise above adversity when confronted with the mysterious death of a diver and the rumor of sunken treasure.

The Lady of Tarpon Springs by Judith Miller
judithmccoymiller.com

Annalise knows painful memories hover beneath the pleasant façade of Gossamer Grove. But she is shocked when she inherits documents that reveal mysterious murders from a century ago. In this dual-time romantic suspense novel, two women, separated by a hundred years, must uncover the secrets within the borders of their town before it's too late.

The Reckoning at Gossamer Pond
by Jaime Jo Wright
jaimewrightbooks.com